A Blessing & a Curse

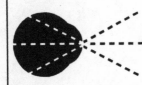

This Large Print Book carries the
Seal of Approval of N.A.V.H.

A Blessing & a Curse

ReShonda Tate Billingsley & Victoria Christopher Murray

THORNDIKE PRESS

A part of Gale, Cengage Learning

GALE
CENGAGE Learning·

Farmington Hills, Mich • San Francisco • New York • Waterville, Maine
Meriden, Conn • Mason, Ohio • Chicago

GALE
CENGAGE Learning®

LIBRARY OF CONGRESS CATALOGING-IN-PUBLICATION DATA

Names: Billingsley, ReShonda Tate, author. | Murray, Victoria Christopher, author.
Title: A blessing & a curse / by ReShonda Tate Billingsley & Victoria Christopher Murray.
Other titles: A blessing and a curse
Description: Large print edition. | Waterville, Maine : Thorndike Press, a part of Gale, Cengage Learning, 2017. | Series: Thorndike Press large print African-American
Identifiers: LCCN 2017014086| ISBN 9781410497895 (hardcover) | ISBN 1410497895 (hardcover)
Subjects: LCSH: Bush, Jasmine Larson (Fictitious character)—Fiction. | African American women—Fiction. | African American churches—Fiction. | Large type books. | BISAC: FICTION / African American / General. | FICTION / African American / Christian. | FICTION / African American / Romance. | GSAFD: Christian fiction.
Classification: LCC PS3602.I445 B58 2017 | DDC 813/.6—dc23
LC record available at https://lccn.loc.gov/2017014086

Published in 2017 by arrangement with Gallery Books, an imprint of Simon & Schuster, Inc.

Printed in Mexico
1 2 3 4 5 6 7 21 20 19 18 17

A Blessing & a Curse

CHAPTER 1

RACHEL JACKSON ADAMS

"I think Jasmine is your sister."

Rachel Jackson Adams cocked her head. To the left. Then the right. She studied her father, zoning in to see if his eyes were dilated, his speech slurred. Something. It was obvious her father was on the brink of a stroke since he was uttering complete nonsense.

"Jasmine? As in 'Jasmine all-those-last-names' Jasmine?" Rachel asked her father. Maybe he'd been outside working in his garden. The Houston heat was enough to make anyone delirious.

"She only has one more name than you."

"Okay, Dad, you've got jokes." Rachel stood up from her spot on the sofa, where she'd been sitting with her father watching their now-defunct reality show, *First Ladies*. When she'd walked into his house this afternoon, she'd been shocked to see that

7

he'd had that show on. Again.

When Rachel had joined the reality show on the OWN network last year, she had dreams of syndication, endorsement deals, and becoming a household name. Not to mention that she'd mapped out how she had planned to take Gayle's place as Oprah's BFF. They'd only done one season of the show — reality TV had proven to be too much for even Rachel, who considered herself a reformed drama queen. But her father, the Reverend Simon Jackson, was watching that show like it was the only thing on TV.

"Really, Dad?" Rachel asked, grimacing as she looked at the TV. It was the scene where she, Jasmine, and Rachel's husband's one-time mistress, Mary, had visited a church for Women's Day, and Rachel had been forced to deliver a Word. For some reason, Rachel had drawn a blank, so she'd just started reciting her favorite song lyrics. It had been the most embarrassing thing ever.

"I like this show," Simon said, finally smiling after delivering his cockamamie announcement. "Wait, here comes the part where you talk about if loving God is wrong, you don't wanna be right."

Rachel rolled her eyes. "I'm glad you find

it amusing."

He chuckled. "I thought you were gonna break out with 'Meeting in the Ladies Room' next."

"Back to this sister madness." Rachel picked up the remote and pressed pause. The television froze with Rachel's mouth wide open in the middle of a sentence. She shook her head at the image. "Ugh." Then, she pushed the button to turn the TV off altogether.

"I know you think I'm talking crazy." Simon's tone was serious again.

"You are." She tossed the remote back on the table.

"No . . ." he said, scooting to the edge of his seat. Simon began sifting through a bunch of photos strewn all over the coffee table. Rachel hadn't given them a second glance until now.

"Why do you have all of these pictures out?" She picked one up.

"I was looking for something."

"Oh, my God," Rachel said, laughing as she looked at the picture. "Is this you?" She turned the tattered black-and-white photo of a much skinnier Simon Jackson in a multicolored button-down shirt and bell-bottom jeans. "Look at that Afro."

"I was superfly," he replied as he continued to sift through the pictures.

"Where's Mom?" Rachel said, leaning over to peer at the piles. While she had given her mother, Loretta, major grief in her teen years, Rachel loved her something fierce. She'd died when Rachel was just nineteen, and her father had married his current wife, Brenda, shortly after, but Rachel's love for her mother had never wavered. "I want to see some pictures of her."

"You can go through the pictures later. I need to talk to you about Jasmine. I have questions." He glanced down at a tattered photo clutched tightly in his hand. "A lot of questions."

"Daddy, what is going on? You're really not making sense."

"I told you, I really do believe Jasmine is your half sister."

"The only way that would be possible is if you were getting busy with Jasmine's mother." Rachel busted out laughing, but quickly ceased when her father didn't laugh with her. "Umm . . . which is ludicrous since you don't know Jasmine's mother . . . right?" She studied her father, who suddenly couldn't look her in the eye. "Right?"

Instead of answering and with the slowness of a child waiting for his punishment, Simon extended his hand — and the photograph he was clutching — in Rachel's direction.

"Who is this?" Rachel asked, taking the picture. The black-and-white photo was also tattered, but the tall, stunning beauty in the picture looked familiar. Rachel's heart dropped just a little. She looked . . . like Jasmine. "Who. Is. This?" she repeated.

"That's my first love . . . the first woman who ever captured my heart." His eyes locked with his daughter's. "And the woman I think is Jasmine's mother."

Rachel studied the picture again. No. All the *no*s in *no*-dom. This was not Jasmine's mother. This was a woman who bore a resemblance to Jasmine and her father had watched their reality show so much that his brain was making him see something that wasn't there.

Rachel handed the picture back to her father. Her parents had met in college, so the thought of him being seriously in love with another woman had never even been in the realm of possibility. "I'm not entertaining this. Your first love was my mother. You've always said that."

"No, I said Loretta was my *greatest* love. Doris was my first love."

Doris. Rachel's mind raced, trying to recall Jasmine's mother's name. She was coming up blank.

"So, you cheated on Mom?" Just the thought gave Rachel a sinking feeling in her gut. Her father had been a lot of things over the years — neglectful, strict, judgmental — but she never would have taken him for a cheat.

"No," Simon said, inhaling. "This was before your mom." He shifted as if he was uncomfortable. "Do you want something to drink? I can have Brenda bring you some tea or someth—"

"No, Daddy. I don't want anything to drink." Rachel cut him off. "I want you to tell me what's going on."

"Sit." He motioned toward the sofa and she eased back into her seat. Simon leaned back, ran his hands through his salt-and-pepper hair, and said, "Where do I begin?"

Sweet Home Baptist Church in Smackover, Arkansas, might have only boasted a membership of seventy-three, but they quadrupled that number when it came time for the annual Bible Revival. Reverend Horace Jackson may not have been able to pack folks into his church on any given Sunday, but they came from all over for his two-week-long Revival.

That's why when the rickety bus with the words *Pilgrim Rest Missionary Baptist Church,*

Mobile, Alabama, emblazoned on its side rolled into the dusty parking lot, none of the kids playing in front of the church batted an eye. There were already churches visiting from Mississippi, Louisiana, and Texas for the annual event.

Then, a vision of loveliness stepped off the bus.

Simon had been playing kickball with some of his friends and all of them stopped. The young woman had the longest jet-black hair he'd ever seen, the prettiest doe eyes, and a smile that got off the bus before her.

All the boys stared at the girl like she'd just stepped out of the pages of their favorite book.

"Doris, you wait right here," an elderly woman said to her. "I'm gonna go see where pastor wants us to go."

"Yes, ma'am," Doris said, before turning toward the group of boys. "Hi."

"Hi," several of them mumbled. Simon couldn't seem to find his voice.

"What's your name?" Her eyes zeroed in on Simon, or at least he thought they did.

"I'm Clevester," Simon's friend said, jumping in front of the young woman. Simon should've known he would lay first dibs on the pretty girl. Clevester got all the girls.

"Actually," she said, leaning to the side and

pointing directly at Simon, "I was talking to him."

"And why you need to know his name?"

Simon groaned as Minnie, his Amazon of a sister, stepped in front of him, blocking his view of the pretty stranger.

"Oh, sorry, didn't mean to say anything to your boyfriend," the girl said.

"Ugh! I'm not his girlfriend," Minnie replied. "I'm his sister."

That brought the smile back to the girl's face and she stood up tall as she twirled her ruffled skirt. "I'm Doris. Doris Young." She stuck her hand out to shake. Minnie didn't take it. But Doris just kept grinning.

"Why you always grinning? You special? Something wrong with you?" Minnie asked, her arms folded across her chest as she gave the girl the once-over.

Doris shrugged. "Guess I'm just a happy person." She leaned over to look again at Simon, who was all but hiding behind his sister. "Does your brother have a name?"

"Maybe," Minnie snapped.

"It's, um, it's S-Simon Jackson," he said, finally stepping out of his sister's shadow.

"My brother is shy." Minnie rolled her eyes. "Unless, of course, you put a Bible in front of him. Then he turns into Martin Luther King Jr. or something."

"You a preacher?" Doris asked.

Simon shook his head. "Nah. I-I just like spreading the gospel."

"The gospel is good," Doris said. "My grandfather is a preacher. You kinda young, though."

Simon stood erect. "I'm about to turn fifteen."

"I'm fourteen," she said.

"And that makes you too young for him," Minnie said, stepping back in front of Simon.

Simon pushed his sister aside. "Minnie, go somewhere."

She cut her eyes at him. "Fine. I can tell when I'm not wanted." She grabbed Clevester's hand. "Come on, Clevester. I want you to come pick me some plums off this tree."

After Minnie dragged Clevester away, Simon relaxed and before he knew it, he and Doris were inseparable. She was everything he was not — vibrant, social, funny, and beautiful. If ever there was such a thing as love at first sight, Simon Jackson definitely thought he'd found it.

"We spent every day, all day together for the revival," Simon said, wrapping up the story. "But then she went back home and, of course, we didn't have cell phones or email, but we wrote to each other constantly. Every letter, I fell more and more in love with her."

"Okay, cute story," Rachel said, eyeing her father strangely. "But just because some woman from your past looks like Jasmine, doesn't make her Jasmine's mother."

He motioned for her to be quiet. "Would you let me finish?" The nostalgic smile returned to his face as he continued. "Doris came back to the revival the next summer and our love only grew stronger. And then, the summer after that, we were already making plans to one day get married.

"But when she returned home after that, she stopped answering my letters. Just stopped. I was devastated." Simon shook his head like even recalling that time of his life was painful. "I never could get a straight answer," he said. "My sister's nosy behind did some digging. She wrote one of the boys who had been at the revival from Mobile. He told us Doris had a baby."

"A baby? So her parents made her stop communicating with you because she had a child?" Rachel's mouth dropped open as if a realization had set in. "Wait. Was it your child?"

Simon shrugged. "I don't know," he said, his tone softer. "I tried to get some answers, but my father was adamant that I 'leave well enough alone.' Doris wouldn't answer my letters, and in fact, they started being

16

returned to me as undeliverable. My parents convinced me that the pregnancy was just a rumor and that I needed to go on about my life."

"Maybe it *was* a rumor."

"That's what I convinced myself." He was quiet for a moment, then, as if he was talking to himself, he added, "Until I got a good look at Jasmine. She favors my grandmother and . . . I tried looking on that Internet, but I can't find out Jasmine's exact date of birth because all the stuff that's on there is conflicting."

"That's because she's always lying about her age," Rachel grumbled. "But I think she's like fifty or sixty, so she couldn't be your daughter."

Simon shook his head. "No. No. She looks just like Doris."

Rachel stood to leave. She couldn't process this conversation any longer. "Yes, this Doris woman resembles Jasmine. But I assure you that's a coincidence. I mean, Daddy, you're really reaching. Because if Jasmine is your daughter, that . . ." Her words trailed off, then she took a minute to gather herself before she continued. "That would make her my half sister." The thought made Rachel shudder.

"Do you know anything about Jasmine's

mother?" Simon asked.

It was Rachel's turn to shake her head. "I don't know anything. Except you must be getting senile in your old age. Either that or you're feeling some kind of nostalgia. But Jasmine is from Florida, not Alabama."

"Well, her mom could be from somewhere else," Simon said. "I need to talk to Jasmine. I need to ask her some questions."

Rachel blew out an exasperated breath. Maybe her father was in the early stages of Alzheimer's or one of those other debilitating mind diseases, but she could tell from the look on his face that he wouldn't rest until he got some answers. "What do you need to know, Dad? I'll find it out."

"You'll talk to her?" His voice was full of relief.

"Yes, I'll ask her her mother's name and when she was born. I will get all the details you need so that we can shut this foolishness down." Rachel chuckled. "You need to lay off that prune juice because it's messing with your mind." She leaned in and kissed her father on the forehead. "But if it'll make you feel better, I'll call her so we can nip this in the bud."

Rachel stared at her father, let out a small laugh again, then grabbed her purse and said, "Me and Jasmine related? Oooh,

Daddy, you need to be a comedian." Her laughter trailed after her as she walked out the door.

CHAPTER 2

JASMINE COX LARSON BUSH

Jasmine had one foot out of the cab, but she looked up and wondered if she should get right back in. It was the two women stepping out of Melba's who made her have that thought. Two women who threw a glance her way.

"What are you doing, Jas?" her sister, Serena, asked. "Get out."

Slowly, Jasmine eased out of the taxi, but as the women kept their stare on her, she cringed. It was coming. She could see it in their eyes. First, they frowned, then the look of shock when complete realization set in.

In her head, Jasmine counted; *One, two, three, four, five . . .*

"Oh, my God! Jasmine Cox Larson Bush," the two women said together as if they'd practiced for this moment.

Then they giggled like schoolgirls, even though Jasmine was sure both were at least forty, maybe even fifty years old.

More "Oh, my God" before the taller one, who looked like she could have been an on-fire basketball player back in her day, raised her hand above her head and snapped her fingers. "That's what divas do and I'm done!"

The two busted out laughing as if Jasmine's catchphrase from her reality show was something they'd just created.

Jasmine fixed a smile on her face and attempted to step around the strangers. But the two had formed a blockade, preventing Jasmine and Serena from entering the restaurant.

"Excuse me," Jasmine said.

"Oh, we're sorry," the shorter one, who was decked out in all things leopard, said, though neither made any effort to move out of Jasmine's way. The woman kept talking. "You were absolutely awesome on the show."

"Yeah, you were my favorite," the other said. "That Rachel chick was always throwing shade 'cause she was jealous of your class, you know?"

"Right?" Ms. Leopard said, as she high-fived her friend.

Jasmine was not the president of Rachel Jackson Adams's fan club, but it was like

21

some kind of sister/girl thing — she could talk about Rachel, but no one else could. Yes, what these women said about Rachel was true, but they didn't know that for sure.

That's what Jasmine wanted to tell them, but she wasn't about to get into a debate on the corner of 114th and Frederick Douglass Boulevard in Harlem with two people who didn't matter. So, all she said was "Thanks" as she once again tried to maneuver around the women.

But even as she moved, they didn't.

"Can we just have your autograph?" Ms. Basketball Player asked. Before Jasmine could respond, the girl snatched a brown paper bag from inside her bootleg designer purse and thrust it in Jasmine's face.

A paper bag? And these two had the nerve to question Rachel's class?

Pulling a pen from her purse, Jasmine shook her head. This was not how it was supposed to be. When she set out to do *First Ladies,* Jasmine was all about the fortune she was sure to amass. She cared not one bit about the fame. But the fortune had evaded her and fame was what she had found. She couldn't believe the number of people who recognized her. It didn't matter where she was — today it was her favorite restaurant, yesterday it had been in the shoe department in Saks.

As Jasmine signed the bag, the girls glanced at Serena.

"Are you anybody?" Ms. Leopard asked.

"She's my sister." Jasmine shoved the bag into the lady's hand before she turned away once again.

"Wait, I got one more question," Ms. Basketball Player said.

Jasmine was two steps away from the front door and had no intention of saying another word, until the woman asked, "Do you think you can hook us up with Oprah?"

She couldn't help it; Jasmine stopped. "What?"

"You know, can you hook us up?" she asked, pointing first to herself and then to the shorter one. "Can you call Oprah and tell her that you know two women who really need to have their own show."

"Yeah," Ms. Leopard joined in. "Oprah needs to give us a show 'cause we'd be better than the Housewives and the Basketball Wives and the Hip-Hop Wives combined. We'd do that!"

The tall sidekick added, "Not that y'all weren't good, but we're the real deal. We'd bring all the drama and make her network number one."

"Yeah. And she'd get even more money

after we signed a book deal, and then made a movie, and traveled to other countries like Europe and Africa."

For a moment, Jasmine stood there waiting for one of them to shout out, "April Fools," even though summer was just a couple of weeks away. She waited for them to tell her that they didn't really expect her to call Oprah (even if she'd had her number) and vouch for two women she'd met on a street corner in New York. And she waited for them to say that of course Europe and Africa were not countries.

But they just stood there, their eyes wide with anticipation.

"Okay," Jasmine said.

The two women cheered, high-fived each other once again, and began skipping down the street. Jasmine watched Dumb and Dumber for a second, then she and Serena exchanged a glance before they busted out laughing. Just as they stepped into the restaurant, though, one of the women shouted from halfway down the block, "Wait, you don't even know our —"

The door closed on their words and when Louis, one of the restaurant's managers, greeted them, Jasmine explained the situation in fewer than twenty words.

He laughed. "Don't worry, I got you," he

said as he began to lead them across the room filled with afternoon diners. "I got a table for you already."

Already? She had no idea what he meant by that since she hadn't called ahead. But then, as she neared the group of tables in the far corner, her steps slowed while her eyes widened.

"Mae Frances?" She whispered the question as if she couldn't quite believe what she was seeing. "Mae Frances!"

Jasmine trotted the rest of the distance, leaned over, and wrapped her friend in a hug. "What are you doing here? When did you get back? How did you know that I'd be here?"

"Jasmine Larson," Mae Frances began, even though she was still inside Jasmine's embrace. "Don't you know you're not supposed to touch people when they're eating?"

"I'm sorry," Jasmine said, not sounding sorry at all. "I'm just so glad to see you. What are you doing here? When did you get back?" Then, she grabbed Mae Frances in another tight squeeze. "And how did you know I'd be here?"

"First of all, I thought you recognized by now that I know everything."

"You must've spoken to Hosea." Jasmine laughed.

"And second of all," Mae Frances snarled as she wiggled away from Jasmine's arms, "why are you acting like this?"

Jasmine scooted onto the long leather seat next to Mae Frances. "Why? I haven't seen you in . . . how long has it been?"

"Three weeks, one day" — Mae Frances glanced at her watch — "and nine hours and about twenty-three minutes."

"Hi, Mae Frances." Serena laughed as she slipped into the chair across from them.

With a grin that made her cheekbones rise high, Mae Frances reached for Serena's hand. "It's good to see you. How are you, baby?" she asked in the gentlest of voices. Then, Mae Frances turned to Jasmine and her gravelly tone was back. "See, that's the way you're supposed to greet people. Just say hello, not ask them fifty-eleven questions."

Jasmine leaned over and kissed her cheek.

"That's better," Mae Frances said.

"So, now are you gonna tell me what you're doing here?"

Mae Frances sighed. Then with movements that made time seem like it had slowed down, Mae Frances pushed her plate filled with fried catfish fillets aside, wiped the corners of her mouth with her napkin, then cleared her throat. She looked into Jas-

26

mine's eyes and said, "I came home because I need you."

Jasmine and Serena both leaned forward.

"Mae Frances" — Jasmine took the hand of the woman who, over the last decade, had become like her mother — "what's going on?"

Mae Frances lowered her eyes and that set Jasmine's heart pounding. Was something wrong with her friend?

"I had to come home," Mae Frances began.

Jasmine's imagination took flight. Mae Frances was sick! What kind of illness did she have? How much time had she been given? Tears rose within her. She'd lost her biological mother; she couldn't lose this second one whom had been such a blessing from God.

"I needed my family." Mae Frances's voice was still soft.

The tears reached Jasmine's eyes.

"I wasn't sure that I could get through this without you, Hosea, and the kids." She looked up at Serena. "And you, too, honey. You're my family, too."

"Mae Frances." Jasmine's voice, like the rest of her, trembled as a tear rolled down her cheek.

"I had to come home because . . ."

27

Jasmine wanted to close her ears; she didn't want to know.

"Muhammad Ali died!"

Jasmine sobbed, "Oh, no!" But then the words Mae Frances just uttered reached her brain and Jasmine blinked a dozen times. "Wait," she said, her voice still shaking with emotion, "what?"

"My Muhammad Ali." Mae Frances pressed her hand on her chest. "He passed away," she wailed.

"I'm so sorry," Serena said. "You knew Muhammad Ali?"

Mae Frances nodded, her own eyes glassy. "I met Cassius right before he was leaving for the Olympics. But we spent the most time together when he was about to fight Joe Frazier. Everyone thought he was sure he was gonna win because of all the things he said. But that was his public persona. In private . . . he just wasn't sure."

"Wait!" Jasmine held up her hand. "Do you know how scared I was? I thought something had happened."

"Something did happen! You didn't know he'd passed away and now he's lying in the arms of the Lord?"

Jasmine swiped the wasted tears from her face. "So, you're telling me this is about Muhammad Ali?"

She nodded.

"You knew him."

It wasn't a question, but Mae Frances nodded anyway.

"And you came back here because he passed away?"

She nodded again.

Jasmine's trembles had turned to anger. "There's just one problem with that: you're in New York, his funeral is going to be in Kentucky."

"Don't you think I know that, Jasmine Larson!" she snapped. "I'm not going. It would be too emotional. And I just want to be home here with my family because it's times like this when I just want to hug and be close to the ones who mean the most to me."

All her anger began to roll away. How could she be mad at that? And she didn't need to waste any time being mad anyway. Jasmine had missed this woman who was to her what Maya had been to Oprah.

For the past year and a half, she'd only seen Mae Frances every three weeks or so, since Mae Frances had been splitting her time between New York and Atlanta. She'd moved down to Atlanta part-time to take care of Natasia Redding, Hosea's long-ago ex-fiancée, who was suffering from ad-

29

vanced stages of lupus.

"Wow! You knew Muhammad Ali," Serena said as if she were impressed.

Jasmine was not. At least not anymore. From the moment she'd met Mae Frances, she'd learned that this woman had connections. She knew everyone from Newt Gingrich to Herman Cain, and when Jasmine had asked her why she didn't know any Democrats, Mae Frances had picked up the phone and, seconds later, Jasmine was talking to Joe Biden. She'd danced with Alvin Ailey and had helped Martin Luther King write some of his speeches — or so she said.

There was little that surprised Jasmine about her friend anymore. "So, how long are you going to be here?" she asked.

"You are always up in my business, Jasmine Larson," Mae Frances said. But then she continued, "I'm home permanently."

More blinks from Jasmine. "What?"

Mae Frances cut a little piece of catfish and slipped it into her mouth as she shrugged. "I'm not going back to Atlanta. That roommate thing with Natasia didn't work out."

"So, you just moved out? And left her there?"

Mae Frances leaned back and snuggled into the leather cushions like she was get-

30

ting comfortable, so she could tell a story. "See, what had happened was Natasia called me out of my name. And you know I don't play that."

"What'd she call you?" Serena asked.

"An overbearing fool. She said I was an overbearing fool who needed to get some."

"Wow!" Serena said. "That's so rude."

"And so wrong. I told that heffa that all that screaming she'd heard the night before hadn't been from my TV; I was getting some, and what she needed to get was going so I could get some on the regular."

Jasmine cracked up. Not because of Mae Frances — she was used to her friend's adventures — it was the look on her sister's face that had her buckled over with laughter. Serena was one of those good Christian girls who kept her words, thoughts, and deeds clean and pure. Serena had been a widow for almost two decades and Jasmine was sure she hadn't "gotten some" since her husband passed away.

Mae Frances shrugged again, and popped another piece of catfish into her mouth. "That was last week. And Natasia is gone."

"Where'd she go?" Serena asked. Even with all her shock, she was into what Jasmine had come to call Mae Frances's Fantastic Stories.

"I don't know and ask me if I care."

"Wow." It was like that was the only word left in Serena's vocabulary.

"What are you ladies having today?" The young waiter interrupted them, and for a moment Jasmine wondered what he was doing there. She'd been so into her friend she'd forgotten about ordering.

Jasmine didn't need to glance at the menu; there was only one reason why she trekked up to Harlem every chance she had to feast at Melba's. "I'm going to have the grilled jerk shrimp as an appetizer, the pecan-crusted tilapia as my main course, and for my sides, cheddar-grits cakes and candied yams."

Serena gave her own order: the salmon salad.

When the waiter left them alone, Jasmine asked, "So, is Natasia back in Chicago or what?"

Mae Frances took her time putting down her fork and wiping her lips before she said, "Didn't you get the memo — I don't care. Living with that" — she glanced at Serena — "that *young woman* was enough for me." She paused and, with a sideways glance, added, "I'm sure if she has any problems, she'll be calling your husband."

Mae Frances laughed, but Jasmine didn't

find a bit of humor in those words. The problem was, Mae Frances was right. Hosea's heart was too caring, and for a moment, Jasmine's thoughts turned to Natasia. That woman had brought more than enough drama into her life. She was going to have to find a way to keep Natasia from Hosea.

"But I don't want to talk about her anymore." Mae Frances waved her hand in the air, her words forcing Jasmine back to the present. "I have more exciting news." She pushed her plate aside as if she didn't want anything to get in the way of what she had to say. She looked at Jasmine, then Serena, and back to Jasmine.

She took a deep breath, then exhaled. "I was contacted by a literary agent. Someone saw me on your show and now . . . they want me to write a book!"

"Oh, wow!" Serena said. "Congratulations!"

There was no cheer in Jasmine's voice when she said, "Write a book? About what?"

"What do you think, Jasmine Larson? They want me to write a book about my life."

"That's fantastic, Mae Frances!" Serena said.

But Jasmine's thoughts were just the opposite: No. There was nothing fantastic about this. Mae Frances would never tell anyone anything about any part of her life. She had more secrets than she had connections and Jasmine had always believed that one or two of those secrets could land her in jail.

Still, Mae Frances said, "I think the title will be *The Autobiography of Mae Frances.*" She grinned. "What do you think about that, Jasmine Larson?"

Inside, Jasmine said, *Whatever.* But on the outside, she gave Mae Frances what she wanted to hear.

She said "Wow" before she took a long sip of water.

CHAPTER 3

JASMINE

Jasmine stood on her toes to get a final glimpse of Serena before the top of her sister's head disappeared down the escalator leading to Track 11. And even though hurried New Yorkers bumped her on her left and right, she stood in place for a moment. Just in case Serena changed her mind, just in case her sister decided to stay for just one more day because one week had not been enough.

But, after a couple of minutes and too many shoves, Jasmine pivoted and headed toward the Eighth Avenue exit. Tears spilled from her eyes, but she knew no one in Penn Station would notice. This was New York. Maybe if she were walking down the street crying *and* naked, someone would see her tears.

Outside, the June sun still hung high and bright, even though it was after six. As rush-

35

hour commuters pushed past her, Jasmine searched for the end of the taxi line.

"Excuse me, miss. What's your name?"

If there was one thing that Jasmine hated most about the city she loved, it was that there was always some strange dude stepping to her in the middle of the street. She'd cursed out plenty of construction workers, messengers, and ordinary guys just hanging out on a corner as if harassing women was their job. With the way she was feeling today, all kinds of curses were ready to spew from her mouth.

Except Jasmine knew this voice. And just the tenor of his tone made her crying heart sing.

She spun around and though her eyes were still filled with tears, she smiled.

"Baby!" she said as she wrapped her arms around Hosea's neck. "What are you doing here?"

He held her tight and his embrace wiped her tears away. "I knew you'd be feeling some kind of way with Serena leaving. I just wish I could've been there when you two left the apartment."

"I knew you had that meeting," Jasmine said, stepping back. "No worries. But you came all the way down here to get me?"

He nodded. " 'Cause I knew you'd be crying." With his thumb, he wiped a single tear from her cheek. "And, I can't have my darlin' crying in the middle of New York City."

That brought new tears to Jasmine's eyes, but this time there was no sadness.

"I love you so much," she said, holding on to her husband once again.

"Okay, enough making out in the street. Remember, I'm a famous pastor. We'll handle this tonight in our bedroom."

Jasmine laughed as he took her hand and led her to the curb, where the taxicab line was so long it wrapped around the corner. But he stepped past the waiting people, and that's when Jasmine noticed the stretch limousine. When Hosea grabbed a door handle, Jasmine said, "All of this for me?"

With a smile, he nodded and motioned for her to get inside.

She stepped in, looked up, and gasped. "Mae Frances!"

Her best friend leaned against the door on the other side. And with an attitude, she said, "Would you get inside, Jasmine Larson? We're blocking all this traffic!"

Jasmine scooted across the seat. "What are you doing here?"

Settling into the seat across from them, Hosea answered for Mae Frances. "Nama came by the church and scooped me up because she said you needed us."

"Yeah," Mae Frances said. "I knew you'd be a mess, so I figured you could take me out to dinner." Then, to Hosea, she said, "Tell the driver where you two are taking me, Preacher Man."

Jasmine chuckled the way she always did when Mae Frances called Hosea by the name she'd given to him more than a decade ago. And she chuckled because as she sat in the back of this limousine with these two, her heart didn't hurt as much as it had five minutes before.

"So, you called for a limo? Just for me?" Jasmine asked as she placed her hand over her heart.

"No." Mae Frances shook her head and frowned as if she couldn't figure out what Jasmine was talking about. "Didn't you hear what I said? I called the limo so you could take me out to dinner." Then she did a little wiggle, snuggling into the seat. "And I called it 'cause I got it like that now."

Jasmine frowned.

"The book I'm writing. Remember?"

Sitting back in his seat, Hosea said, "Nama, you're writing a book?"

Jasmine's first thought: had there even been a time when Mae Frances's grin had been so broad? Even though she smiled

38

back at Mae Frances, in her mind, Jasmine rolled her eyes.

"Yeah, you didn't know?" To Jasmine she said, "Why didn't you tell Preacher Man, Jasmine Larson?"

Jasmine folded her arms. "Because I can't believe you're gonna write a book."

"Why not? I can read, you know. I got a couple of college degrees."

The way Jasmine pushed her eyebrows together made her forehead hurt. But she ignored the pain because Mae Frances had just shared something she'd never told Jasmine — she went to college? Had a couple of degrees? Even though Jasmine had known this woman for more than ten years, even though Mae Frances was Nama (the name for grandmother that her children had made up for Mae Frances) to Jacqueline and Zaya, even though she had been a mother-sister-friend to Jasmine, there were so many holes in her life, so much that Jasmine didn't know and Mae Frances never shared. And Jasmine reminded her of that.

As the limousine inched forward in the Seventh Avenue congestion, Jasmine said, "How're you gonna write a book when you have so many secrets?"

"Secrets? What kind of secrets does Nama have?" Hosea asked.

That quickly, Jasmine had forgotten about her husband.

Mae Frances didn't give Jasmine any space to answer. "I don't know what she's talking about," she said to Hosea. Then, she turned squinted eyes to Jasmine. " 'Cause I don't have any secrets . . . do I, Jasmine Larson?"

Jasmine wanted to spew out everything she knew about the woman. She wanted to tell Hosea how it was Mae Frances who had helped her lie to him about their daughter's true paternity, making Hosea believe that the baby Jasmine was carrying when they got married was his. She wanted to tell Hosea how Mae Frances had all kinds of strange connections. How Mae Frances had dated everyone from politicians to pastors, probably dating a couple of them at the same time.

But Jasmine said none of these things because, first of all, Mae Frances and her connections had gotten Jasmine out of every bind she'd ever been in, so she owed her for that. And . . . she was afraid of her. Not physically. Jasmine was (almost) sure that she could take this woman who was at least twenty years her senior (no one knew Mae Frances's age for sure). But it was the other kind, the nonphysical damage that Mae

Frances could do, the secrets (Jasmine's secrets) that Mae Frances could tell, that left Jasmine with her lips pressed together.

So, all she could say was, "I don't mean you have secrets. I just mean you're a private person."

Mae Frances gave her a nod as if she approved of the way Jasmine had handled that. "That I am. Private. But since I'm the one writing the book" — she paused and waved her hand in the air — "I don't need one of those ghost-writing people . . . I will be the one who decides what goes on those pages and what doesn't."

"So, what kind of book are you writing, Mae Frances?" Hosea asked.

"A novel," Jasmine spoke up before Mae Frances could say a word. "It's all fiction."

She glared at Jasmine. "You know I'm not writing any fiction. I'm writing a true story — the story of my life." She kept her stare on Jasmine for just a little longer. Then, "That's right, Preacher Man. I'm going to tell the world about Mae Frances."

Hosea grinned. "Well, I think that's a beautiful thing, Nama. I bet you it'll be a *New York Times* bestseller."

Mae Frances giggled and Jasmine turned to the window. Even though the sun was bright, she searched for the full moon that had to be rising. Mae Frances writing a book? That would never happen.

The ringing of her cell phone pulled her thoughts away from this craziness of Mae Frances the author. But when she grabbed it out of her bag and glanced at the screen, she felt like she was in the twilight zone. There was definitely going to be a full moon tonight because the wolves were out. And this one, whose name appeared on her screen, would be the first wolf out there howling.

She pressed the ACCEPT icon. "Rachel?"

"Hey, Jasmine. What's up?" Rachel said as if the two were friends who spoke often.

Really, Jasmine didn't consider Rachel anywhere near a friend. Yes, when they found themselves in the same space together, they always seemed to have to team up — them against the rest of the crazies out there. But when Jasmine and Rachel were apart, Rachel was just one of those crazies to Jasmine.

"What do you want, Rachel?"

"Dang! Is that how you greet a friend?"

"No, I greet my friends differently. So . . . what do *you* want?"

"You know what? See, this is why I hate talking to you."

"Well, I didn't call you, Rachel. You called me."

"Oh. Yeah," she said, as if she'd forgotten.

Jasmine took a deep breath. She'd thought that a little bit of her intelligence would have rubbed off on Rachel after all the time they'd spent together.

"Anyway," Rachel continued, "I was calling to get some information from you."

"What kind of information? And why?"

"Well, see . . . um . . . there's this newspaper down here that wants to do an interview about us."

"For what?"

"For the American Baptist Coalition. They were impressed with me on the show and I told them to include you, too."

Jasmine's eyes narrowed. As much as Rachel lied, she really should have been more proficient at that sin by now. There was no way Rachel would ever include Jasmine in an interview. She wasn't about to share any kind of spotlight.

But in order for her to find out what Rachel was up to, Jasmine had to keep her talking. "So, what newspaper?"

"The *Baptist Herald;* it's this big paper down here in Houston."

Liar! "So why didn't they just call me?"

"Because it's a short article, and they're

43

really busy and so they asked me to ask you a couple of questions and then I'll get back to them."

Liar! "So what do they want to know?"

"Um . . . they need to know, where are your people from?"

Now Jasmine's frown was so deep, the creases in her forehead looked as if they'd been carved into her skin. "My people?"

"Yeah, your people. Your parents' family. Your ancestors."

"Well, my ancestors are from Africa."

"Ugh!" Rachel blew out an exasperated breath. "Can you just answer my question? Your people . . . aren't they from Florida?"

"Yes," Jasmine said. She and Rachel had just talked about this during the last taping of their reality show. Jasmine had been so proud to say that her father's family was from Pensacola, Florida, after Rachel had said that *her people* were from a place called Smackover, Arkansas.

Jasmine was sure Rachel had lied about that. Really? A place called Smackover.

"Whew!" Rachel exhaled. "That's what I thought."

"Why do you sound so relieved?" Jasmine asked.

"Because that's what I told the *Houston Herald*."

"I thought you said the article was for the *Baptist Herald*?"

Rachel paused. "No, you must've heard me wrong."

Pants on fire!

"Anyway, I told them that your mother and father were from Florida, so we're good," Rachel said.

"Wait. I didn't say my mother's family was from Florida."

"You . . . didn't?"

"No. My mom was born and raised in Mobile."

There was a pause. "Mobile . . . California?"

Jasmine rolled her eyes. "No, Alabama."

"Mobile . . . Alabama?"

Jasmine sighed. Why was Rachel talking like a robot?

So many quiet seconds passed that Jasmine finally said, "Hello?"

"Uh . . . yeah, I'm here. You know, I think one of my aunts lives down there."

That was her cue. It was time to end this call because the last thing she wanted to do was listen to Rachel go on about her people in Alabama, or Arkansas, or wherever they were from.

"Yeah, my aunt Doris . . ."

Jasmine froze for a moment.

"Doris . . . Jenkins," Rachel finished.

This time, a long breath of relief flowed through Jasmine's lips. "That's kinda funny. My mother's name was Doris, but Jenkins was not her last name."

More dead air. Why did this girl call her if she wasn't going to talk? "Rachel?"

"Yeah," she responded, sounding as if she was about to cry. "I gotta go, Jasmine. Talk to you later." In the next second, all Jasmine heard was the sound of silence.

She stared at her phone for a couple of seconds.

"Who was that?" Hosea asked.

"Rachel."

"What did Rafina want?" Mae Frances said, calling Rachel out of her name like she always did.

"I don't know," Jasmine said as she tucked her phone back inside her purse. Rachel was up to something, but those questions didn't give her any kind of hint at all. "She asked me a couple of questions and then hung up."

"Well, who cares about that Ralonda woman, anyway," Mae Frances said. "We have better things to talk about. Like my book. Where should I begin my story?"

Jasmine took a deep breath and exhaled. Mae Frances had never been the easiest person to get along with. But now that she thought she was about to be a star, Jasmine was sure life would be bordering on miserable.

Why couldn't her life be simple? Why couldn't Mae Frances go back to just being her friend and Rachel go back to being her enemy? Why couldn't she just have peace?

Peace . . . that's what Serena always talked about. Maybe she needed to move to Florida with Serena so that she could have peace, too. Yeah, that's what she needed to do. Because between Mae Frances and Rachel, she had a feeling that peace might be a long way away.

CHAPTER 4

RACHEL

Doris.

Jasmine's mother's name was Doris. But that was a common old person's name; surely there were hundreds of Dorises in Mobile, Alabama. Surely this was not her father's Doris.

Then what about the resemblance?

"No, no, no," Rachel muttered to herself. Because if that Doris was her dad's Doris, then that meant her father was right and Jasmine really was her . . . Rachel couldn't even form the thought in her head again.

"Hey!"

Rachel jumped at the sound of her husband's voice as he tapped on her car window. She took a deep breath and rolled it down. "Lester, you scared the bejesus out of me!"

"Umm, why are you sitting in the car talk-

48

ing to yourself?" Lester asked as he eyed her.

"I, ah, um, I . . . I, ah . . ."

He leaned in and examined the car, like he was expecting to find something to explain her strange behavior. "Are you okay?"

No. I'll never be okay again. Not if I'm related to that hag, Rachel wanted to say. Instead, she simply said, "Yeah, I was just a little distracted."

"A lot distracted." He pointed to the gear then opened her driver's-side door. "You want to put the car in park, please?"

Rachel hadn't even realized she was idling in her driveway with the car in reverse. She'd hung up the phone with Jasmine and literally hadn't moved.

Her mother's name was Doris.

Rachel adjusted the gearshift to park, rolled up her window, turned off her car, and waited on Lester so she could step out. "Sorry, I'm a little stressed."

"What's wrong?"

Before she could answer, her cell phone rang and the "Dance With My Father" ringtone reverberated through the air. Without thinking, Rachel pressed IGNORE.

Lester raised an eyebrow. "Are you really going to ignore your father's call?"

49

"Yeah, I can't deal with him right now." She was frazzled and had no idea what to say to her father.

"Rachel, what's going on?"

"I can't talk about it right now." She finally noticed his keys and that he'd pulled his car up beside hers. "Where have you been? Who's with the kids?"

"David came by right after you left. He offered to stay with them while I ran up to the church."

Her brother! Rachel needed to talk to her brother about this. She couldn't tell Lester just yet, because he would give her the whole "family is a blessing" spiel and she wasn't about to hear that, especially since learning she was related to Jasmine was a definite curse. But David would help her figure this nightmare out.

Rachel didn't say anything else to her husband as she turned and made her way up the brick walkway to their lavish seven-thousand-square-foot home. Rachel could feel her husband's eyes studying her from behind, but she ignored him as she made her way to the den.

" 'Sup, ma," Rachel's son, Jordan, said from his usual spot on the sofa. David was sitting next to him, the two of them engaged in some PlayStation football game.

50

"What did I tell you about that gangsta talk in my house?" Rachel asked.

Jordan pressed pause on the video-game controller that seemed to be permanently attached to his hands and turned to David. "Unc, *'sup* is gangsta?"

David laughed as he kept pushing the controller.

"Yes, in this house, it is," Rachel replied.

"It must be her time of the month," Jordan whispered.

If Rachel wasn't in such a mood, she'd pop her fourteen-year-old son in the mouth. He must be going through puberty because he was always making these crass comments lately. She made a memo to get him in check, but right now, her mind was somewhere else.

"Where is everyone?" she asked.

"Brooklyn and Lewis are asleep and Nia is upstairs playing that Movie Star Planet game," David said.

Lester was standing over the bar, going through a stack of mail. Rachel leaned in and whispered, "David, can I talk to you? Out back."

David narrowed his eyes at her, but didn't respond. The silence made Lester look up.

"I just need to talk to David about something real quick," she told her husband.

Lester continued studying her, but Rachel ignored him and grabbed her brother's hand, making him drop the controller to the floor. "Come on."

They walked out onto Rachel's deck and David took out his pack of Kool's. He tapped the package and removed a cigarette. It was strange seeing her brother smoke. He used to be an athletic health nut. But that had been before a bone-crippling injury had ended his NBA career before it had ever really started. He'd turned to drugs after that and it had taken him years to get clean, so she'd gladly put up with a cigarette any day.

David took his time as he lit the cigarette. He inhaled then said, "So, what's going on?"

Rachel took the Kool from her brother, took a puff, and broke into a coughing fit.

"Uh, what is that about?" he asked, snatching the nicotine stick back from her.

"I thought those things were supposed to relax your nerves," Rachel said. The smoke had flooded her nose. She squeezed her nostrils to try to remove the smell. "That is disgusting."

David took a long drag and slowly blew out circles.

"You got too much time on your hands if you've learned how to do tricks with the smoke."

"Yeah, leave the smoking to the big dogs. Again, what's going on with you, pulling me outside all secretive and stuff?"

She inhaled and began pacing the deck. "I don't know how to say this."

David stopped his cigarette in midair. "You're cheating with Bobby?"

Rachel spun around. "What? Where did that come from?"

He shrugged. "I don't know. That's the love of your life."

"He *used* to be the love of my life when I was young," Rachel snapped. "I'm a First Lady now. I wouldn't dare think of cheating on my husband."

David smirked. "Yeah, okay, li'l sis. Whatever you say. Then what's got you all worked up?" He paused, waiting. "Just say it," he snapped when she just stood there.

It's like the words wouldn't even form in her mouth. Finally, she said, "I . . . I think we may have a half sister."

"What?"

She sighed, then turned to look out over their two acres. "Yeah. Dad thinks he has a daughter."

"Daddy was creeping?" David all but yelled.

"Shut up and lower your voice," Rachel

said. She blew a frustrated breath. "No, this was before Mom."

"Rachel, what are you talking about?"

Rachel turned to face her brother head-on. "I don't know how to say this. Daddy thinks he got an old girlfriend pregnant when they were teenagers."

"How do you know this?"

"Daddy told me."

David ran his hands over his head like he was thoroughly confused. "So do we know who this half sister of ours is?"

Rachel rolled her eyes. "We don't know anything for sure. But we think it's Jasmine."

"Jasmine who?" David huffed, like he was getting irritated. Then, his eyes grew wide. "Oh my God. *Your* Jasmine?"

"She's not my Jasmine," Rachel snapped.

And then David doubled over with laughter. "You have got to be kidding me," he said, as he tried to catch his breath. "Jasmine is your sister. Ha ha ha ha!"

Rachel swatted his arm. "She would be *our* sister if this is true. Daddy thinks he got somebody named Doris from Mobile, Alabama, pregnant. He said she looked just like Jasmine. I'm thinking it's another Doris."

"Yeah, I'm thinking it's not," David said, still laughing.

"You know what? I don't know why I thought I could talk to your silly behind," Rachel snapped. She should've called Jonathan. Her other brother was much more rational than David.

"Okay, okay," David said, trying to rein in his laughter. "Sorry. But you gotta admit, that's hilarious."

Rachel folded her arms and glared at her brother. "No, I don't have to admit anything. But I do need to know for sure before I tell Daddy anything. I want to do a DNA test, but I don't know how to make it happen."

David looked like he was thinking for a minute. "I know. You remember when you were trying to find out if Lewis was Lester and Mary's son? You pulled that baby's hair straight out of his head so you could get some DNA."

David was getting some kind of perverse enjoyment in all of this. That's because he didn't know Jasmine. If he knew Jasmine like Rachel knew Jasmine, he wouldn't find anything funny.

"No," Rachel said, shaking her head. "This is just a weird coincidence. We just need to tell Daddy that Jasmine's mom's name is Eartha or something. So he can just drop this."

"So, you're just gonna lie to our dad, the minister?"

Rachel looked at him like he was crazy. "Like you've never done it." She released a heavy sigh. "I just don't want to give him false hope until we know for sure."

"Then you gotta find out for sure."

"How am I supposed to do that, David?"

He went back to puffing on his cigarette then said, "Next time you see Jasmine, pull a piece of her hair."

"For what? It's not like it's hers. It belongs to some lady in India."

"Oh, my bad." David laughed. "Just ask her to take a DNA test."

"Oh, yeah, like she's going to go for that." Jasmine and Rachel had an up-and-down relationship, and after their stint on reality TV, they'd been more down than up, so having a heart-to-heart talk would get them nowhere.

"If you want to know if the girl is our sister, just sit her down and talk to her."

"So, call her?"

David shook his head. "No, that's a conversation you need to have face-to-face. Isn't Lester going to New York next week anyway?"

Rachel had forgotten all about that. Lester was scheduled to speak at a church in

Queens. He'd asked her if she'd wanted to go and she'd said no. Maybe she needed to change her mind.

"Okay, I can do that," she said, nodding, finally feeling better about this situation. "I'll get some of Daddy's DNA, go to New York, get Jasmine's DNA. And I'll run the test without anyone being the wiser."

David flicked his cigarette on the ground, then picked it up when Rachel gave him the side-eye. "Look, I know I don't know much about Jasmine, but I doubt if you can show up on her doorstep and say, 'Hey, can I have some of your DNA?' "

"I know how to be creative, I watch *Law & Order.*"

"Rachel. Just ask the woman."

Yeah, David didn't know Jasmine at all. She was as difficult as they came. Nothing was as simple as just asking. But Rachel decided she'd figure out the *how* later. Right now, she needed to go tell her husband that she would be making the trip with him to New York, and come clean about how she needed to prove once and for all that she was absolutely not related to Jasmine Cox Larson Bush.

CHAPTER 5

JASMINE

Jasmine hung up the phone, plopped down onto the sofa, and then clapped her hands. "It's all set," she said to Hosea and Mae Frances. "We're going to Pensacola."

"So you gave Serena the dates and everything?" Hosea asked, as he looked up from his tablet.

"Yup. We're going to go before the end of July. You and me and Zaya and Jacquie will be heading down there for a two-week vacation."

"That's great, darlin'."

"Great?" Mae Frances growled. She tossed the newspaper she'd been reading onto the floor and glared at Jasmine. "I can't believe you're excited about going to Florida." She shook her head as if that was the worst idea she'd ever heard. "If you want to go away, go and see the world. Go to where I've been: Paris, Patras, or Palermo. Or if you just can't see yourself as international, visit someplace as pedestrian as Palm Springs. But Pensacola?" She shuddered.

Jasmine had to press her lips together so she wouldn't say a word. Mae Frances was acting brand-new, as if she'd always had lots of money, as if she'd always traveled the world and dined in nothing but five-star restaurants. Well, maybe it had been that way before Jasmine had come into her life. But when Jasmine had met Mae Frances back in 2006, she had been barely surviving in her East Side apartment with her ratty old furniture and bare cupboards.

But Jasmine loved the woman who had become her best friend too much to go at her like that. So all she said was, "Hosea and I have plans to take Jacquie and Zaya all around the world, but this, right here, right now, is about family."

And Jasmine meant that. Although she'd spent most of her adult life putting her lower-middle-class upbringing far in the past, being around Serena always gave her a new perspective on their family and her upbringing. As they had spent that week together reminiscing about pajama parties and Christmases, birthday gifts and Thanksgiving dinners, Jasmine finally realized that the love for and pride in her that her parents had felt was far more valuable than all the material possessions she'd longed for growing up.

She'd never have the chance to thank her parents on this side of Heaven, but she could do something they would love. She was going to take Jacquie and Zaya down to Pensacola to meet Uncle Jethro, and Uncle Ben, and Aunt Em. And their cousins Lucas, Joe-Joe, and Willard.

She wished that she could connect her children with her mother's side of the family, too, but everyone except one aunt had passed away before Jasmine was born. But, her father's family, even with their country names and countrified ways, were going to be a part of her life from now on.

Turning back to Hosea, Jasmine added, "Serena's excited, but I don't think she really believes we're going to do it."

"She doesn't think we're going to make that trip? Why not?"

"She said there aren't very many five-star hotels in Pensacola."

"Your sister knows I'm not that guy."

"And I'm not that girl, either."

Both Hosea and Mae Frances stared at Jasmine as she turned from one side to the other, looking at both of them.

"What?" Jasmine asked. "I mean, yeah, I

love staying in the nicest of places, but this isn't about luxury hotel suites or gourmet restaurants. I already said this is about family."

Hosea grinned. "And that's what's most important."

Mae Frances hmphed once again, but Jasmine ignored her as Hosea stood. "Mae Frances, it's time for us to head uptown," he said.

Jasmine frowned. "You're going to the meeting, too?"

Hosea answered for her. "Pops asked her to sit in and take notes since Mrs. Whittingham is on vacation."

"Your father wants *her* to take notes?" Jasmine asked. Turning to Mae Frances, she said, "You don't even know how to use a tablet."

"I'm going to take notes the old-fashioned way. I'm going to take dictation," she said proudly.

Jasmine had never seen Mae Frances hold a pen or a pencil in her hand, so this wasn't about taking any kind of dictation. This was all about the esteemed Reverend Samuel Bush. Mae Frances planned all kinds of ways to spend time with Hosea's father.

Not that Jasmine ever thought anything would happen between those two. First, though she didn't know her age, Jasmine was sure that her friend had at least a good decade on her father-in-law. Now, of course, age would never matter to Mae Frances. Based on the men in her life she had talked about, she'd been a cougar from way back.

But Mae Frances's fiery attitude and her take-no-prisoners manner were a clear indication that she didn't have a settling-down-with-a-pastor kind of personality, no matter how much she liked to flirt with Samuel Bush.

"Well, however you're going to take notes," Hosea said, "we better get a moving. Let me get my portfolio from the office."

As Hosea traipsed from the living room, Jasmine glanced at Mae Frances and shook her head.

"What?" Mae Frances asked.

"Why are you going to this meeting? You don't know how to take dictation."

She grinned. "I'm going to spend a little time with Papa Bush."

Jasmine rolled her eyes as Mae Frances did a little jig, sashaying around the sofa. "I'mma get me that man one day," she sang.

Jasmine was just about to tell Mae Frances not to hurt herself when the phone rang. The concierge greeted her.

"Mrs. Bush, a Rachel Adams is here to see you."

Jasmine frowned. "Rachel? What's she doing here?"

"Uh . . ." The concierge hesitated as if he had no idea how to answer that.

"I'm sorry." Now it was Jasmine who hesitated. What she really wanted to do was ask Stanley to put Rachel on the phone. It wasn't like she wanted that woman in her home, since trouble always followed her.

On the other hand, she didn't want the concierge or any of her neighbors who happened to be in the lobby to hear her and Rachel talking because there was no telling what that nut was going to say.

"Okay, Stanley. Send her up, please."

Jasmine hung up just as Hosea came back into the room. "Ready, Nama?" he asked.

"I was ready," Mae Frances said. "But now, I just might have to stay. It seems that Raquisha has popped in for a visit."

"Who?" Hosea frowned.

"She means Rachel," Jasmine said, still looking at the phone. "She's on her way up."

"Rachel Adams? That's a long way to come for a pop-in visit."

"Exactly," Jasmine said. "Rachel is up to something." She was sure of that. First there was that call last week about some bogus magazine interview and now she'd flown all the way to New York? For sure, something was up. And it was serious.

"What do you think it is?" Hosea asked.

The ringing doorbell stopped Jasmine from responding. She rose, but Mae Frances was at least ten steps ahead of her and she was through the living room, into the foyer, and at the front door first.

When she swung it open, Jasmine heard Rachel before she saw her. "Dang! Do you live with them?" Rachel asked. "I thought you were in Atlanta."

"You been here thirty seconds and got sixty questions." Mae Frances slammed the door, leaving Rachel standing in the hallway.

"Mae Frances!" Jasmine shouted as she rushed to the door. She opened it and came face-to-face with her friend, her enemy, her frenemy.

"You really need to find yourself some better friends," Rachel said as she stepped past Jasmine, not waiting for an invitation. She glared at Mae Frances.

Closing the door behind her, Jasmine asked, "Why are you here?"

Rachel turned back to her. "Dang, is that any way to say hello to a friend?"

"Let me help my wife out," Hosea said as he joined them in the circular foyer. He

64

hugged Rachel. "What brings you to New York?"

"Lester's speaking at a church in Queens this weekend."

"Wow, I didn't know that. How long are you going to be here? Maybe the four of us can get together for dinner."

Jasmine wanted to raise her hand and ask if she had a vote. Because if she did, she wouldn't be spending any time at any dinner with Rachel. Where would they go, anyway? Knowing Rachel, her favorite restaurant was probably Red Lobster.

But Jasmine wasn't going to protest too much right now. She'd put Hosea's suggestion to break bread with the Adams family to rest later. Right now, she wanted to know what Rachel was doing in her apartment.

"Well, I'd love to stay and chat," Hosea said, "but Mae Frances and I have to get going."

"Like I said, Preacher Man, I just might have to stay here and —"

"No, Nama. You're coming with me. Remember, Pops asked you to do this."

"Oh . . . yeah . . . well . . ." She eyed Rachel up and down, then said to Jasmine, "Call me if you need backup." Then she strutted out the door like she was some kind of OG.

All three of their glances followed Mae Frances; all three of them shook their heads.

Hosea kissed Jasmine's forehead and said a final good-bye to Rachel before he disappeared out the door. Jasmine locked it behind them then faced Rachel. Crossing her arms, she asked again, "Why are you here?"

"Can we at least go inside? I mean, can I sit down and get a glass of water or something?"

Jasmine stood in place; her stance was her answer. But then when Rachel took the same stance — folded her arms and glared at her — Jasmine acquiesced.

She didn't say a word as she turned, but Rachel followed her into the living room. Rachel paused at the arch. "Wow!" she whispered.

Jasmine watched as Rachel strolled into the room, clearly impressed by the grandness of it. Rachel's eyes first took in the massive glass windows, which framed the million-dollar view of Central Park. Then she scanned the room itself, her eyes finally settling on the parlor grand piano in the corner.

"Wow," she said again.

If it were any other time, Jasmine would have basked in Rachel's surprise. She'd always bragged about her seven-thousand-square-foot home on two acres. And Jasmine had always told her that was nothing but country living. Come talk to her when she could live like this with the big boys, in the big city.

But right now, Jasmine's thoughts were only on the meaning of Rachel's visit. "Rachel, have a seat so you can tell me why you're here."

Rachel sighed but did as she was told. She sat on the sofa and Jasmine lowered herself onto the chair across from her. Rachel's eyes still roamed around the massive room. And while she checked out Jasmine's home, Jasmine checked her out. She hoped that Rachel felt the heat of her stare. She didn't move her eyes away until Rachel finally faced her.

"So, what have you been up to?" Rachel asked, as if she really had just stopped by for a friendly visit.

"Are you kidding me? You asked to come into my home, you asked to sit down. Now stop playing and tell me what's up."

"Okay." She clasped her hands together and brought them up to her chin like she was about to say a quick prayer.

"I came by to ask . . . to see . . ." She stopped and then, with surprise in her tone, asked, "So, you cut your hair?"

"What?"

"The last time I saw you, your hair was longer."

There had been many times in the past when Jasmine had questioned Rachel's intelligence; now she wondered about her sanity. "If you came all the way here to talk about my hair . . ."

"I was just asking. I was thinking about cutting mine. Wearing it short, like yours. You know, going natural . . ."

"Rachel . . ." Jasmine dragged out her name like it had six syllables.

"May I have a glass of water?"

"What?"

"You know, that stuff that comes out of the faucet. May I have a glass, please?" Rachel coughed and tapped her throat. "I feel a little parched."

Jasmine raised an eyebrow, surprised that Rachel even knew that word. She wanted to tell her she'd give her a drink after she told her what was up. But Jasmine needed a moment to get away. Maybe if she had a couple of minutes, she could figure out what Rachel was up to, then throw her out.

"I'll be right back." She stood and wished that Mae Frances had stayed. Two minutes with Rachel and Mae Frances would've known what was going on.

Inside the kitchen, Jasmine grabbed a bottle of Perrier from the refrigerator, but then she paused and reflected on all the questions going through her mind. What in the world did Rachel want?

She thought back to the questions Rachel had asked her when she'd called last week. About her mother. And her father. About where her family was from. She was sure this visit was about those questions.

But what did it all mean? And why? And why was Rachel even . . .

A crash stopped Jasmine's thoughts. She put down the bottle of water before rushing into the living room. She paused. Unless Rachel was playing hide-and-seek, she was not there.

Where had that girl gone?

Jasmine stayed still until she heard more noise coming from . . . her bedroom? She ran down the long hallway, pausing in the doorway. The room was empty, but she heard the clatter of jars and bottles clanging together.

"What in the world?" She took slow steps toward her bathroom and then stopped. The sight in front of her made no sense — Rachel on her knees, surrounded by what looked like the contents of her medicine cabinet.

"What in the world . . ."

"I'm sorry," Rachel said, not even looking at Jasmine as she placed one bottle after another on the counter.

Jasmine shouted, "What are you doing?"

"I was looking for an aspirin and your cabinet came crashing down. You should really check into this. This building is old; it might be falling apart."

Without thinking, Jasmine reached down and grasped Rachel's arm. She pulled her from the floor and swung her around until she faced her.

"What are you doing? Why are you in my bedroom? Why are you going through my things? Why are you even in New York? What is going on, Rachel? What . . . is . . . going . . . on?"

"Okay." Rachel jerked her arm away from Jasmine's grasp. "I'll tell you."

"You better tell me now," Jasmine said, sure smoke was seeping from her ears. "I'm not playing any more of your games."

"I said okay." Rachel took a deep breath and then tears sprang into her eyes.

Was she getting ready to cry? Why?

"I came to New York to get your DNA."

"What?"

"Your D-N-A," she repeated. "I didn't want you to know, but I have to have your DNA for a test."

Jasmine shook her head as if she were trying to get Rachel's words to compute. "What kind of test? And why?"

"A paternity test. Because the worst thing in the world could be happening. Every bad thing that I've ever done could be coming back down on me. I could be cursed."

"What in the hell are you talking about?"

"I'm cursed, Jasmine. At least, I will be if I find out this is true."

"If you don't tell me right now what's going on . . ."

"You could be my sister!" Rachel cried. "You could be my sister!" she shouted again. Then she rushed to the commode and leaned over the toilet as if just saying those words made her sick to her stomach.

CHAPTER 6

RACHEL

Growing up, Rachel had always prayed for a sister. When her brothers were torturing her, she'd bargained with Jesus. She'd be good all the time if she could get a sister. When she had to play with her Barbies all by herself, she'd prayed harder. But, nothing. Until now.

God sure had a strange sense of humor.

"Are you sure you're okay?"

Rachel was lying back on Jasmine's sofa, a wet towel across her face. She knew this whole situation was nauseating, but had it really made her physically sick?

"Yeah, I'm good," she finally managed to say as she sat up and removed the towel. "I guess I just ate something bad."

Jasmine stared at Rachel, studying her. Their eyes met and Rachel's heart warmed. Gone was her anger over Rachel's snooping; gone was the usual attitude, Jasmine simply looked concerned — like a concerned big sister.

That thought snapped Rachel back to reality.

"Sorry about that in there," she said, pointing down the hallway to the bathroom. "I just . . . I was . . . um . . ." She took a deep breath. This was no time for games, shenanigans, or smart remarks — she had to shoot straight. Rachel had tried her best to mature over the years and while Jasmine had a way of bringing out the worst in her, now was not the time. "Look, Jasmine, I need to talk to you. Woman to woman."

"No," Jasmine said, slowly, as if she was still concerned about Rachel, "you need to talk to a doctor because you're acting real strange — snooping around my house, throwing up, and talking crazy."

"I'm not talking crazy."

"Umm, yeah, you are." Jasmine folded her arms across her chest. "Talking about I could be your sister. What does that even mean? I'm barely your friend."

Rachel managed a half smile. It wasn't often that Jasmine acknowledged they were friends. As much as they fought, Rachel had her moments when she really enjoyed being around Jasmine. The bickering was just who they were. They taunted each other, called each other names, argued incessantly, but when either of their backs were against the wall, they stepped up for each other. When Rachel had gotten caught up in a murder investigation in Chicago, Jasmine had been right there by her side the whole time. When Mary had tried to regain custody of Lewis, her biological child who Rachel had adopted, Jasmine had stepped in to help Rachel keep it together. And while they could get ugly with each other, they wouldn't stand for someone else doing it. It was like they were . . . sisters.

"Rachel, why are you just staring at me?" Jasmine snapped, the edge back in her voice. "You are creeping me out. Now, you'd better tell me what's going on."

"Can I have that water?"

"We don't have any more," Jasmine said, glaring at her.

"Please?" Rachel said. "Then I'll tell you everything."

Jasmine blew a frustrated breath then said, "Fine," before spinning and stomping out of the room.

Rachel sat, gathering her thoughts, trying to come up with the perfect words. A part of her wanted to get up and run, pretend she'd never been here, or come up with some excuse; but now her curiosity was piqued just like her father's had been. On the plane ride here, Lester had been supportive of her mission, encouraging her and telling her she was doing the right thing by going to get answers. In fact, he'd wanted to come with her, but Rachel wanted to do this alone. So, she'd left Lester in the hotel room.

Now she needed to do what she'd come to do.

"Here," Jasmine said, walking back in and handing Rachel a green bottle.

"Umm, Perrier?" Rachel said, taking the bottle and examining it. "Seriously? You don't have any Aquafina or something?"

"I just grabbed a bottle of water."

"But this stuff is nasty."

"Rachel," Jasmine said, her voice stern like she was somebody's mama.

"Okay, okay," Rachel said, unscrewing the top. "I'll drink your bougie water." She took a long gulp and grimaced at the fizzy taste. "Ugh, this stuff is disgusting."

"Rachel, if you don't —"

"Fine." Rachel set the bottle down, then motioned to the wingback chair across from her. "Have a seat, please."

"I don't want to sit down."

Rachel fought back her snappy retort and simply said, "Okay, but I think you'll want to sit for this." Another deep breath, then she blurted out the words. "I think you may be my sister. My half sister."

Jasmine narrowed her eyes in Rachel's direction, then managed a terse laugh. "Really, Rachel? That's not even funny."

Rachel looked at Jasmine, her eyes relaying just how serious she was. "And I'm not laughing. Your mother is Doris Young from Alabama, correct?"

The smile disappeared from Jasmine's face and she slid down into the seat she'd previously declined.

Rachel continued. "I know this sounds crazy — shoot, I swore my dad was crazy when he told me. But my dad, well, he thinks . . . he thinks your Doris was his Doris. His girlfriend, his first love."

"Well, your dad is mistaken," Jasmine said matter-of-factly.

"That's the same thing I said," Rachel replied. "But he's adamant."

"No disrespect, but maybe your father is getting dementia or something."

Any other time, that comment would've pissed Rachel off, but since it had been Rachel's initial thought as well, she gave Jasmine a pass.

"I mean, I've met your dad," Jasmine continued. "Remember, in Los Angeles at the American Baptist Convention? Surely he would've said something then."

"But you only met him briefly," Rachel said. It was Lester who had initially pointed that out, at the same time reminding Rachel that her father had been exhausted from traveling, so he wasn't fully focused in Los Angeles. He'd even left the election results meeting early because he wasn't feeling well, so his contact with Jasmine had been minimal. "It wasn't until my dad started watching our reality show that he got a really good look at you. He watched it over and over and I never understood why. Until he finally told me. He said you looked so much like his first love. Doris."

Silence briefly filled the room, then Jasmine said, "So, I look like someone your father used to know."

Rachel reached into her purse and pulled out the tattered photo she'd swiped from her father's house. She held it out in Jasmine's direction.

Jasmine froze at the sight of the photo. "W-why do you have a picture of my mother?" She snatched the picture and studied it. "Where did you steal this from?"

"Turn it over," Rachel said. "I can tell you what it says because I've read it a thousand times." Jasmine turned the picture over as

Rachel recited the words she'd committed to memory. "To Simon, forever my love. Doris."

More silence. Rachel gave Jasmine a moment to stew in her disbelief before she said, "We can solve this — either confirm it or shut it down."

"How?"

"By going on Maury," Rachel replied and Jasmine's head shot up.

"I'm kidding, trying to lighten the mood." She scooted toward the edge of the sofa. "Jasmine, this is a shocker for both of us. And my dad wants nothing more than to know the truth. He says not only do you look like your mother, but you also bear a striking resemblance to his grandmother. He did the math and he's convinced you're his."

"I'm my father's child." Jasmine's tone was firm, like this wasn't even open for discussion. "Even if your father knew my mother, I come from Charles Cox."

"I hope that is the case, and I hope my father is wrong," Rachel replied. "But there is only one way to know for sure. I brought some of my father's hair." She pulled a small baggie out of her purse. Inside the bag was a hairbrush. "I already called a testing facility in Manhattan and they can do it. I just need your DNA and we can settle this once and for all." When Jasmine didn't reply, Rachel added, "I mean, I want to know. I can deal with being your friend, but can you imagine if we were really sisters?" She laughed. Jasmine didn't. And the look on her face told Rachel that Jasmine was still in shock. It wasn't until that moment that Rachel realized this was bigger than just knowing whether the two of them were related. For Jasmine, finding out Simon Jackson was her father would mean that her life as she knew it had been built on a lie.

Now, Rachel knew, they didn't have a choice. They had to find out the truth.

CHAPTER 7

JASMINE

No!

That was the only word that filled Jasmine's mind.

No!

It reverberated straight through to her soul.

No!

That's what she'd told Rachel when she'd kept talking about some stupid paternity test to prove some ridiculous theory about the two of them being sisters.

No was what she'd kept saying to Rachel, right before she told her to get out of her apartment and never come back.

And then *no* was what she'd just told Hosea after he'd come home and she'd blurted out Rachel's absurd story.

"Sisters!" Hosea said. He laughed . . . at first. But then he watched her pacing back and forth in front of him, her heavy steps leaving imprints in the plush carpet.

It was her glare that made his smile fade fast. "Sisters?" he repeated.

"No!" And then she repeated the word again when Hosea just sat on the sofa, pensive, his hands folded beneath his chin as if he were giving credence to such a thing.

"No! She's not my sister! Stop thinking that!"

"It sounds insane," Hosea said. "But why would Rachel come here and say that?"

"Because she's batshit crazy. And she takes jokes too far."

Hosea shook his head and then he was the one who said *no.* "She wouldn't come all the way to New York to tell a joke. There's got to be more to this."

Jasmine whipped her head from side to side. And with every part of her body, she was still saying *no* when Hosea stood from the sofa and wrapped his arms around her.

"It's going to be all right," he said as if she needed comfort.

But she didn't need him to tell her it was going to be all right, because there was nothing wrong. The only wrong thing in her life was Rachel — and the fact that she'd let that woman inside her apartment. She should've just left her standing in the hall when Mae Frances slammed the door in her face.

"So what are you going to do about this?" Hosea asked.

"About what?"

"About what Rachel said."

"What do you want me to do? Have her committed to some mental hospital?" She plopped down onto the couch. "Her sanity is her husband's problem, not mine."

"You know that's not what I mean. I'm just asking, are you going to check out what she said? Are you going to talk to Rachel some more? Maybe talk to her father?"

Jasmine stared at her husband as if he'd just sprouted two heads. Then she moved to the edge of the sofa, and with hard eyes she glared at Hosea. "Listen to what you're saying." She paused. "Are you really saying that my father is not my father?" And with just her stance, she gave him a warning.

"Of course I'm not saying that . . ."

"Well then, there's no need for me to talk to Rachel, or her father. There's no need for me to talk to anyone."

Doubt was etched all over Hosea's face. "I don't think Rachel would lie about this."

"She was born a liar. She'd lie about the day of the week if there was something in it for her."

"Maybe she has some of the facts wrong,

82

maybe something is confused, but lying about being your sister? Why would she do that?"

"It's either a lie or she's trying to punk me. Either way, I'm not playing along."

"But suppose . . ."

Jasmine jumped up and blew out an exasperated breath. "Don't you get it? She made this up to get to me." She held up her hand, stopping him from interrupting her. "Think about all the things she's done to me in the past." Jasmine counted on her fingers. "She hired that stripper to embarrass us at the American Baptist Coalition Conference when you were running for president, then she kidnapped Jacquie . . ."

"She didn't . . ."

Jasmine spoke over his words. "She showed up to Oprah's show and locked me in that room." She shook her head. "This is just another middle school trick from a woman who never progressed mentally out of the sixth grade. And I'm not going to play into it. I'm going to ignore her and if she ever has the audacity to come around me again, I'm going to give her such a beating that . . ."

"Jasmine!"

"What?"

"If you don't believe Rachel, fine. Ignore

her. But all this other talk . . ."

She waved her hand. "Okay, maybe I won't beat her down."

Hosea gave her a half smile. "That's my darlin'."

"But I don't want to talk about this anymore."

"All right."

"And I don't want you to ever mention it again," she said, pointing her finger at him.

"Okay."

"I just want to pretend that Rachel Jackson Adams never came here today. In fact, I want to pretend that we never met; really, let's act like she was never born. She no longer exists to me. In fact . . ." Jasmine grabbed her cell, scrolled down to where she had Rachel's name, then pressed DELETE. "Now she's gone forever," she said, holding up the phone for Hosea to see.

Hosea pressed his lips together and Jasmine could tell her husband had something he wanted to say. She didn't want to hear it, didn't want him to say another word about how there was more to this. But curiosity made her ask, "What?"

"I'm just thinking, if you think this isn't true, why are you protesting so much?"

Her glare made him hold up his hands. "Okay, I got it. No more talk about Rachel . . . or this. So . . . let's go pick up the kids," he said, making a quick change of subject. "Remember, we're taking them to Shake Shack tonight."

"I forgot, but that's good. That'll be fun," Jasmine said, though there was not a bit of cheer in her voice.

She'd banned Rachel from existence, but as the hours passed, she couldn't get thoughts of her or her words out of her mind. Not even her children with their chatter and their laughter could take Jasmine's thoughts away from Rachel.

She kept going back to the scene in her apartment, to the picture, to the words Rachel had spoken. And it was as if she were trying to interpret another language.

Through the hamburgers and shakes they had for dinner, through returning home, through getting her children ready for bed, Rachel and her cockamamie story remained with her.

Even when Jasmine kissed Hosea good night and closed her eyes as he held her, Rachel wouldn't go away. She was waiting for Jasmine, right there in her dreams.

I think you may be my sister. My half sister.

Over and over, Rachel taunted her.

I think you may be my sister. My half sister.

She kept saying it, at first serious. Then

her tone filled with laughter.

I think . . . ha ha ha . . . you may be . . . ha ha ha . . . my sister!

"No!" Jasmine sprang up in bed, her arms flailing as she reached for Rachel's throat. She pressed her thumbs as hard as she could against her skin. If she could just kill her, that would shut her up!

"Jasmine!" Hosea shouted, grabbing her hands.

Jasmine blinked, then blinked again. In the darkness her eyes adjusted. And she saw her hands, around her husband's neck.

"Oh my God!" Jasmine exclaimed, pulling back. "Babe, I'm sorry."

Hosea clicked on the light, then massaged his neck.

"Are you all right?" she asked.

"I don't know." He coughed. "I might never be the same."

"I'm so sorry!" she cried.

"Darlin', I was just playing with you. I'm okay, don't worry about it." It was the distress on her face that made Hosea pull her into his arms. "It was only a dream," he said. Then he held her as they lay down together. And in her ear he whispered, "It was only a dream," over and over again.

But even as she settled down, and even as she heard the soft snore of her husband returning to sleep, Jasmine wouldn't close her eyes. Because what Hosea said wasn't true. That hadn't been a dream. It was a nightmare. The worst nightmare she'd ever had. And if she closed her eyes, she might have that nightmare again.

No, she couldn't let that happen. Even if she had to stay awake for the rest of her life, she was never going to let Rachel Jackson Adams invade her sleep again.

CHAPTER 8

RACHEL

Some things are best left buried.

Rachel remembered her mother used to always say that, but she'd never really given it much credence. Until now.

Regardless of whether Jasmine was her half sister or not, Rachel was now just fine with that information staying buried. After Jasmine threw her out like she was common trash, Rachel was livid. Jasmine had the nerve to call her a liar and literally push her out the door. As if Rachel would lie about something like that. As if she really *wanted* to be related to Jasmine.

Nope. As far as Rachel was concerned, that move was the final straw and her frenemy had officially reverted to being her outright enemy.

The question now was: what in the world would she tell her father?

"Sister Adams, you hear me?"

The sound of the elderly woman raising her voice snapped Rachel out of her thoughts. Rachel had zoned out ten minutes ago when the woman first began rambling on and on. They were in the dining hall of the church for a private reception following Lester's sermon.

"I'm sorry, what did you say?" Rachel replied. She really hadn't meant to be rude, but the woman's incessant babbling was nerve-racking.

"I was just saying that Pastor Adams really showed out today." The woman glanced over at Lester, who was talking with some of the church elders. She had a totally inappropriate look on her face — like if she was thirty years younger, Rachel would definitely have to check her. But this woman and her sagging, wrinkled skin and snow-white hair was no threat. Besides, Rachel had bigger issues taking up space in her head.

"I mean, we got to get him back here soon because he is definitely God's messenger," the woman continued.

Rachel nodded, although she couldn't tell you two words Lester had said during his sermon. She could tell he'd done a good job, though, based on all the hooting and hollering going on in the sanctuary. Lester had come a long way from the red-mop-headed little boy who had a crush on her. Being a pastor had given him confidence. Being the president of the American Baptist Coalition had given him *juice*. And although sometimes she longed for the old Lester, the one who did anything she said, there was something about the confident Lester that she found attractive. He could check her with ease, yet give her just enough space to do her thing. Some people felt he was still a pushover, but she liked that he had found a balance.

"Just know that you all are welcome at Greater Macedonia anytime," the woman said, still looking at Lester like he was the gravy and she was the biscuit.

"Thank you so much for having us, but I must get going." Rachel flashed an apologetic smile and quickly made her escape. She was so ready to get out of there and get home. When Jasmine had put her out, Rachel had wanted to hop on the first thing smoking and get home. But Lester had managed to calm her down and convince her to attend the service. Still, she was leaving this evening on a five o'clock flight and she was set to go.

"Excuse me, may I steal my husband away?" Rachel said to the group of men standing around Lester. "Just for a moment."

They all nodded as Rachel draped her arm through Lester's and led him to a corner.

"Are you okay?" he asked, pushing a tendril of hair out of her face.

"I am," Rachel replied. "I just want to go. And the car should be here."

"Are you sure you don't want me to come back with you? I know you're trying to act like this whole thing isn't bothering you, but I can see in your eyes that it is."

She feigned a smile. "I'm good. Just tired and need to figure out what to say to my father. But hopefully I'll come up with something between now and the time I get home."

"Well, you call me if you need anything and I'll see you on Tuesday." He leaned in and kissed her lightly on the lips. "Love you and make sure you let me know you got on your flight."

Ten minutes later, Rachel was settled in the backseat of the town car, replaying the whole scene at Jasmine's. Her cell phone vibrated, jolting her out of her thoughts. Rachel smiled when she saw her brother's name pop up on the screen.

"Hello," she said.

"Hey, li'l sis," Jonathan replied. "I was just

calling to check on you. See how everything went. David filled me in and I was really worried about you. I can only imagine what you're feeling."

Rachel released a heavy sigh. Jonathan was much more levelheaded than David and she really could talk to him about what she was truly feeling. But what was the use? Jasmine had refused the test. And now they were officially no longer friends.

"What did you find out?" Jonathan asked when she didn't say anything.

"I found out we aren't going to find out anything," Rachel finally replied. "Jasmine is being her usual difficult self and it's just not even worth it."

"So, you couldn't get her to take the DNA test?"

She slid her Gucci sunglasses on. Her *real* Gucci sunglasses. A few years ago, it would've been nothing for Rachel to wear some knockoffs. But that was one thing she'd picked up from Jasmine, how she was worthy of the real thing (even though she still bought her designer stuff at a discount, unlike Jasmine, who paid exorbitant costs for everything). "Nope, but it's for the best anyway," Rachel replied. She needed to stop letting her mind wander to anything positive Jasmine had brought to her life, since she would no longer be in it. "I need to just shut this down with Daddy and move on."

"You know he's going to want to talk to her and convince her to take the test himself."

"I know. That's why I'm thinking of telling him that we took the DNA test and confirmed that he was not her father."

"So you're going to lie?"

"I'm not going to lie. I just want to protect Daddy. Jasmine doesn't care about anybody but herself."

"I imagine this can't be easy on her," Jonathan said.

"Yeah," Rachel acknowledged. As mad as she was, and as much as she didn't want to admit it, she hadn't lost sight of that fact. "I know. I actually get that. If she turns out to be Dad's child, there would be so many questions. Her whole life would've been a lie."

"What are you going to do?"

"I don't know." Rachel felt some of her anger seeping away. What would she do if someone showed up talking about Simon not being her father? She'd probably throw them out of her house, too.

"How are you taking it?" Jonathan asked.

She shrugged like he could see her, then when she realized he couldn't, she said,

"I'm cool. I wanted to know for sure, but she threw me out of her house, and after the ugly way she acted, I don't even care."

He laughed. "You know you care. But I'm proud of you. The old Rachel would've been ready to turn things up if someone threw her out."

"I know, right?"

"I really am proud of you."

"Thank you, Jonathan." Rachel leaned back in her seat and smiled. She might not have any sisters, but her brothers had always shown her unconditional love. Even when they were bickering, they had her back. Her whole family — even her crazy extended family — was full of love. If Jasmine didn't want to be a part of that, then it was her loss.

CHAPTER 9

JASMINE

Jasmine yawned as the plane made its final descent.

"Flight attendants, prepare the cabin for landing."

There was no beckoning skyline as she glanced out the window. Only the tallest building, the fifteen-story Crowne Plaza Hotel, shone welcoming lights. The sight of Pensacola made Jasmine yawn once again.

It was because she hadn't slept in three days that she was making this trip. Truly, Jasmine felt like she hadn't really closed her eyes in seventy-two hours, catching short naps, a couple of hours at a time. But trying to stay awake hadn't helped. Even with her eyes open, she had nightmares. Rachel wouldn't go away, and neither would her nonsensical words.

Last night she'd decided she had to do something, so she'd begun to think about

95

taking this trip. Because Serena would call Rachel all kinds of crazy, too. She wouldn't be like Hosea, who had actually given a moment's credence to Rachel and whatever scam she was trying to pull.

She hadn't called her sister to tell her she was coming, though. Hadn't said a word since she'd made the final decision this morning and hadn't even purchased a ticket until she'd arrived at the airport this evening.

That wasn't a concern. She wasn't worried about Serena being away or anything. Her sister had such a mundane life: she went to work and came home. There wasn't much more than that since her daughters had decided to stay on campus at Hampton University for the summer.

Jasmine couldn't imagine how boring her sister's life had to be without her daughters and without a man. Even though she had tried to hook Serena up a few years ago, it seemed Serena hardly dated, never getting over the death of her husband all those years ago.

So, she knew her sister would be home — almost waiting for her — ready to tell Jasmine all she wanted and everything she needed to hear.

The moment the wheels touched the

tarmac, Jasmine switched her phone from airplane mode and texted Hosea: *just landed. will call later. love u.*

Two seconds later, his text came back: *love u more. b safe, b well.*

Jasmine sighed. Safe she was. But well? She wouldn't be well until she told Serena and then the two of them figured out Rachel's angle. That was what concerned Jasmine the most. What was Rachel up to with this asinine story?

As soon as the seat belt sign clicked off, Jasmine jumped from her first-class seat, grabbed her carry-on, and maneuvered through the Pensacola airport. Her steps were strong and determined as her thoughts stayed on her mission. Once she figured this out with Serena, she was going to war. Rachel Jackson Adams had never seen what Jasmine had in store for her. She was going to make that trollop pay for her sleepless nights.

Jasmine jumped into the first cab in the line and as the car pulled away from the airport, her thoughts took a break and she allowed her mind to wander. It was only a little after nine, but it easily could have been the middle of the night in Pensacola with the way every business was shut and every street was deserted. As the cab zipped by the darkened storefronts, Jasmine marveled at the fact that she'd actually lived here for two whole years.

Pensacola was her bridge between her younger days in Los Angeles and her grown-woman life in New York. This small town had served its purpose for her, though. She'd moved here searching for what? She did not know. She'd found it, or rather, she'd found Him. She'd accepted the Lord here, though there was little evidence of a change in her life at first. And then she'd moved to New York in search of something else. And she'd found him — Hosea Bush.

God had saved her soul; Hosea had saved her heart.

Now she was living a queen's life, with a prominent husband and two children who could already grace the cover of any top-selling magazine. Maybe that was why Rachel had come to toss a torpedo into the middle of her nirvana. Maybe that's what jealousy and envy did to people who didn't have many accomplishments or much of a life of their own.

She sighed. Couldn't she keep her thoughts away from Rachel for even ten minutes? It was a relief when the car began to slow its roll as the driver eased in front of the house that had been passed down from her grandfather, to her father, and now to her and Serena. All the lights were out, even though it seemed a bit too early for Serena to be asleep.

"That'll be fourteen dollars," the driver said.

She tossed him a twenty and slid out of the cab. Even when the car moved away, Jasmine stood in the darkness, staring at the house that held so many memories.

Here was where she'd spent most of her childhood summers, with her grandparents who cared more about chores than letting children have their fun. Here was where her family's idea of a great evening was sitting in front of the television and playing a game of dominoes.

Jasmine had wanted to get so far away from this place that when their father had died, she'd told her sister to take her name off the deed.

"You can have this house," Jasmine had told Serena right before she moved to New York. "I want no part of this."

Serena had shaken her head. "You say that now, but this house belongs to both of us. This is our family legacy . . . the Cox legacy."

Jasmine had scoffed then, but as she stood staring at the two-story, block-shaped house that looked like all the other homes on this street, the memory of her sister's words had never been more comforting.

Yes, this was her father's legacy. *Her* father. She was a Cox.

She moved toward the house and stood at the top of the steps right in front of the door. She placed her bag down on the wooden planks and let more memories flood her mind.

She thought about how her father had run up and down this street with her one Christmas when they'd come to Florida and her grandparents had given her a bicycle (albeit used) as a gift.

She recalled the summer before she went to college, and how her father had sent her five hundred dollars (more money than he'd given her in all her years of life combined) and told her to go on a shopping spree because clothes were cheaper in Florida and he wanted her to be the best-dressed girl on the UCLA campus.

And she remembered when she'd moved here from Los Angeles (following her father and sister who had relocated years before) how he'd welcomed her broken soul with arms that stayed open.

"You made a terrible mistake," he'd said once she'd told him the real reason she'd

left LA — that she had slept with her best friend's husband. *"But terrible mistakes don't make you a terrible person unless you keep doing that same mistake over and over."*

Then he had held her and loved her until she came back to life. Jasmine had no doubt that only a father, a real father, could help a daughter rise from the ashes that had been her life back then.

"I am a Cox," she whispered. "I am a Cox." She made that her mantra, repeating it over and over, faster and faster, until the words meshed together forming a senseless stream. And then, without any warning, she burst into tears.

Only seconds passed before light hit the porch, shining bright on Jasmine as if she stood in the center of a stage. She heard Serena's voice before she looked up and saw her.

"What in the world? Jasmine?" Serena pushed open the screen door and at the same time tightened her robe. "What in the world?" she repeated. "Come in. What are you doing here?"

"I . . . I . . ." Jasmine sobbed.

As if she were the elder, Serena wrapped her arms around her sister's waist and led her inside to the sofa. Once Jasmine sat, Serena went back to the porch for Jasmine's bag before returning to her sister.

Sitting down, Serena pulled Jasmine's hands away from her face. "What in the world is going on? What are you doing here?"

Jasmine's shoulders shook as she whimpered.

"Is it Hosea? Oh my God!" Serena held her hand against her chest. "Is something wrong with the kids?"

Jasmine shook her head, then took a few breaths before she answered. "No, everything is fine."

"Clearly everything is *not* fine. Because look around . . . you're in Pensacola. Unless you were headed to Jamaica and you got off at the wrong stop."

Jasmine's lips curled into the tiniest of smiles. "Didn't I tell you that I was going to come and visit?"

"Um, yeah. You and the kids and Hosea . . . next month."

Before Jasmine could explain more, she heard the sound of slow footsteps coming down the stairs. Now Jasmine's smile widened. She hadn't expected her nieces to be home and as she waited for one or both to appear, she tried to remember the last time she'd seen them. It was a sin and a shame that she couldn't recall.

But then Jasmine's smile collapsed when the legs that descended were those of a man. And then she saw the rest of him. A grown man. Wrapped in a bathrobe, just like Serena's.

"Is everything okay, baby?" the man asked, as he glanced at Serena.

Jasmine's eyes became the size of silver dollars as the man stepped into the living room.

"Carl?" Jasmine said his name as if she were asking a question. Her eyes moved from the man who had been her coworker when she lived in Pensacola to her sister. But no matter how many times Jasmine looked back and forth between the two of them, she could not get this picture to compute.

He nodded. "What's up?"

What's up? Somebody needed to say more to her than "what's up"!

Carl asked, "Is everything okay?"

Jasmine felt like she should be the one asking the questions. "I didn't know you and Serena were still seeing each other." Her words were meant for Carl, even though her eyes were on Serena.

"Uh, yeah. I don't know why you would think anything else. From the moment I met Serena, I knew she was the one."

"Awww, baby."

Awww, baby?

Thoughts of sleepless nights and why she'd made the trek to Pensacola skipped right out of Jasmine's mind.

Carl said, "Is everything all right down here?"

"Yeah," Serena answered. Then she looked at Jasmine. "I think we're good."

Jasmine nodded, just because she couldn't think of anything to say.

"Okay, well, I'll be upstairs if you need me."

"I'll be up soon, baby," Serena said before she blew Carl a kiss.

Then with a mere nod to Jasmine, Carl trotted up the steps. Jasmine's eyes followed him until she couldn't see him anymore and then she turned to her sister, staring at her as if she'd never seen her before.

"Really?" Jasmine said. "You're involved with this man?"

"Uh . . . yeah. Why would you have a problem with that when you're the one who introduced us?"

"I introduced you, but that was how many years ago? I didn't know this was still going on."

"I never told you that we stopped, did I? We're still going on and going strong."

"And you never told me" — Jasmine leaned over and flipped up the hem of Serena's robe — "that all this was going on." She shook her head. "You? The church girl? And isn't he a church boy?"

"Don't get it twisted. We still love the Lord. It's just that it had been so long." Serena shook her head. "I'm telling you, with Carl I understand that scripture about the spirit being willing but this danggone flesh . . ." She shrugged. "But we'll be getting married soon."

Jasmine leaned back and raised a single eyebrow. "Really? Without me knowing about it?"

"Please, you're my big sister. You will always know about everything."

Big sister!

Serena's words stopped cold the interrogation that Jasmine planned. And those tears she'd been fighting welled up in her eyes once again.

"Okay, you're going to have to tell me — what in the world is going on?"

"It's Rachel. Rachel Adams. She's come up with some crazy story."

"What kind of story could drive you to tears and to Pensacola?"

Jasmine inhaled, then exhaled the words: "Rachel says that I'm her sister; that her father is really my father." She paused and waited for Serena to jump up and exclaim her outrage at the complete ridiculousness of that statement.

But all Serena said was "Go on. Tell me what she said to you."

Maybe she's in shock. So Jasmine told her sister the story of how Rachel showed up at her home, tore down her medicine cabinet, and then told this psycho story of her father and their mother.

As Jasmine spoke, she waited for that moment when Serena would laugh, wave her hands, and tell Jasmine she was right — Rachel was some kind of psychotic sociopath who got a kick out of playing with other people's feelings.

But all Serena did was sit there and listen, pensive, the same way Hosea had listened the first time she told him. Serena listened as if she were giving credence to what Rachel had said, too.

She just needs to hear more. So Jasmine told more, and the more she told, the more she expected her sister to jump up, cry foul, and demand that they fly to Houston right then to give Rachel the beatdown of her life.

But Serena just sat on the edge of the sofa, listening . . . and thinking. She said nothing, letting Jasmine get all the way to the end.

And then, there was silence.

With a frown that was much more about Serena's reaction than the story itself, Jasmine said, "Isn't this all crazy?" Maybe she needed to give Serena a hint of what she was supposed to say. "Can you believe Rachel?"

Now was the moment. Serena was supposed to scream out her righteous indignation. But still, all Serena gave her sister was silence.

Jasmine jumped up. "You've got to be kidding me!" she said as she stomped back and forth in front of the sofa. "Are you saying you believe her? Are you saying that Daddy wasn't my daddy?"

"I haven't said a word." Serena held up her hands. "I was just listening."

"But it's the way you were listening. Like you believe . . ."

"So when are you going to have the test?" Serena asked.

Jasmine stopped moving and stared at her sister. But there was no anger in her eyes; it was almost as if Jasmine felt sorry for Serena. As if she were watching her sister lose her mind. "You know that's ridiculous, right?"

Serena gave a half shrug, moving only one shoulder. "I'm just sayin', why not have the test?"

"Why would I waste time and money on a lie?"

"I'm just thinking that you should have the test."

"For. What. Purpose?"

"For the purpose of knowing for sure."

"I know for sure."

Serena's eyes were filled with sadness as she glanced up at her sister and held her gaze.

Slowly Jasmine lowered herself back onto the sofa. "What? What do you know?"

This time Serena shrugged for real. "I don't know anything. It's just that this sounds surprising, but not crazy to me."

"So you think we're not sisters?"

"That's not what I'm saying because no matter what, that bond can never be broken. And anyway, Rachel is saying that Mama was your mother, right? But . . ."

Jasmine swallowed hard, as if she were afraid to ask the next question. "Do you know something? You need to tell me."

Now it was Serena's turn to give a hard swallow, as if she wanted to hold back the words. Finally she said, "I've just been wondering for a long, long time."

"About what? About me?"

"No, not you. About Mama. It kinda started when she passed away. Remember when Aunt Virginia came to LA for the funeral?"

Jasmine nodded.

"Well, right before she left, she gave me this box that she said belonged to Mama. And in there were a bunch of papers, like some old report cards and some letters and stuff like that." When Jasmine frowned, Serena said, "And there was her birth certificate, too."

"Okay."

"Well, when Mama died, I thought she was forty-seven. But according to her birth certificate, she was only thirty-seven."

Jasmine shrugged. "So? She lied about her age. That just makes me my mother's child because I used to lie about my age all the time."

"Yeah, but most people shave ten years off, not add ten years."

Jasmine paused and thought about the numbers. "Well, that's impossible anyway because I was twenty when Mama passed away. She couldn't have been thirty-seven." She waved her hand. "That birth certificate was wrong; they make mistakes like that all the time."

"But it wasn't just the birth certificate," Serena said. "When I saw that, I started thinking about things I used to think about as a little girl. Like why we never knew any of Mama's people."

"We knew Aunt Virginia."

"Yeah, but she was the only one. And she wasn't really related to Mama. Remember we found that out? She was the lady who used to watch her when she was little, a friend of Mama's mother."

"Well, everyone else died."

"That's what Mama said."

"And you don't believe her?"

"It's just that *everybody* died? Her mother, her father, her brothers, her sisters . . ."

"Mama was an only child."

"That's what Mama said."

"I don't know why this sounds strange to you. Lots of people have small families."

"Yeah, small, but nonexistent? There has to be some relative left. Somebody. Someplace. Didn't it ever bother you as a child that we only spent time with Daddy's family?"

Jasmine answered her sister, but only in her head. That never bothered her because she never even wanted to spend time with her father's people. So why in the world would she think about going to Alabama?

Serena said, "I just used to wonder where Mama's family was. And once Mama died, it made me wonder even more. I wanted to ask Daddy about it, but I was only fifteen and I didn't really know what to do."

"So, why didn't you say something later on?"

"I don't know. I was just gonna let it all go away. But now . . ."

"Well, I don't see what any of your questions have to do with me."

Serena waited a moment before she said, "I went through those papers and I think this family has some secrets that were supposed to die with Mama and Daddy. But, for some reason, they've come alive now."

"And you think the secret is that I'm a bastard child," Jasmine said, as if she were accusing Serena.

"No, because you're not. No matter what comes out of this, Charles Cox was your father. He loved you; he raised you; he was your daddy."

"Exactly. He was my daddy. I was . . . I am his daughter." And then a memory hit her. Of a time when she was about six, standing in the kitchen making cookies with her mother . . .

"When we finish, can we take some cookies to the baby?" Jasmine asked.

111

Doris Cox looked down at her daughter and smiled. "Your sister is too little to eat cookies. And anyway, these are for you 'cause you're my extra-special baby."

"But I'm not a baby anymore and you have a new baby."

"Your sister is special, too. But you'll always be extra special to me." Then she kissed the top of Jasmine's head. "You will always be my extraspecial, very special Mama's baby."

"And I'm Daddy's baby, too, right?"

Her mother smiled again. "Don't tell anybody, but you're Mama's baby more. You're Mama's special gift from God . . ."

Over the years, her mother had often said those words — that she was a special gift from God — but to Jasmine those were just the loving sentiments of a wonderful mother who adored her firstborn. But could there be another reason behind those words?

"All I'm saying" — Serena's words dragged Jasmine back to this place where she didn't want to be — "is go ahead, have the test, let's put this to rest."

"An unnecessary waste of funds."

"Then have them pay for it, but do it so you can have your questions answered."

"I don't have any questions."

"Yes. You do. Or else you wouldn't have gotten on a plane and flown three hours to see me for validation."

Slowly, Jasmine closed her eyes and pushed back the new tears she felt forming. Of course, Serena was right. She did have questions and she hated that she did. But she had questions because she couldn't figure out Rachel's motive. And since she couldn't figure that out, she had to face the fact that maybe Rachel had brought this absurdness to her because there was some semblance of truth in her story.

"Just do the DNA test," Serena urged. Even though her voice was softer, her tone was more insistent.

In her head, Jasmine still said no, but in her heart, she knew she had to do it. She had to get those questions answered. Those questions that she hadn't allowed to seep from her heart, but those questions that had now been unleashed: How in the world could something like this even be possible? Was her life a total lie? If this was true, then her daddy wasn't her daddy and her name wouldn't even be Cox. So who would she be?

This time she couldn't stop the tears that felt fiery hot as they seeped through her closed eyes. Just as she leaned her head back onto the sofa, there was a knock at the door.

"What in the world?" Serena said. "I

haven't had this many people come to my house in the last two years."

She scurried across the living room and when she opened the door, Jasmine felt the force before she even opened her eyes.

"Jasmine Larson, I cannot believe you left New York without me."

Mae Frances dumped her bag onto the sofa then held her arms open wide. "Come here," she said. "You know I'm going to make this all better, right?"

Jasmine sat still for a moment, looking up at her friend. What was Mae Frances doing here? But then, she wasn't really surprised. This was just who her best friend was.

She pushed herself up, walked a couple of feet, and by the time she collapsed into Mae Frances's arms, she was sobbing once again.

Serena joined them and the two held Jasmine. They just stood there with their arms wrapped around her. And they just let her cry and cry until Jasmine couldn't cry anymore.

CHAPTER 10

RACHEL

If Rachel weren't sitting there, witnessing this herself, she'd swear it was impossible. She fiddled with her purse strap, tapped her foot, then stood and paced nervously around the waiting room. Even though the room was adorned with contemporary furniture and a state-of-the-art television, it still felt cold and uninviting.

Rachel made her way over to the receptionist's desk and tapped on the window.

"Yes, ma'am?" the receptionist asked, not bothering to hide her irritation.

"How much longer?" Rachel asked the woman.

The young woman pushed her cat-eye glasses up on her face and sneered, "Ma'am, like I told you the last three times you asked me in the past thirty minutes, it shouldn't be much longer."

Rachel gritted her teeth in an effort to stay

calm. She wanted to school this girl on her customer service skills, but right now Rachel's thoughts were focused on something much more important. Right now, she simply wanted to know what was happening on the other side of that door.

"Fine," Rachel said, but the girl closed the window before she finished the word.

Rachel stood, taking in the surroundings. Her eyes stopped on the sign above the front door: DNA TECHNOLOGIES: WE HELP YOU GET TO THE TRUTH. That's all she wanted. The truth.

Rachel still couldn't believe she was here. That *they* were here. She turned just as the lobby doors opened.

"I simply detest public restrooms," Mae Frances said as she wobbled her old frame back over to the chair in the corner. "I need to call up Ben and ask him to prescribe something for my bladder."

Not that she cared about this old woman's bladder, but Rachel asked anyway. "Who is Ben?"

"Carson. He's a world-renowned doctor. Well, he wouldn't be if I hadn't helped him get into that good school. But now he done lost his mind, all on TV talking a whole buncha foolishness when he was trying to be president, so on second thought, I don't think I'll call."

Rachel sighed. She had no desire to entertain this woman and her delusions. Granted, Mae Frances had proven she was well connected, but there was no way she knew all the people she claimed to know.

"Excuse me," Rachel said, turning back to the receptionist's window and tapping again.

The receptionist snatched the window open. "Yes?"

"Does it always take this long?"

The girl slammed her hand on her desk. "Look, lady!"

Rachel had had enough. She was exhausted and her tolerance level was past its limit. Jasmine had called her early yesterday, agreeing to take the test, so Rachel had taken the first flight out and come to New York. Jasmine was adamant that the test be done in New York and Rachel was adamant that she, Rachel, find the lab, just in case Jasmine got any bright ideas about paying someone off to get the results she wanted. Rachel had spent all yesterday doing that, had flown out the first thing this morning, and hadn't even been to the hotel to drop her suitcase off. So she was not in the mood for this rude, nine-dollar-an-hour teenybopper.

"No, you look. Your job is to sit here and answer questions, and if I have a question, you need to answer it. You got one more time to snap at me before I lose my religion and show you what happens to disrespectful little twerps!"

Mae Frances spoke up before the girl could reply. "Rachelle, just come over here and have a seat. The girl doesn't know any more than she's already told you."

Rachel's nerves had reached their boiling point. She spun around to face Mae Frances. "My name is Rachel and tell me again why you're even here? This has nothing to do with you."

Mae Frances glared at Rachel for a minute before saying, "Little girl, you're lucky I know Jesus now. And you need to be thanking Him that I am here because if I wasn't, Jasmine Larson wouldn't be here, either. The only reason she agreed to have this test is because I told her to. I could've told her that you really were a crackpot and if I had, you'd never have the answers you so desperately crave."

Rachel inhaled, trying to calm herself. She didn't need to be snapping at Mae Frances. When Jasmine had called her and agreed to the test, Rachel hadn't even bothered to ask what had changed Jasmine's mind. She should've known it was Mae Frances. Rachel didn't know what kind of hold that woman had over Jasmine. After all, who in their right mind wanted to be best friends with Moses's grandma? But at that very moment, Rachel was grateful for whatever Mae Frances had done. Jasmine was here and soon they'd know the truth. Soon they'd put this ridiculous notion of being sisters to rest.

"I'm sorry, Mae Frances," Rachel said, genuinely apologetic. "I really appreciate you helping us get to the bottom of this."

"Hmph" was all she replied.

"I mean, I'm just on edge. And I'm exhausted. I had to drop everything and get back to New York. I wish we could've done this in Houston. I already had a clinic set up to rush the results."

"Chile, please, so you can have one of your hoodrat friends fix the test?" Mae Frances laughed.

This woman had better be glad she was dealing with a different Rachel now. Because back in the day . . . "Number one, I don't have hoodrat friends," Rachel said. "Anymore. And number two, I want to be Jasmine's sister about as much as she wants to be mine."

A small smirk crept up on Mae Frances's face.

"What?" Rachel asked.

"I think you want the test to be positive."

"Are you crazy?"

"Just a little. But the fact remains, you and Jasmine Larson act like sisters anyway. It wouldn't surprise me none. Although it would be quite funny."

"Whatever," Rachel said as she went back to pacing.

"Don't be mad at me because your poppa was a rolling stone."

"He was not!"

Mae Frances chuckled. "Laying his hat at Jasmine Larson's momma's home."

"Really, Mae Frances?" Rachel said, irritated. "Now, you're biting off Temptation lyrics, trying to make jokes."

"Actually, those are my lyrics. I gave them to Smokey Robinson one night when he —"

"Ugh," Rachel said, shaking her head as she walked back over to the reception desk to demand some answers about what was taking so long. But before she could ask the receptionist again, the door swung open and Jasmine walked out. Her eyes were puffy, like she'd been crying and she looked . . . scared.

"Are you okay?" Rachel gently asked.

"Yes," Jasmine said. Rachel waited on some smart remark, some condescending comeback, but Jasmine said nothing as she pulled her sweater around her like she'd suddenly gotten a chill.

Jasmine swallowed, then her voice quivered as she said, "I've been done for a while. I just had to take a moment to myself."

Rachel could only imagine how Jasmine was feeling and she knew now wasn't the time to give her grief. "Jasmine, I'm sorry you have to go through this. I know we both just —"

"Look, you got your stupid DNA test," Jasmine snapped, cutting her off. "They are rushing the results and will courier them over tomorrow, so tomorrow we can put an end to all of this foolishness and you can leave me alone."

Rachel didn't say anything, but only because she didn't know what to say.

"Come on, Jasmine Larson," Mae Frances said, appearing at Jasmine's side. "The car is outside. Hosea has been blowing up my phone. He's at the apartment."

Jasmine nodded, then looked over at Rachel. "I'll call you tomorrow when the courier arrives."

"Can . . . can you wait so that we can open them together?"

Jasmine released a long sigh. "Fine, Rachel."

Mae Frances took Jasmine's arm. Rachel wanted to ask if all that was necessary since they'd only drawn a little blood, but the look in Jasmine's eyes said she was in much more pain than a needle prick could ever deliver.

"Let's get you home to your family," Mae Frances said as she led Jasmine out of the lobby.

Rachel stood, watching them leave. *Could I be her family?* Rachel found herself wondering.

She shook off that thought. No sense driving herself crazy. One more day. Tomorrow, they'd know the truth.

CHAPTER 11

JASMINE

This view alone was worth a million dollars. At least that's what the realtor had said when she first showed this apartment to Jasmine and Hosea all those years ago. It was this view that had made Jasmine beg with everything inside her. She'd told her husband she would never be able to live her life without living in this Central Park South apartment.

It had been a huge investment, but worth every million. There were so many days when Jasmine sat in the chaise in front of this massive window, stared at the park below, and found peace in the beauty of this man-made (with a lot of help from God) creation. But the solace that usually blanketed her when she spent a few moments taking in this view didn't cover her today. Instead, as she gazed out at the park in its luscious summer glory, Jasmine's mind filled with questions: Were the trees in the park really green? Were the people who strolled below Russian spies? Was this really Central Park? Was she even in New York?

Maybe this was all just an illusion.

Silly questions, of course, but now she felt like she had to question everything. Because clearly life wasn't what it seemed. What had been real was not. Not anymore.

That was all she could think about. For the last two days. Since Mae Frances had appeared at Serena's door and explained that Hosea had called and told her what was going on. Then Mae Frances, Serena, and Jasmine had talked. Well, it was more like Mae Frances and Serena talked and Jasmine just listened as they both told her the same thing.

"You have to have the test. You have to know."

The two of them had talked to her well into the morning hours, though it didn't really take all that time. Jasmine had been convinced before Mae Frances had shown up. Really, she'd probably made her decision before she even got on the plane to Pensacola.

So, the next morning she'd made the call to Rachel — with Mae Frances's help, of course, since Jasmine had deleted Rachel's number with the expectation that she'd never again in this life speak to Rachel Jackson Adams. But that, along with so much in her life, wasn't true. And so Mae Frances had called one of her connections, gotten Rachel's number, and Jasmine had made the call.

"I'll do the test," she'd said to Rachel without even saying hello. "But I'm not going through any trouble. We'll do it in New York and you'll pay for it."

Then Jasmine hung up. She hadn't been sure how Rachel would respond, and if Rachel had never contacted her again, that would've been fine. Jasmine would have gone on with her life, knowing that Rachel had made it all up.

But about an hour after she'd ended the call, Jasmine had received a text from Rachel with a place to meet yesterday morning.

And Jasmine had shown up. Because she just had to know.

The tap on her shoulder made her jump inches off the chaise and she twisted around. "Oh my gosh! You scared me, Hosea."

"I don't know why; I called you three times."

She looked up at her husband and he leaned down, softly kissing her forehead.

She said, "My mind was . . ."

He finished her sentence for her. "In another place. I understand."

After a few minutes of silence, she said, "I wish I'd never taken that test."

"Why?" He eased down onto the chaise, sitting shoulder-to-shoulder with her.

"Because what difference does it make now? My mother and father are dead, so there's really no need to stir up something when I know all the way down to my soul that my father was my father. He raised me, took care of me, loved me. If I wasn't his daughter, then he was a damn good actor."

"And nothing will change that, darlin'. Whether you carry his DNA or not, he's still your father."

"That's my point. So what is the purpose of knowing any of this?"

"Because you have questions. And all questions deserve to be answered."

"Maybe these are questions that I don't need to have and answers that I don't need to know."

"No, you need to know . . . because if you hadn't taken the test, every night when you laid your head down on your pillow you would wonder."

"No matter what happens with this test, I'm going to wonder. Like, why did Rachel's

126

father even think that he could be my father? What happened between him and my mother? Did anything ever really happen with them? Did he even know my mother or is he a liar like his daughter?"

Hosea was silent for a moment, nodding his head just a bit as he considered Jasmine's questions. "You need to know the answers to all of that. You need to know for family's sake."

Now, she was thoughtful. "These results could show that I have no family. I might end up not knowing who I am."

"Well, if you forget, I'll tell you — you're Jasmine Cox Larson Bush," he said, emphasizing each syllable the way Jasmine did when she introduced herself.

But while Hosea smiled, Jasmine didn't. "We may need to take out the Cox and I may end up putting something in there . . . like Jackson." She shuddered. "Jasmine Jackson." Shaking her head, she added, "That sounds ridiculous. Too close to Jermaine Jackson."

Hosea chuckled.

"I'm serious, babe. A name like Jackson . . . what's special about that?"

"What's wrong with Jackson?"

"Who important ever had the last name Jackson?"

"Well, I could ask you the same thing about Cox."

"You might not know anyone named Cox, and that would make the name special enough. But Jackson? No one special was ever named Jackson."

"What about Andrew Jackson?"

"He doesn't count. He was white."

"But he was the president. That's pretty special."

"He doesn't count," she repeated. "No one even remembers him. People remember folks like Jesse Jackson and his son, Junior. And we know what kind of Jacksons they turned out to be."

"Well what about Mahalia Jackson or Maynard Jackson?"

Jasmine paused for a moment, then nodded.

"And then, you can always tell people you're related to Curtis Jackson."

She frowned.

Hosea answered her question before she asked. "You know him as Fifty Cent."

"Ugh! See what I'm sayin'?"

Hosea chuckled. "Come on, darlin'. None of this is important. No matter how the test comes back today, let me tell you who you are." He took her hands into his and kissed her fingertips. "You are a woman who loves

128

God, you are my wife, and you are the mother of the two most amazing children on earth. And I'm not just saying that about Jacquie and Zaya. That's a scientific fact."

"Oh, really? There was some kind of test done that proved this?"

"No, but if there were a test, that would be the result."

She smiled, but then she thought about Hosea's words — *test, result* — and her smile faded away.

He pulled her into his arms, letting her rest her head against his chest. "The most important thing you need to know today is that I love you with everything in me. And I will be with you on this entire journey, no matter where the road leads."

Before she could thank Hosea for being in her life, before she could thank God for blessing her with this man, the doorbell rang.

And Jasmine shook. "Oh my God." She pressed her hand against her chest because she was sure her heart was about to pound its way out. "That must be the courier . . . with the results."

"No," Hosea said, squeezing her hand, "because the concierge would have called to let him up."

Together they stood and Hosea made his

way to the front door. When he disappeared into the foyer, Jasmine squeezed her eyelids together. "Please, Father God. Please, Father God. Please, Father God." She didn't think she needed to say anything else. God knew the desires of her heart; and didn't the Bible say that He would give her what her heart wanted? Well, what she wanted was to be who she always was.

When she opened her eyes, Mae Frances stood in front of her. "Good morning," she sang as if this was somehow the cheeriest day of the year. "How are you this glorious morning, Jasmine Larson?"

"I'm good," she said, breathing once again. "Just a little anxious. I thought you were the courier."

"So is Rawanda here yet?"

"No." Jasmine shook her head.

"What time is she coming?" Mae Frances asked.

"I texted her this morning and told her that the results were going to be here at three."

Hosea said, "I thought you said they'd be here before noon."

"Yes, but I didn't want Rachel here when they came. I'm going to need some time — without her." She glanced down at her watch. "It's almost noon now. I thought the

130

courier would be here."

Mae Frances slipped a padded package from her purse and held out the envelope to Jasmine.

Hosea moved to Jasmine's side as they both frowned. Jasmine asked, "What's that?"

"The test results you're waiting for."

"You went down to the clinic to get them?" Jasmine didn't give her friend a chance to respond. "Why? And why would they give them to you?"

"I didn't go down there. When I walked in, the courier was in the lobby on his way up and your doorman told him to give me this package since I was coming up here."

"He's not supposed to do that!"

Mae Frances twisted her lips. "Stanley knows me. He knew me before you even moved into this building."

Jasmine had no time to listen to how Mae Frances knew yet another person. Instead, her eyes were on the package her friend held. "Did you open it? Do you know the results?"

"Who do you think I am, Jasmine Larson? I wouldn't get in your business like that."

If this were any other time, Jasmine would have had all kinds of retorts for Mae Frances. But this wasn't any other time. This was now, and all Jasmine could do was stare

131

at the package, which Mae Frances still held.

Mae Frances added, "Only you need to open this envelope."

Her hands were shaking, her knees were trembling as Jasmine reached for the news that could change her life. But as her fingers touched the envelope, Mae Frances pulled it back. "What about Rachel?" Mae Frances asked.

That question made Jasmine quiver more. When was the last time Mae Frances called Rachel by her given name? If this was that serious to Mae Frances, then Jasmine just wanted to cry.

Mae Frances finished with, "I think she needs to be here."

"I don't want her here!" Jasmine snapped. She left out that she didn't even want Mae Frances or Hosea there. She wanted to open this by herself, to have a private moment of celebration or complete sorrow. Whichever it was, she really wanted to be alone. But she knew that would never happen; these two would never leave her alone for this. So, all Jasmine said was, "Please, Mae Frances. Please give that to me."

Just as Mae Frances handed her the envelope, the doorbell rang again and Jasmine paused. Who was invading their space now?

Without a word, Hosea rushed to the door and Jasmine and Mae Frances stood, staring at one another. Seconds later, Hosea walked back into the living room, followed by Rachel.

Jasmine's eyes widened. "What are you doing here?"

"I'm here for the results."

"I told you they were coming at three."

"And that's why I'm here early, because I know how you are." Her eyes moved to Jasmine's hands. "Are those the results?" When Jasmine didn't answer, Rachel crossed her arms. "Have you opened it yet?" she asked like she had a major attitude.

Jasmine wondered why Rachel was upset. No matter the results, her life wasn't going to change too much. Either Jasmine wasn't her sister and they could go back to being enemies, or she was and that would be the biggest blessing Rachel would ever receive, while Jasmine would know for sure that she was cursed.

Jasmine shook her head. "I was just getting ready to open it."

Rachel poked out her lips. "Then do it!" she said, like she was in charge.

Jasmine took her eyes away from Rachel

and glanced at Mae Frances, and then turned to Hosea, who gave her a reassuring nod. All three kept their eyes on her and for a moment, Jasmine wanted to tear the package to shreds so they would never know. But, with hands that were still shaking, she ripped it open.

She took her time unfolding the single trifold paper and read the words slowly, so she could understand completely.

It was difficult to read everything, the way her body quaked. But still she took in every word, every letter.

The results were in and there was no mistake.

Her knees could no longer hold her upright and she collapsed, wilting to the floor.

"Jasmine!"

She heard her name called, but she didn't want to open her eyes.

"Jasmine!"

With a deep breath, she did what she didn't want to do. She opened her eyes. And stared into the eyes of Rachel Jackson Adams . . . her sister.

CHAPTER 12

RACHEL

Rachel released a long sigh as the Houston skyline came into view. She'd been out of it from the moment the car service had dropped her off at JFK and now she just longed to see her children. This was the first time she'd allowed her mind to think of anything other than Jasmine since she'd left New York.

Rachel had known in her heart that Jasmine was her sister. She'd known the minute Jasmine confirmed her mother's name. But now she *knew.* There was a 99.9 percent probability that Jasmine Cox Larson Bush was indeed her half sister.

Rachel finally managed to smile when she recalled Jasmine's desperate look at Hosea as she said, "But there's a point one percent chance that I'm not." Even Mae Frances had looked at Jasmine with pity when she'd said that.

Under regular circumstances Rachel would have been offended. Did Jasmine not want to be related to her that bad? But again she remembered that Jasmine's whole world had been turned upside down. That's why Rachel had quietly told everyone good-bye, with the promise to be in touch after Jasmine had time to process the news. She eased out of the house without any fanfare, without any theatrics. She knew Jasmine would never be the same again and that was tough.

Fifteen minutes later, Rachel had just made it to baggage claim when she heard someone calling her name. She looked up to see her husband. She'd called Lester on the way to the airport and despite her attempts to tell him she was fine, Rachel guessed he could hear in her voice that she wasn't.

"Hey, honey," she said, leaning in and kissing Lester before he took her in a comforting hug.

"Hi. How was your flight?" he replied.

"It was okay. Just seemed longer than normal."

Lester stood back and examined her. "Are you sure you're okay? I've been worried sick because you don't sound okay."

Rachel handed her husband her bag, then

said, "Yeah, I am. It's Jasmine who I'm worried about."

"Well, it's been a few hours since you've seen her. Do you want to call and check on her?"

Rachel thought about it for a minute. Did she want to call her *sister*? If she was worried about Jonathan or David, she'd blow up their phones until she knew they were okay. But she and Jasmine weren't there. A small pang filled her heart when she wondered, given their history, if she and Jasmine would ever be there.

"No," she finally said. "I'm gonna give her a little time."

Lester didn't say anything more as he took her hand and led her into the short-term parking garage. They'd talked over the phone and had agreed that they'd go straight to her dad's from the airport.

On the drive to her father's house, Rachel rode in silence. Lester caressed her hand, squeezed it at just the right time. He'd asked her again if she was okay and then, thankfully, had left her to her thoughts.

It had taken thirty minutes to get to her father's house, but now that they were here, standing on his front porch, Rachel still didn't know what to say.

Her stepmother met her at the front door,

a nervous look on her face. Rachel had called and told Brenda that she was on her way. She didn't tell her why she was coming, but given all the questions Rachel asked about what kind of mood Simon was in and how he was feeling, she knew Brenda had an idea of what this conversation was about.

"Hey. How are you?" Brenda said.

"I'm fine."

Her hands were clutched over her chest as if she knew the answer to the lingering question.

"Well, your dad's inside," Brenda said. "I told him you were coming by because he was trying to go for a walk. I played it down, though. I didn't mention . . ."

It's like she couldn't even bring herself to finish the sentence. Rachel nodded her understanding as she stepped inside the living room.

"Hey, Ms. Brenda," Lester said, kissing Brenda on the cheek. She closed the door behind them and the three of them made their way back into the den.

"Hey, baby girl," Simon said from his favorite rickety recliner, watching his favorite show, *Sanford & Son*. "To what do I owe this pleasure?"

"Hey, Daddy," Rachel said. She leaned down and quickly hugged her father.

138

He lowered his feet off the ottoman.

"Um, what's going on?" he asked, studying her.

"I can't hug you?" She tried to fake a smile.

"Yes. Now, what's going on?"

"I just wanted to come by and talk to you."

Simon studied her harder, like he was looking through her. Then he glanced over at Lester, then at Brenda, and then he picked up the remote and turned the TV off.

"You talked to Jasmine." It was a declaration. Not a question. Dang, her dad was good.

"I did," Rachel said, easing onto the sofa across from her dad. "At first she thought the idea of you being her father was ridiculous."

Simon nodded. "That's understandable, and it may be hard for her to process, but if I could talk to her, I could convince her to have the test and then we could know for sure."

Rachel swallowed, trying to gather her words. "We know for sure, Daddy. We had a test done so that we could know."

Simon fell back in his chair.

"So?" he asked.

Rachel's hand went up and Lester took it

to give her strength to continue.

"Well, it turns out you aren't as senile as we thought," she said, trying to manage a laugh, but it came out as a muffled cry. Rachel swallowed her words, composed herself, and said, "Jasmine is your daughter."

Silence filled the room as Simon sat on the edge of his seat in shock. A glaze covered his eyes and it was a full minute before he spoke.

"I . . . I need to see her."

"I think we need to give her a little time, Dad. Like you said, this is very hard for her to process right now."

Simon nodded his understanding. "Well, when will I get to talk to her?"

"I don't know, Daddy."

Those words seemed to tear at his heart. "Baby girl, I don't know how much time I have left."

"I thought you said you weren't sick," Rachel said, feeling a race of nervousness.

"No, I don't mean it like that," Simon said. "I'm still in remission from the prostate scare, but none of our days are promised. I'm getting older and I've already lost years, decades, with Jasmine. I don't want to wait another minute to keep from getting to know her."

"Well, let's give her at least a week. Maybe

you can fly up to meet her after that," Rachel said.

"Oh, no, you know he's not gonna fly," Brenda spoke up. She was right about that. It had taken an act of Congress to get her father to fly to Los Angeles for the American Baptist Coalition Convention. He'd been so nervous and had sworn he'd never fly again.

"We will just drive to New York," Simon said.

"Daddy, you can't drive across the country," Rachel said. "That's a twenty-four-hour drive."

Lester finally spoke up. "Aren't we going to Arkansas in two weeks for the family reunion? Why don't you guys just see if Jasmine and Hosea will come there?"

Simon's eyes lit up at that suggestion and Rachel's mouth dropped. She loved her country relatives and had been looking forward to the family reunion, but the idea of Jasmine commingling with that crazy side gave Rachel chills. Jasmine thought she had enough to harass Rachel about now? Meeting her crazy family would give her ammunition for days.

"Yeah, that's not gonna happen," Rachel said. "Jasmine in Smackover, Arkansas? If you looked up *city girl* in the dictionary, you'd see Jasmine's picture. No way is she coming to the country." Rachel laughed. Simon didn't.

"You think you can make it happen?" Simon asked, his eyes full of anticipation.

"Daddy, Lester's just talking," Rachel said, cutting her eyes at her husband. "There's no way Jasmine's going to agree to come to Smackover." She left off the part about how she didn't want Jasmine there.

"Why not?" Simon responded. "We're her family. She needs to get to know her family. All of us."

"Well, if you ask her, she has a family," Rachel replied. If she had known this suggestion was a possibility, she would've waited until after the reunion to break the news to her father.

"And we're her family, too." Simon reached over to the coffee table and picked up the cordless handset. "What's her number? I'll call her."

"No, Daddy. Not yet," Rachel said. She knew her dad was excited, but he didn't need to go there just yet. The anticipation in her father's eyes made her heart sad. Rachel would just have to find a way to ask Jasmine to go to Arkansas, because if Jasmine said the wrong thing to her daddy, or said something smart or sarcastic, or hurt his feelings, they were going to be two sisters fighting. No, Rachel would convince Jasmine to come, or maybe she'd convince Hosea or even Mae Frances. Regardless, if that's what her dad wanted, she'd do it for him. She'd find a way to get Jasmine to Smackover, Arkansas.

Hell will freeze over first, a little voice in her head muttered. *No, I can do this,* Rachel thought. *I can.* Then she pushed aside the little voice that was now laughing hysterically at the idea. Rachel wouldn't rest until she got Jasmine to come to the Jackson Family Reunion.

Chapter 13

Jasmine

"Mommy, you're squeezing me!" Jacqueline shrieked like a seagull. She squirmed to loosen herself from Jasmine's grasp. "I can't breathe." Then the nine-year-old coughed as if she were choking.

It was Jacqueline's normal over-the-top drama, though Jasmine had held her daughter so tightly she could almost feel the bones through her thin frame.

Jasmine released Jacqueline and turned to her son. "Mama," Zaya said before she could squeeze the life out of him. "Why are you crying?"

"I'm not crying," Jasmine said, though tears dampened her cheeks. "I'm just a little sad 'cause I'm gonna miss you."

"But we're just going to camp," Jacqueline said. "We'll be home later."

"I know," Jasmine said, standing up and sniffing back more tears. "Silly me."

144

"Well, buh-bye," Jacqueline said as she opened the door. Then she shouted, "Nama!" And she jumped into Mae Frances's arms as if she hadn't just seen her yesterday.

"How's my big girl?" Mae Frances said as she hugged Jacqueline.

"You know you're gonna have to stop calling me that. I'm more than a big girl; I'm almost a teenager." Then she turned to her brother. "Zaya, come on! Daddy's waiting for us downstairs!" She gave Jasmine a final glance and another "Buh-bye!"

But even though his sister rushed into the hallway, Zaya lingered behind. "Are you gonna be all right, Mama?" The concern was written all over his six-year-old face.

"Yes, baby," she said. "I'm going to be fine."

"Maybe I should stay home today," Zaya said, and that made Jasmine cry even more. "Just to make sure."

Jasmine pressed her palm against her son's cheek. Her sweet, sensitive son. He was just like his father. "No, you don't have to do that. You go on," she said. But he didn't move until he heard his sister shouting from the hallway, "Come on, Zaya! The elevator's here!"

And then there was Jacqueline, who was

just like her mother.

Zaya scurried out of the apartment before Mae Frances closed the door. Once they were gone, Jasmine let her tears flow.

When she turned toward the living room, Mae Frances followed her. "You can get poisoning from all that crying, you know."

Jasmine blew her nose into a tissue and flopped onto the couch. Tucking a pillow beneath her head, she stretched out on the long sofa — her plan was to stay there and cry until the children came home.

"Jasmine Larson!" Mae Frances planted her hands on her hips. "What are you gonna do? Just stay in this apartment and cry until you die?"

That was a good question and a good suggestion. Maybe that would be what she'd do. Stay right here in the apartment and grow old. Of course, she'd never feel the sun again, never hang out in the wonderfulness of New York again, never attend any of her children's events again. She'd never see a graduation or see her children get married. Those thoughts were so ridiculous . . . or not. Because if she stayed behind these four walls, she'd never have to come face-to-face with the reason for all these tears.

"You need to get up and get over this," Mae Frances said. Then she raised her hands and added, "I don't understand. Why are you so upset?"

Those words made Jasmine sit up straight. "You don't understand. Suppose you found out that your father was not your father?"

She shrugged. "I never knew my father."

Jasmine paused. Another rare moment when Mae Frances spoke about herself. If her heart wasn't aching so much, she'd ask a couple of follow-up questions.

But right now, this was all about Jasmine and her pain. So she kept her focus there. She said, "Well, how would you like it if you found out your mother wasn't your mother?"

"I'd feel like I'd won the lottery."

Another pause from Jasmine. These little comments from Mae Frances were almost enough to take her focus away. Almost, but not enough. "Well, I don't feel that way. I don't feel like I've won a thing; I feel like I've lost everything."

Mae Frances lowered herself to the sofa and shrugged. "I'm not trying to be insensitive."

Jasmine gave her a side-eye.

Mae Frances continued: "Okay, maybe I'm insensitive, but it's only because I don't get all the tears. Yeah, I get that you're surprised, but all that's happened is that you found out that you came from some-body else's sperm. So what? The man who raised you is still your daddy and your mama is still your mama."

"But how did all this happen? And why?" Jasmine cried. "And why didn't anyone tell me? I mean, I don't know anything. I don't understand. Hell, was my mother really my mother?"

"Seems like you've got questions."

"I do!"

"Then you need to get some answers."

"From where?" Jasmine whined, then she flopped back onto the sofa, resuming her position.

"From your aunt Virginia. I know she'd want to talk to you."

Slowly, Jasmine lifted herself up, head first, with her eyes on Mae Frances the whole time. In the first six months of know-ing Mae Frances, Jasmine had realized her friend knew everyone. If Mae Frances told her she'd raised Barack Obama, she would've believed that. But to this point, Mae Frances had known all of these public figures. Was she saying that now she knew one of Jasmine's relatives?

Her eyes were still on her friend as she wondered: Who was this woman? How did she know Aunt Virginia? And if she knew

148

Aunt Virginia, did she know her mother? Did Mae Frances know this story?

"How do you know about Aunt Virginia?" Jasmine asked in a whisper.

Mae Frances frowned as if she didn't understand the question.

Jasmine said, "You just told me that I need to talk to my aunt. How do you know her?" When Mae Frances stayed quiet, Jasmine jumped up. "Mae Frances, you better start talking. What do you know? Who do you know? And how is it that you always know everybody?"

Mae Frances folded her arms. "You know what you're doing right now? You're deflecting. You're trying to take the attention off of yourself and turn it on me. But I'm not gonna let you do that."

"And *I'm* not gonna let you sidestep my questions, Mae Frances. How do you know my aunt Virginia? And while we're talking about that, how do you know everybody who's important on earth? The living and the dead." Jasmine stopped and faced her. "How do you know . . . every . . . damn . . . body!"

Mae Frances put her hand on her heart as if she were taken aback by Jasmine's language.

"I'm serious," Jasmine asked, sounding

like she was pissed. "How do you know my aunt Virginia?"

"Well." Mae Frances paused. "I know her because . . . Serena told me about her when we were at her house! How the hell you think I know her?"

For days Jasmine had been crying, but then looking at Mae Frances glaring at her, Jasmine couldn't do anything but laugh. "Serena told you about our aunt?"

"Yeah. You fell asleep and she told me why she thought there was something to Rachel's story. She told me about your aunt and your mother's birth certificate. So what were *you* thinking?"

"I don't know. You know everybody else. I was thinking maybe you knew my aunt. Maybe you knew my mother."

"No, I didn't know either one of them. I'm just sayin' that you need to take the trip down to Mobile to get some answers."

Jasmine thought for a moment. "And what am I going to do with those answers?"

Mae Frances shrugged. "I don't know, but it'll be a start, Jasmine Larson, so you can move forward. Unless you really do want to just stay on this couch and cry till you die."

With a sigh, Jasmine sat back down and propped her chin up with her hands. After a moment she said, "All right, Mae Frances.

All right."

"And we need to do this soon, 'cause I have to work on my book, and once I start writing, I'm not gonna have time for all of this extra drama."

Jasmine rolled her eyes.

"But I'm not writing a word until everything is all right with you, Jasmine Larson. 'Cause whoever is your father, whoever is your mother, you're like a daughter to me."

It was instant the way the tears filled Jasmine's eyes once again. But this time it wasn't because she felt like she didn't fit in. This time it was because she knew she did.

Chapter 14

JASMINE

Jasmine slipped out of the car and stood in front of the gray house. Behind her, she heard Mae Frances's voice as she spoke to the driver, but Jasmine paid no attention to her friend. Instead she stood at the edge of the curb, taking in the houses on the street.

The homes looked like war-worn soldiers, older structures that had seen too many years. This probably wasn't the poorest neighborhood in Mobile, but it certainly was far from the richest.

Was this where her mother had grown up? Had her mother lived on this street?

"All right," Mae Frances said. "What are you standing here for?"

Mae Frances marched up the uneven walkway, not noticing that Jasmine hadn't moved. She wanted to, but she was overwhelmed by so much, trying to imagine what life had been like for her mother grow-

152

ing up in this city. Jasmine had new questions now. Why did her mother leave Mobile? How did she get to California? And the one that plagued her the most: is this where she met Rachel's father?

Mae Frances raised her hand to knock on the door, but then a quick glance over her shoulder made her pause. "Jasmine Larson, come on up here," she said. Her tone was gruff, though her face was soft with understanding.

Jasmine did as she was told, moving on shaky legs, and once she stood by Mae Frances's side, her friend knocked hard on the wooden door.

As they waited, Jasmine's thoughts shifted from the past to the present. She thought about what she was about to hear and she grabbed Mae Frances's arm. "Let's go. Let's get out of here."

"What?"

"I want to go home."

"No, Jasmine Larson. We came too far."

"It doesn't seem like anyone is home. Maybe this is a sign."

"We'll just wait."

"I don't want to wait," Jasmine said, sounding like tears were not far away. "I don't want to know. I just want to —"

The door swung open before she could

finish and Jasmine looked into the eyes of the woman she could only remember seeing three times in her life; the last time more than twenty years ago, when Virginia had made the trip to Los Angeles for Jasmine's mother's funeral.

The silver-haired woman was bent over slightly, her frame weary with age. She peered through eyes that Jasmine wasn't sure could see much, but then her head reared back. "Jasmine Cox," she said as if two days, not two decades, had passed between them.

"Hi, Aunt . . ." And she paused. "I hope you don't mind me dropping by. I know you weren't expecting company and I should've called."

Aunt Virginia shook her head. "I've been expecting you."

Jasmine frowned. "Oh, did Serena call you?"

"No. I've just been expecting you for a long, long time now." She stepped aside and motioned with her hand for Jasmine to come in.

They were inside when Jasmine remembered. "Oh, Aunt . . . Virginia. This is my friend, Mae Frances. She flew down here with me."

Aunt Virginia and Mae Frances exchanged

nods and then the two visitors followed Aunt Virginia farther into the house. "I was in the kitchen, baking up a few things for the sale we're having after church tomorrow. So y'all come on back here."

They moved behind Aunt Virginia as she took slow steps, but Jasmine didn't mind. This gave her time to scan the living room with the extra-long brown crushed-velvet sofa and mismatched wingback chairs. In the long hallway, the walls were covered with dozens of frames holding faded photos.

In the kitchen, Jasmine and Mae Frances sat at the small round table and Aunt Virginia asked, "Do you want anything to drink?"

Jasmine shook her head, but Mae Frances said, "What you got?"

Before Aunt Virginia could respond, Jasmine blurted, "You said you'd been expecting me. How did you know that I was coming?"

Aunt Virginia's glance moved from Mae Frances to Jasmine, then back to Mae Frances before she sat down at the table.

"I knew you would be here one day," she said, lowering her eyes. "Either your mama was going to bring you back" — then she looked up — "or you were going to make this trip on your own."

"How did you know?"

"Because secrets never stay down low. Secrets are like cream: they always rise to the top. Only cream can be sweet, but secrets rarely are."

"I don't know about any secrets," Jasmine said. "I'm just here to ask you some questions."

"About your mother."

Jasmine nodded.

"And your father," Aunt Virginia added.

This time Jasmine paused, not sure which father Aunt Virginia was talking about. Was she talking about the man who raised her? Or was she talking about Simon? Did Aunt Virginia know Simon?

"I just want to know . . . I never knew anything about my mom, not really. I knew she was from somewhere in the South, I knew she was from Mobile. But beyond that, I never cared. Not really. Serena cared, but I didn't."

Aunt Virginia chuckled, just a little. "Yeah, Doris told me you were just like her. Wanting to be part of the bigger world. She said you were always antsy, never content. Always wanting more than you had."

"I didn't know that you talked to my mother all that much."

"Oh, we talked. Not often, but often

enough so that I always knew that she was all right. That was my girl. I loved her like she was my own daughter."

"So you raised her? After her parents died?"

Aunt Virginia frowned. "Is that what she told you?"

Jasmine paused as if she were trying to recall. "I don't remember; I just knew that her parents were dead."

Aunt Virginia released a long breath. "The truth is, when Doris told you that, her parents were very much alive. But they treated Doris like *she* was dead."

Jasmine squinted and shook her head. "What? Why?"

"Maybe instead of you asking me a million questions, it would be better for me to just tell you what I know."

Jasmine nodded because there were no words left inside her. Or maybe it was because she needed every bit of energy she had to keep her pounding heart from breaking out.

"Somehow, you found out that your mama had to leave Alabama . . . because of you."

She paused and Jasmine waited for more. When Aunt Virginia said nothing more, Jasmine shook her head. "I didn't know that. All I know is that this girl told me that her

157

father thinks he's my father."

"Not 'think,' Jasmine Larson." Mae Frances spoke up for the first time. Turning to Aunt Virginia, Mae Frances said, "We *know* that the man who raised her is not her dad, 'cause this dude over there, the report came back that he's the daddy."

"The report didn't say that," Jasmine protested.

Mae Frances raised an eyebrow.

Jasmine said, "There's a ninety-nine-point-nine percent chance that he's my father, but there's still that point one percent . . ." Her voice trailed off, as if her protests were beginning to sound silly even to her ears.

Aunt Virginia patted her hand. "Let me tell you all the parts I know and then you can ask me any questions I don't answer. Is that all right with you?"

Jasmine gave her another nod.

"All right, then. Your grandmother, Doris's mother, was my best friend. From the time we were little bitty things, Ada Mae and I were great friends."

Ada Mae. Jasmine couldn't recall ever hearing her grandmother's name.

"We grew up next door to each other."

"Right here?" Jasmine said, her eyes darting around the room as if she were looking for clues from the past.

"Not here, just a couple of streets over. But all through school, till we graduated, when you saw one of us, you saw the other. We were that close.

"Then your grandmother got married; she married Boone Young, the most eligible bachelor, the most handsome man in Mobile, Alabama."

Boone Young.

"And not long after that, they had your mama. It was like the whole city, at least the black part, celebrated, 'cause the Youngs were big here back in the forties. Boone Jr. and his family owned just about every business in town: the barbershop, the beauty salon, and the funeral parlor. And everybody loved them 'cause they gave back, too. When it was time for school, they gave out school supplies to the kids who couldn't afford them. If a family didn't have money for a funeral, they could pay it over time. Or if someone was sick and 'bout to die, the family could start making payments on layaway. Yup, the Youngs took care of black folks in Mobile.

"And Ada Mae's folks were real respected, too. Her daddy was the pastor at Pilgrim Rest Missionary Baptist Church, and his daddy before him was the pastor there, too.

So when Doris came along, she was the next generation of Youngs. Everybody loved that little girl; though it was sure easy to love her. Doris popped out of Ada Mae with a big ol' smile on her face. Yup, that's what Ada Mae told me. And Doris never stopped smiling. She was like a ball of sunshine . . . for everybody."

"So then, why would her parents treat her like she was dead?"

"I'm getting to that part. You gotta let an old lady take her time." Aunt Virginia took a deep breath. "Now, you've got to understand that your grandparents were good people. Boone and Ada Mae loved their little girl."

Ada Mae. Boone. Just from their names, Jasmine tried to imagine the grandparents that she'd never met. "If they were so good . . ."

"Let me tell the story now! It started when your mama went to a church revival in Smackover, Arkansas, and she met this young man. When Doris came home two weeks later, she couldn't wait to tell me all about the cute boy she met. I thought it was just a schoolgirl crush; I mean, she was only fourteen. I knew it wasn't going to last more than a couple of weeks after she came back. But she ended up writing that boy just about every week; she was so smitten. And she showed me some of his letters, too. He was just as smitten as she was! The two of them were talking 'bout Doris moving to Smackover, getting married, and having a big ol' family. And that was after only spending two weeks together! Your mother couldn't wait to get back to Smackover that next summer.

"But your grandmother almost didn't let her go; she was so worried about this boy Doris kept talking about. But I talked Ada Mae into it. 'It's just a little crush,' I told her. Well, your grandmother let her go because of me. And your grandmother let her go the next summer, too, even though she was even more worried. 'Doris is getting older, you know,' Ada Mae said. But like the summer before, I talked her into it. Then Doris came back, and that was when everything changed. A few months later, we found out that Doris and that boy had been serious." Aunt Virginia paused. "*Very* serious."

"Ohhhhh!" Mae Frances said.

But Jasmine just frowned, having no idea of the definition of *serious* in that sentence.

Without her even asking, Aunt Virginia explained: "Your mama came back in a family way."

"What does that mean?" Jasmine asked.

"Oh, Lawd, Jasmine Larson. Does she have to spell it out for you?" Mae Frances shook her head. "Your mama came back from a *church revival* pregnant. Lawd have mercy! What kind of Word were they preaching there?"

"I don't know, but Doris was sixteen and pregnant." Aunt Virginia paused as if she wanted to make sure that Jasmine understood. She added, "And that baby was you, Jasmine."

Jasmine swallowed. Her mother was a teenage mom? That couldn't be true.

"There was no way she could have that baby here," Aunt Virginia continued. "That would've been too much of a black mark on the Youngs. Not to mention on her grandparents. No, the pastor's granddaughter could not be pregnant. So they sent her away to have the baby with an old family friend who Ada Mae and I had grown up with. They'd arranged for her to have the baby, give it up for adoption, and then come back home. The adoption agency had been chosen and everything. Your grandmother and grandfather had it all worked out.

"But I knew the moment Doris left that she would never be back, at least not back here to Mobile. I guess I knew her better than Ada Mae and Boone. She was never going to give up her baby." She paused. "She was never going to give you up."

Jasmine inhaled, trying to take in all of this.

Aunt Virginia said, "Ada Mae went to California when you were born to do the final adoption for you and then to bring Doris back here. But Doris told her to go home without her because she wasn't leaving California without you."

"She didn't want to leave me." It wasn't a question, but a statement that Jasmine knew was the truth. She closed her eyes for a moment, and imagined all that her mother had given up for her. Just to keep her.

"Doris never planned to leave you. She was never gonna do it and there was nothing that Ada Mae and Boone could do. No matter how hard they tried. They both went to California to talk to her, but they had raised an independent, think-for-herself daughter, and right then, she was being independent and thinking for herself."

"So, they just left her there?" Jasmine asked, trying to imagine herself as a baby, alone with her teenage mother, wandering around a city she didn't know. Had her mother been scared? Had her mother wondered if keeping her baby had been the right thing to do?

"Believe me, Ada Mae and Boone loved their daughter; they didn't want to leave her. But short of moving to California themselves, there was nothing they could do."

"So, that was it? They just left her in California? By herself?"

"I'm telling you, there was nothing they could do. Your mama was sixteen when she was pregnant and seventeen by the time she had you, but she was a headstrong woman. And really, I think it was more on her that she was estranged from Ada Mae and Boone. The more they insisted that she give up the baby, the further Doris pushed them away. After a while, I think she was the one who stopped communicating with them."

"So, what did they tell people? I mean, they had a child! Nobody wondered? Nobody cared that my mother had disappeared?"

"They just said she was in school in California and after a while, people stopped asking."

"I can't imagine that. Those people just gave up their child?"

"Oh, yeah, Jasmine Larson," Mae Frances interjected. "That happened all the time in those days. There were at least three or four girls who just disappeared when I was in high school. Never to be seen again. But we all knew what had happened."

"I just can't imagine," Jasmine repeated. Her heart ached as she pictured her mother, barely seventeen and all alone with a baby.

"Well, that's what happened," Aunt Virginia said.

Jasmine waited a moment as if she needed to muster up some kind of courage to speak the next words. "So then, it's true. The man who raised me . . . he's not my father?" Her voice cracked.

It was as if she didn't want to do it, the way Aunt Virginia slowly shook her head. "I know this is hard on you, but you came for the truth. And the truth is all I'm going to give you."

Jasmine swallowed. "Simon Jackson is my father?"

"Now, I don't remember his name. But that sounds about right. After you were born, Doris never mentioned him in all the years I stayed in touch with her, though I have to admit I was surprised she didn't go back to Smackover to find him. The way she talked about that boy, the way she talked about that town, I still don't know why she didn't go back there to marry him. I don't even know if he knew she had his baby.

Then, after a while, she met your father."

Jasmine paused for a moment, thinking about those words. And then she figured it out. Sitting right there in Aunt Virginia's kitchen, she knew what had happened. Her mother had probably loved Simon, just like Aunt Virginia said. But then when her mother told Simon that she was pregnant, he had dumped her, and she'd never heard from him again.

That man had just left her mother . . . and her . . . all alone.

It must have been the look on Jasmine's face that made Aunt Virginia quickly add, "But I want you to know that your mother was happy. She met Charles Cox, married him, and made herself a mighty good life in Los Angeles."

"But what about my father? I mean . . ." Jasmine paused. What was she supposed to call Charles? "What about my daddy? Did he know I wasn't his daughter?"

Aunt Virginia shrugged. "Those are some of the things that I just don't know. I know your mama was married about a year after you were born. I don't know if she met your daddy before or after. And I don't know what she told him. All I know is that when I went out to Los Angeles to visit her when you were about two years old, your mama

166

and your daddy were so happy. They belonged together and everything had worked out the way God intended." She pressed her hand against her chest. "I believe with all my heart that everything worked out the way it was supposed to."

There were tears in Jasmine's eyes when she nodded. She wanted to believe that, she had to believe it. "So . . . what about my . . . grandparents?" Jasmine asked, though she wasn't sure that they deserved to be called anything more than Ada Mae and Boone. "Are they alive?" And then, she held her breath. Because suppose they were alive — would she want to see them? And if she did, what would she say to them? And then she imagined how much she'd have to repent because she knew exactly what she'd say.

But before she could come up with all the ways that she would curse them, Aunt Virginia squashed her thoughts: "No, they're not alive. I done outlived all of them. It's been more than a spell with Boone; he didn't even make it to the three score and ten that the Bible promises. But Ada Mae." She shook her head. "We just lost her last year."

A tear rolled down Jasmine's cheek and her heart ached when she asked, "So, they were alive when my mother died? And they didn't even come to her funeral?"

Aunt Virginia shook her head. "Jasmine, you've got to understand that by then, everyone was so deep into the life and the lies they'd created. Your grandparents knew about you and Serena and your . . . dad. I told them everything. But once they'd decided . . . once your mother decided that it was going to be a certain way, it just stayed that way."

With her palm, Jasmine wiped her tears away. "I don't understand."

"Well, just because you don't understand, that doesn't mean that wasn't the way it was. You ain't gonna understand all the ways of this world and you're never gonna understand all the people. You may have made a different decision, but for Ada Mae, Boone, and your mama, this was their decision. And it seemed to work for all of them."

A single sob passed through Jasmine's lips, and she fought hard to push back the rest of her sorrow. Mae Frances placed her hand on Jasmine's shoulder as if she knew her soul needed to be calmed.

"So . . ." Aunt Virginia said. But then she said no more.

"I don't know what I'm supposed to say."

"I just gave you more than a lifetime of

information. You don't have to say anything else."

Jasmine nodded. "Well, now at least I know more about my mother."

"And now maybe it's time for you to find out about your father," Mae Frances said.

It took a moment for those words to register and when they did, Jasmine jumped up and glared down at the woman she thought was her friend. "I know everything that I need to know about . . . that man," she growled, thinking once again about how Simon Jackson had deserted her mother.

Both Mae Frances and Aunt Virginia pressed their backs against their chairs. "You don't know anything more than one side," Mae Frances said. "You need to know the other side of the story. You need to find out everything you can about your father."

Jasmine raised her hand as if she wanted to slap somebody. But she held back, and instead all the tears she'd been fighting poured forth. She screamed, "I will never claim that man as my father! Never!"

And then she ran from the kitchen, leaving Mae Frances and Aunt Virginia both with their mouths wide open.

CHAPTER 15

RACHEL

You can't choose your family. The words Rachel's mother used to always mutter filled her head. That was so true, because there is no way she would've ever chosen to be related to the monstrosity standing in the middle of her father's living room.

"Lookie here!" her cousin Teeny said, wobbling his six-foot-three, four-hundred-pound frame over to her, picking her up and swinging her around like she was a rag doll. "Girl, I ain't seen you in ten years," he bellowed.

"I. Can't. Breathe," Rachel said, squirming, trying to get out of her cousin's massive grip.

Teeny dropped her, laughing like he was some kind of clown. Rachel shot her father an evil eye. She had just come over because her father had needed her to sign some papers for his new life insurance policy. But he should've warned her that Teeny was here — and she would've definitely taken a U-turn and signed the papers later.

Simon smiled, like he found the whole situation amusing. Growing up, Rachel used to be entertained by Teeny's over-the-top antics. He was the complete opposite of his criminal brother, Buster. And as her aunt Minnie's youngest child, he always had to be center stage. But as she'd gotten older, Teeny had become an embarrassment — loud, boisterous, sloppy — and Rachel had been thrilled when Aunt Minnie packed her family up and moved back to Arkansas.

Rachel had only seen Teeny one other time since they had moved, at her mother's funeral, when he showed up with his anorexic girlfriend. He was so happy, talking about how "she completed him." She completed him all right, Rachel had thought. They were a complete number ten.

"So, I hear you big-time now!" he exclaimed, playfully punching her in the arm a little too hard. "Let me hold a hun'ed dollars." He released a crow-sounding laugh and didn't seem fazed that he was the only one laughing.

"Teeny lives in Baton Rouge now. He just stopped through on his way to Arkansas,"

Simon said, stepping up and rescuing Rachel.

Teeny pulled his pants up. Rachel wanted to tell him to try a belt but they probably didn't make them in his size.

"Yep, I'm taking my time. Since my Emily ran off with the UPS man, I ain't got nothing but time." A flicker of sadness passed over him, but the smile quickly returned. "Well, I'm like U-Haul, I gots to keep it movin'. So I'm driving big rigs now. Dropped a load off in Waco, now I'm gonna go pick up Mama in Pine Bluff and then we gon' meet y'all at the family reunion," he said. He narrowed his eyes, zooming in on Rachel. "I am gon' see y'all at the family reunion, right? You know Uncle Bubba's the last of grandpa's siblings. He's turning eighty and he wants us all there."

"Don't worry," Simon said. "We'll be there." He patted Rachel's forearm. "All of us." He shot her a sly smile, then added, "Matter of fact, we may have a new relative to introduce you to."

Rachel inhaled. It wasn't written that Jasmine would show up in Smackover, so the last thing her dad needed to do was get his hopes up and go telling folks about his "newfound daughter."

"New relative? Whatchu talkin' 'bout, Unc?"

"Nothing," Rachel quickly interjected, but Simon ignored her as he kept talking.

"I said, I can't wait for you to meet your new cousin." He paused, grinning like he was introducing the world to a newborn baby. "My daughter, Jasmine."

That stung Rachel's core. For thirty years, she'd been her father's only daughter. And now, just like that, he was claiming someone else.

"Daughter?" Teeny bellowed. He slapped Simon on the back. "Unc, you ain't tell me you had it like that. I didn't know your little soldiers still had ammunition. Aww, shucky, shucky now. What you look like with a little girl?"

Rachel couldn't help but roll her eyes as Simon laughed.

"Nah, nephew, it ain't like that. And I ain't never stepped out on any of my wives," he said, smiling in Brenda's direction as she sat in the corner, knitting. She returned his smile as he continued. "But I did just discover that my very first love gave me my very first child."

That burning in her heart had escalated into a full-fledged inferno. Her father was acting like Jasmine was the best thing since the invention of the Internet. He already had a daughter. Jasmine was just an additive. Like you add a little bit of seasoning to an already wonderful pot of gumbo. He was acting like Jasmine was the gumbo.

But his words made her thoughts shift in another direction. All this time, she'd been concerned about Jasmine's history being rewritten. This revelation altered Rachel's history as well.

My very first love gave me my very first child.

Rachel mother's, Loretta, was not her father's first true love as she'd always believed. But more than that, Rachel was not his first daughter.

"Wow, Unc," Teeny continued, plopping down on the sofa. "Tell me about my new cousin. Is she single?"

"No, but she's your cousin, nasty behind," Rachel snapped.

"Half cousin," he said with a smirk. "Girl, you know I'm messing with you," he said when he saw the disgust on Rachel's face. "We don't mix up bloodlines. Although I think you gon' have to remind her of that quite often, cuz once she see all this fineness, she gon' be smitten."

"Even if you weren't family, I don't think you ever have to worry about that," Simon said with a chuckle. "She has her a prominent preacher. He's on TV. They are real high class. I even saw an article in *Gospel Today* calling them a power couple. Just google her. All kinds of great stuff on the Internet about her."

Rachel could only stare at her father. He'd been researching Jasmine? She wanted to ask him if he saw the article about how his precious new daughter used to make it rain for singles.

"So, when do I get to meet this high-class cousin?" Teeny asked.

"Hopefully at the family reunion. I called and left her a message. I —"

"You what?" Rachel said, cutting him off.

"I called her," Simon repeated. "I mean, I know you wanted me to wait, but I just can't. I'm just bursting at the seams to see her. I feel like I have decades to catch up on. I want to know her. I want to know about Doris."

"Dad!" Rachel said, pointing to Brenda in the corner, who hadn't looked up.

"Oh, I'm not trying to be disrespectful. Brenda knows how much I love her. But I've told her all about Doris." A nostalgic smile spread across his face. "I was young, but ours was a solid love. She was just as sweet as sugarcane and —"

"Like seriously, I don't want to hear this,

Dad, and I'm sure Brenda doesn't, either," Rachel interrupted again.

"I want to hear it, though, Unc. I always love a good love story. Reminds me of me and Emily before the UPS man stole her," Teeny said.

Simon looked at Rachel, then over at Brenda, before turning back to Teeny. He still wore his smile, but it was like he was trying — but failing — to tone it down.

"I'll tell you about it later. Next week at the reunion."

Teeny patted his legs. "Yeah, I probably need to be gettin' on up the road. Don't like drivin' at night too much." It took about four attempts, but he finally pulled himself up off the sofa. "Cuz, it was good to see you again." He leaned in to Rachel. "But, um, I was serious 'bout that hun'ed. Can you help a brotha out?"

"Ugh," Rachel said in disgust as she turned and headed out the door toward her car. She was so disgusted with her cousin and her father. She ignored her father as he called out after her and she definitely ignored Teeny as he shouted, "Be like that then! I bet my new high-class cousin would give me a hun'ed bucks!"

Rachel wanted to tell him he'd be lucky if Jasmine gave him the time for a conversation, let alone one silver nickel. But she knew that if she turned around and saw her father still looking like some proud papa, she might very well burst into tears.

CHAPTER 16

RACHEL

'Cause I'd love, love, love to dance with my father again.

Rachel's Luther Vandross ringtone filled the air inside her Range Rover. She debated not answering, but she couldn't bring herself to ignore her father's phone call.

"Hello," she said, pushing the talk button on her speaker.

"Hey, baby girl," Simon softly said.

"Hey."

A brief silence hung between them. Finally Simon said, "Did I do something to make you mad?"

Rachel let out a deep sigh. She wanted to say there was no way her father could be so clueless. But there was. She'd grown up without him even realizing how much his actions (everything from missing her dance recitals to his condemnations) hurt her.

"I mean, Brenda said you were mad.

That's why you left," Simon said.

A pause, then Rachel replied, "I'm good."

It was Simon's turn to sigh. "That means you're not. Is this about Jasmine, I mean, what I said about her?"

Rachel choked back the lump in her throat. What was she supposed to say? *I'm upset because you were proudly talking about your new daughter?*

"It's no big deal, Daddy."

He hesitated again. "Well, you left before signing the papers. That's why you came over here in the first place."

Rachel silently cursed. "Dad, can I just do it tomorrow?"

"They have to be signed and postmarked today. Brenda is gonna take them to the post office soon as we're done."

Rachel wanted to tell him to forge her name or something, but she knew there was no way her father would ever do something illegal.

"Fine," she huffed. "I'll be back in ten."

Rachel exited off the freeway and made a U-turn to head back to her father's house.

When she pulled back into the driveway, Rachel hesitated before getting out. Was she being petty? "No," she mumbled. Her feelings were very much real and her father needed to take those feelings into consider-

179

ation when dealing with this situation.

Rachel looked around to make sure Teeny's truck was gone, then she got out and dragged herself up the walkway.

"Are you okay?" Brenda asked, meeting her at the door.

Rachel nodded as she stepped inside. "Where's Dad?"

"Still in the den." Brenda leaned in and whispered, "Talk to him about it, Rachel. You know your father. He didn't mean anything, but he's not going to understand that this affects you, too, unless you tell him."

Rachel gave Brenda a slight smile. After her mother died, Rachel had never wanted to see her father with anyone else. But she couldn't deny how good Brenda was to and for her father. And while she'd never fully embraced her stepmother, the woman still never failed to dispense motherly advice.

As she made her way to the back, Rachel took Brenda's words into account. She had to let her father know what she was feeling. Growing up, she'd held on to bitterness about her father's detachment, but she'd come so far since then. She wasn't about to travel down that road again.

Simon dropped the photo he was looking at and sat up as Rachel walked in. He'd

180

moved it quickly, but Rachel could tell it was that old tattered photo of Doris.

"Baby girl, I'm sorry," Simon said.

Rachel eased onto the sofa next to him. "So am I. I shouldn't have stormed out like that. It's just . . . it's just that . . ." For some reason, she felt like a little girl pleading for love and attention again. "It's just that, well, I'm no longer your only daughter. That's a huge pill to swallow. And then to see your excitement about Jasmine . . ."

Simon scooted up to the edge of his chair and reached out to take her hand. "Rachel, I know we've had some issues, but you will always be my number one girl. Yes, I'm excited about Jasmine, because she's a piece of my first love, but that doesn't discount what I feel for you."

Rachel grimaced as he continued. "Your mother knew that," he added, as if he could tell that was painful to hear. "She knew how I felt about Doris. Loretta knew that while Doris and I were young, our love was very real. I would've married her if I could have. When I lost contact with Doris, it broke my heart. I tried everything, but my letters went unanswered and I had no way to get in touch with her. I wanted to find her so we could spend the rest of our lives together. But that wasn't God's plan. God wanted me to marry your mother."

Rachel hadn't even realized she was crying until a tear fell onto her lap.

"Your mother was okay with that because it was my past," Simon continued.

"But it's like you want to relive the past."

"Why? Because I talk about Doris with fondness? I loved her. And to know that she carried my child, and to think of all she had to endure . . ." Simon's words trailed off as he choked back his words. "I just want to get to know the child I didn't get to know."

His words were profound and tore at Rachel's heart. She took a deep breath and found herself saying, "You really want her at the reunion, don't you?"

"Nothing would make me prouder," Simon said. "I know our family is a little different from hers."

That finally made Rachel chuckle. "A little?"

"Regardless, it's family and I want her to get to know us. Get to know *me.*"

Rachel smiled at her father. "I get that."

"So will you help me? Maybe call her and let me talk to her?"

That wiped the smile right off her face. "What makes you think she will take my calls?"

Simon shrugged. "I don't know if she will.

But I have to exhaust every effort. I *will* exhaust every effort. I'm not giving up."

"Dad, I just don't know. Jasmine is not taking this news well and I just don't like you calling her, because she might say the wrong thing."

"And? Won't be the first time someone said something to me sideways. She has a right to be angry, so it won't bother me none."

Rachel sighed. She knew it would be a moot point to try to convince Simon Jackson of anything else once he set his mind to something.

"Fine."

"Fine? So, you'll call?" He was acting like a kid about to go get his favorite snow cone.

"Yes." Rachel nodded.

"You'll call now?"

Rachel shook her head, but dug in her purse for her cell phone. "Yes, Daddy. I'll call now."

A sense of relief and happiness swept over Simon, while Rachel fought back the stinging feeling in her heart. She scrolled through her phone until she reached the Ts. She swiped "Old Troll" and waited for Jasmine's number to begin ringing. It rang once. Then twice. By the third ring, Rachel was hoping that it went to voice mail, so she almost hung up when Jasmine picked up.

"Yes, Rachel?" Jasmine said, not bothering to hide her irritation.

"Hey," Rachel said, not feeding into her attitude. "How are you doing?"

"I'm fine." Her tone was dry, as if Rachel was getting on her nerves.

"Well, good. I, um, I was calling, well, I'm here with my, our . . . with Daddy," she said, pushing the words out.

Silence filled the phone and Rachel had no idea what to make of it.

"He just, he wanted to speak with you," Rachel continued.

"Rachel, I'm not —"

Before she could finish her sentence, Simon took the phone out of her hand. "Jasmine. It's Simon."

Rachel watched her father intensely. Everything inside her wanted to snatch the phone back. Jasmine wasn't ready. Rachel could hear it in her silence.

"I'm so happy to talk to you. I know this is all a bit much, but I just, well, I need to see you. To talk to you." He paused and it was killing Rachel, wanting to know what Jasmine was saying. Simon continued. "I understand that and I'm sorry to call you like this. But I left a few messages. I have so much I need to say. I'm sure you have questions, too. I mean, there's so much I could tell you about your mother and I know this is difficult, but you were conceived in love and I want to make sure —" He paused again. "I understand, but if you would just give me a chance, I know I could answer some of your questions. I was thinking our family reunion next week would be the perfect time. We'll have almost a hundred of our family members in Smackover, Arkansas, and I could show you where me and your mom met. I could introduce you to relatives." He was rushing his words out as if he was scared she would hang up on him at any moment.

Rachel was on the edge of her seat. Then the deflated look that passed over her father's face told her Jasmine's answer.

"I really wish . . ." He took a deep breath. "Well, take some time and think about it . . . I understand . . . Yes . . . Okay. Thank you for talking to me."

He slowly eased the phone away from his ear and handed it back to Rachel.

"Well, what did she say?" Rachel asked as she took her phone and dropped it back in her purse.

"She said no."

"No? Just no?"

"Just no." Simon stood and Rachel saw

the mist in his eyes. That broke her heart. She could count on one finger the number of times she'd ever seen her father cry. "Excuse me, baby girl," he said. "I need to go."

He scurried out of the room. Rachel knew he needed to be alone so she didn't go after him. But now she was incensed. Jasmine wasn't the only one hurting. They all were, and if there was one thing she wasn't going to do, it was stand by while Jasmine hurt her father even more. She'd put her own feelings aside to give her father this one wish.

Rachel felt a new resolve. Jasmine *would* be going to their family reunion. If she had to, Rachel would use every trick she had to make that happen.

CHAPTER 17

JASMINE

Jasmine pressed END on her phone and wished she could press it again and again so Simon Jackson would get her point. She knew she shouldn't have answered the phone. She'd ignored all the calls from Simon; once she'd heard that first message he'd left on the day she'd flown back from Alabama, she'd saved his number into her phone just to make sure she never answered him, not even by accident.

So then, why oh why had she answered Rachel's call? She had deleted that woman's number, but she recognized it when the phone rang. Still, she'd answered. Why? But Jasmine knew why. Because, while she was ignoring Simon, she wanted to make sure that he *knew* she was ignoring him. And she wanted him to know that she would never speak to him. When she'd answered Rachel's call, Jasmine had wanted to send that message to Simon and then tell Rachel that both of them needed to lose her number.

But then, Rachel had betrayed her, the way she always did, and put Simon on the phone. She'd wanted to just hang up in his face, but her real father had raised her too well for her to behave that way.

"Who was that?"

Hosea's voice snatched her thoughts away from the call. "Nobody," she said.

Hosea raised one eyebrow and glanced around his office. Jasmine followed his gaze to the bookshelves that were stuffed with Bibles in every translation to the singular Holy Book that sat on his desk. And it made her remember that she was sitting in the middle of one of the largest churches in the city.

"All right! That was Simon," she confessed. "But I didn't lie," she added as if she needed to explain that to her husband and to God. "He's nobody to me."

"He's your father."

Jasmine glared at Hosea. "No matter how many times you say that, it's not going to change the fact that he's not."

With a sigh, Hosea rose from his side of the desk and came around. Then he planted himself next to her on the sofa. "Why are you fighting this so much?"

"Because it's just so ridiculous!" She jumped up and paced in front of him. "I mean, really, Hosea. I'm damn near . . . you know . . . just about . . . in my . . . around forty . . . ish . . . and now I find out that not only is my father not my father, but that the woman I hate . . . well, one of the women I hate . . . is my sister? Come on now." She folded her arms. "This sounds like a bad novel where the author couldn't come up with a better plot. This doesn't sound like my life. This doesn't *feel* like my life."

"I can't even begin to imagine how you feel, but that's the reason I really wish you'd at least talk to Simon. Because I know it will make you feel better."

"And how could it possibly do that?"

"Because it'll answer your questions."

"Aunt Virginia answered all my questions."

Hosea nodded. "I think she answered what a young girl told her, but if you were to talk to Simon, you could find out even more about your mother. And I know you've always wanted to know more about her."

Jasmine tilted her head and examined her husband. She had never really told him that. All she'd ever said was that she felt cheated when she lost her mother back when she was in college. She felt cheated because she'd always looked forward to knowing her mother, woman-to-woman. That's something that Doris had always promised her.

I can't wait for my little girl to grow up. Because then I'll be more than your mommy: we'll be friends, best friends. Because you're my special little girl.

Jasmine remembered her mother's words, and she felt cheated once again, the way she always felt when she thought about those lost years with her mother.

If only her mother had lived . . . would life have been different? Would she, Jasmine, have ended up as one of LA's most notorious strippers, would she have cheated on Kenny Larson, her first husband, the night *before* their wedding, and then all those times afterward? Would she have lived a life that had her cheating with every married man she could find?

Maybe she had always cheated because she'd been cheated. Really, if Jasmine thought back, it was her mother's death that had set her on that path.

And now, with this ridiculous revelation, Jasmine felt like she was on the verge of being cheated once again — this time out of a father.

But she wasn't going to let Simon or Rachel or Hosea or anyone do that to her. She'd lost her mother when she was twenty; she wasn't about to lose her father now that she was closer to fifty than forty. No matter what a freakin' test said.

And it wasn't just because to her Charles Cox would always be her father. It was that Simon Jackson didn't deserve to call her *daughter.* Not after the way he'd treated her mother.

"So, what did Simon say?" Hosea asked.

Hearing his name aloud made her cringe all over. "I don't want to talk about this, Hosea."

"Humor me," he said with a smile, but that was just a ruse. He was pretending this was a lighthearted conversation, but her husband was in pastor mode and she hated when he tried to minister to her.

She glared at him. He smiled back. Silent seconds passed between them. And then, God won.

Jasmine sighed. "He said he wanted to talk and explain stuff to me."

Hosea nodded.

"And he said," Jasmine continued, "that he wants me to come to his family reunion."

"In Houston?"

"No, in Smackover." She'd told Hosea

about the conversation with Aunt Virginia and had told him how that town had held a special place in her mother's heart. But what she'd left out, what she hadn't told anyone was that now she felt a tug on her heart whenever she heard of or thought about Smackover. She thought about that place where her mother had first fallen in love. And she couldn't help but think about it as the place where *her* life began. It was the city where she was conceived.

The truth of it was that Jasmine Cox Larson Bush was from Smackover, Arkansas!

But that didn't have anything to do with her and this family reunion. Those people weren't her family.

It was the way Hosea looked at her that made her grab her purse, sling it over her shoulder, and fold her arms. "I swear if you say one word to me about going to Smackover, I'm out of here."

"I thought we were going out to dinner."

"We won't be going anywhere if you say that . . ."

"Oh, come on. You can't tell me you're not curious. I mean, Smackover." He stood and wrapped his arms around her. "Who could pass up an invitation like that?" he asked in a tone that was supposed to make her laugh, but all she wanted to do was cry.

192

"Me! I can pass it up."

"So, you're not even a little bit curious about that place and those people . . . your people?"

"No!" she said, though that was a lie. Her curiosity kept rising and the truth was, she did plan to go down there. She wanted to walk through the town, see what her mother saw, see if it would bring her any kind of connection, bring her any closer to the mother she loved even more now knowing what she had been through for her. Knowing how her mother had kept her against everyone else's wishes.

But she didn't want to visit Smackover with anyone around. Especially not Simon, Rachel, and *their* family. She wasn't even sure if she was going to tell Mae Frances or Hosea when she finally made that trip. She was thinking that her journey to Smackover would be best done alone.

"I want you to do me a favor," Hosea said as he slid the purse from Jasmine's shoulder. "I want you to pray."

"I pray every morning."

Hosea chuckled. "Well, there's no law against praying all day, any day, all the time. I want you to go into the sanctuary and pray."

"Hosea," she said, rolling her eyes.

193

"No, seriously. I'm not saying to pray so that God will tell you to go to Smackover, because even if He did, I don't think you're going to listen to Him. You're not going to listen to anyone right now because your heart is so hard."

"No, it's not."

"And I'm always concerned about anyone who walks around with a hardened heart," he said as if he didn't hear her objection. He stepped away, but even as he walked back to his desk, she stood like a planted tree. He sat down in his chair and picked up his Bible. "I can give you the scriptures about what happens to folks with hard hearts. Check out Romans, chapter two, verse five." And then without even opening the Bible, Hosea quoted, "But because of your hard and impenitent heart you are storing up wrath for yourself on the day of wrath when God's righteous judgment —"

"All right!" Jasmine said, not even letting her husband finish. She marched out of the office and into the hallway that led to the sanctuary. She couldn't say that she'd ever heard that verse before, but it didn't matter. Hosea had said enough to make her think maybe she should pray.

Jasmine stepped through the door that Hosea and his father used to enter the sanctuary during services. And she paused for a moment. City of Lights at Riverside Church always seemed so grand to her, but never more than when it was like this. The rows and rows that held three thousand in both of their Sunday services were empty, and even though dusk was fast approaching, there was no artificial light. The sun that still shone outside streamed through the huge stained-glass windows, creating beams of light throughout.

With reverence, Jasmine moved toward the altar, her slow steps silent on the thick carpet. And as she got closer, she smiled a little. This had been Hosea's idea, but now she was glad that she was here. Because for the first time since she'd heard this news, she felt serene. There was no one in her ear telling her what to do. No one trying to make her feel bad when Simon Jackson should be the one to carry all the shame.

At the front, she stood for a moment, staring at the gold cross that hung high on the wall behind the pulpit. She thought of the times when she'd come here by herself to pray. It still amazed her that she knew God this way. And yes, she did know Him. And He knew her, which was even more of a shock to Jasmine. But she knew she had this relationship with God because when she prayed, she felt Him.

But when she prayed here at the altar, she heard Him.

Using the rail for balance, she lowered herself onto the cushions. Then she bowed her head and her heart and she talked to God. She prayed for peace — that was what she wanted most. And she prayed for God to loosen her heart. Not enough for her to go to Smackover, because Hosea was right — God Himself would have to send Jesus Himself down from Heaven itself to convince her that she should go. And even then, she was sure *she'd* be able to convince God *and* His Son that she didn't need to be near Arkansas right now.

But she wanted her heart loose enough so she could feel peace. And she knew that here, at the altar, God would give it to her.

CHAPTER 18

RACHEL

Rachel studied the digital ARRIVALS SCREEN. JFK flights to Little Rock. 10:40. On time.

A flutter of nervousness passed through her stomach. Jasmine was about to meet her people. Jasmine, who always had something to say, was really about to meet the craziness that was the Jackson family.

Rachel still couldn't believe that she was here. That she'd done it. That she'd actually been able to convince Jasmine to come to Smackover. She smiled, proud of herself. All her life, people had underestimated her. Even Jasmine had underestimated her when their husbands first started running for the American Baptist Coalition presidency. People thought that she could be ditzy. But Rachel wasn't anything close to a fool. She had street sense *and* common sense and she knew how to get what she wanted. That's why after two days of racking her brain, she'd come up with the perfect plan to get Jasmine to agree to come to Arkansas.

Her cell phone rang, snapping Rachel out of her thoughts. She smiled when her best friend's name popped up on the screen. Twyla had all but bet her that Jasmine wouldn't show.

"I was right, wasn't I?" Twyla said before Rachel could even say hello.

"Her flight hasn't landed and as far as I know, she's still coming."

Twyla tsked. She'd never even met Jasmine, but after everything Rachel had shared, Twyla made it clear she didn't care for her. "I just can't believe she's coming. What I wouldn't give to be a fly on the wall."

"It's not that serious," Rachel said.

"Please. That bougie heifer. You make sure your uncle Bubba feeds her some coon."

Rachel laughed. "You know even I don't eat that mess."

"Well, feed it to her anyway. And record it and put it on Facebook."

They laughed and joked some more as Rachel slid into a seat outside of baggage claim.

After a few minutes, Twyla said, "Rachel, all jokes aside. I'm proud of you. When you told me you had thought about lying to get her there, I knew that was the route you were going to take."

Twyla was right. Rachel had been trying to come up with a plan to get Jasmine to agree to come to the family reunion. After the switcheroo with her father, she knew Jasmine would be unlikely to answer any more of her calls. So she'd contemplated lying, telling Jasmine some elaborate story to get her to come, but in the end she just wanted to operate in a place of truth. Her relationship with Jasmine was up-and-down enough. Lies would only shake the foundation even more.

"Yeah, I couldn't do it," Rachel said.

"Well, you found a way to get through to her. But look, Calvin just got back with the kids so I gotta go before he starts trippin'. Call and let me know how it went. Or better yet, post it on Facebook." She laughed.

"Bye, girl." Rachel wasn't about to let this weekend play out on social media for her friends' entertainment.

She leaned back and thought about everything. It was actually her daughter who had helped her come up with a plan.

Rachel had been sitting at her computer, on the verge of giving up on the whole Jasmine family reunion thing, when Nia had come bouncing into her office.

"Hey, Mom. What are you doing?"

"Just working, sweet pea."

Nia leaned in and looked at her computer screen, where she had been reading an article about Jasmine. "Why are you reading about Ms. Jasmine?"

"Just doing some work."

"Ooh, look at Jacqueline's dress, Mom," Nia said, pointing to a picture in the bottom right-hand corner of the screen. Jasmine and her children were standing in front of a building with a bright yellow ribbon around it. It looked like a grand opening. Rachel leaned in closer to read the caption.

"Oh, it looks like that's for her charity, Jacqueline's Hope," Rachel said.

"I hope I can get a fancy dress like that." Nia turned to her mom. "Why don't you open a charity in my name?"

Rachel smiled and shuttled her daughter out of the office. "Little girl, go clean your room."

Nia laughed as she exited. "I'm serious, Mom. I want a charity."

Rachel shook her head at her little drama queen. If only Nia knew why Jasmine had started Jacqueline's Hope. She wouldn't want to have to endure a kidnapping, just to have a charity named after her. Rachel was proud of the traction Jacqueline's Hope was getting. As she finished reading the article, she stopped when she got to one line. A direct quote from Jasmine: "We hope to expand Jacqueline's Hope."

Then, a slow smile spread across Rachel's face.

Expand.

She'd made a few calls, first to her cousin Leo, who directed her to her cousin Wanda, who confirmed that the old Piggly Wiggly building that was owned by her aunt Ruby was still abandoned.

The perfect place to expand.

Simon had been thrilled with the idea and made a call to Aunt Ruby, who would do anything for her brother, including give him a building she had long ago stopped caring about but refused to sell because it had been the one legacy her father had left her.

So Rachel had called, and called, and called, until Jasmine finally picked up.

"Why are you blowing up my phone?" Jasmine had snapped without even saying hello.

"Because I need to talk to you," Rachel replied.

Jasmine let out a heavy sigh. "Rachel, seriously, I can't do this with you. I only answered to plead with you to just leave me alone."

"Jasmine, I understand what you're going through. More than you even know."

"I'm glad you understand, but that doesn't change —"

"We want to open a Jacqueline's Hope in Smackover."

That caused an abrupt silence and Rachel seized the opportunity

"This isn't about you or me. Or even Daddy. This is about the thousands of children all over the South who need something like Jacqueline's Hope." Rachel knew she was laying it on thick, but she would do whatever was necessary. Besides, she believed in the cause, so it wasn't like she was lying. "Don't let your hard heart stop others from getting a blessing. You've been talking about expanding. You don't have any centers in the South. Think of the difference this could make. Building this facility in a place your mother met her first love." She rushed her words out, making sure the sincerity was evident. "My family has a building that would be perfect. My aunt Ruby loves children and would be great to run it. Or you could bring in your own staff. It's a win-win for everyone."

Rachel could tell by Jasmine's silence that she was making progress, so she continued. "Yes, my father wants to see you, get to know you, but he won't push a relationship. If you want to just say hello to our family, then go back to your hotel, we'll even understand that." Rachel didn't bother to tell her the only hotel was the Super 8. "I'll take care of your hotel reservations, contact the media in nearby cities, and since my grandmother used to babysit the mayor, he'll even come out in support."

"And you're doing all of this because?"

"I believe in Jacqueline's Hope, that's why. And I want to make my father happy. Being able to do this for you would bring him joy."

More silence. Then, finally, Jasmine said, "I'll think about it and call you back tomorrow." She hung up the phone without another word.

That had been a week ago. She had indeed called Rachel back the next day and agreed to come. She claimed it was only because of Jacqueline's Hope, but Rachel could tell she had some underlying reasons. It didn't matter, she was coming.

It was at that point that Rachel looked up and saw a diva strutting through the small airport, her oversized designer sunglasses on, rolling Chanel luggage, her face devoid of a smile.

Jasmine wasn't just coming. She was here.

CHAPTER 19

JASMINE

Head high. Steps deliberate. No emotion.

That mantra played in Jasmine's head as she stepped off the escalator. Right away she spotted Rachel to her left, standing next to one of the tables near the windows. Even from so many feet away, Jasmine could tell from the way Rachel clutched her purse that she was nervous.

The polite thing would have been for Jasmine to acknowledge her, and to move toward Rachel. Instead she turned to her right and strutted toward the Starbucks counter. It wasn't that she was trying to be rude. It was just that she needed drugs before she could face her . . . Jasmine paused the thought in her head. She wasn't prepared to call Rachel anything more than Rachel. She needed another cup of coffee before she could even do that.

She stopped at the counter, and behind

her Hosea whispered, "Darlin', Rachel's over there."

Jasmine nodded, though she didn't turn around. "I saw her."

"Don't you think we should at least go over there first?"

"No."

Then, before Hosea could say another word, Jacqueline shouted out, "Auntie Rachel!"

Jasmine whipped around as she watched her daughter dash like an Olympian through the maze of tables and then jump into Rachel's arms.

Ugh! Traitor!

At least Zaya didn't rush over to her. Why did Jacqueline love Rachel so much? And then Jasmine wondered if somehow her daughter knew. She and Hosea hadn't said a word to the children about this situation and Jasmine had no intention of ever saying anything. She wouldn't have even been on the plane, she would've never seen Rachel again if it weren't for Jacqueline's Hope.

She'd been praying to open up a third facility and Jasmine would've thought this was some kind of trick if Rachel hadn't called two days after Jasmine had been in the sanctuary praying. True, she hadn't been praying about Jacqueline's Hope, but wasn't that just like God? Jacqueline's Hope wasn't in her prayers that day, but it had been in her heart. And He'd given her the desire of her heart — even if it had to come through Simon and Rachel. Jasmine didn't care who brought the blessing; she was just grateful that she was being blessed. And so many children and parents would be blessed, too. That was why she had agreed to come to Smackover. Because she would do anything to help a missing child's family and to have the hope of returning even one child to his or her home.

Even though she would do anything for her charity, however, she wasn't going to have a thing to do with . . . this family. She, Hosea, and the children were here only for the business of Jacqueline's Hope and Jasmine had made sure that Rachel (and Simon, through Rachel) understood that.

"I'll come, but only because of my charity." Jasmine recalled the words she'd said on their last telephone call.

"I understand," Rachel had responded.

"I'm serious. I don't want to speak to or see your father."

Rachel had paused before she said, "Jasmine, he's your father, too."

"If you don't understand English, if you don't understand my rules . . ."

"I understand!" Rachel had snapped. "I'm just saying, how are you going to be in the same city and not even say hello to him?"

"I'm hanging up now," Jasmine had said in warning.

"Okay, okay. You're only coming to open up Jacqueline's Hope. Nothing more."

"And you'll pay all of our expenses."

"What?" Rachel had shouted, sounding like she was about to pop a vein.

"We'll need a suite with two bedrooms, preferably three. If there's not a three-bedroom available, Mae Frances will need her own room."

"And why should I pay for all of that?"

"Because that's the only way I'll come."

There was so much silence after that that Jasmine had wondered if Rachel had changed her mind. And if she had, that would have been fine. But even that request hadn't been enough to get to Rachel and when she agreed, Jasmine had hung up.

Though Rachel had finally agreed to cover their hotel, meals, and transportation around Smackover, that didn't mean Jasmine trusted her. And she had her own plans.

Turning away from Starbucks, Jasmine moved as fast as she could toward Rachel and Jacqueline.

"How are you, Jacquie?" Rachel said as she wrapped her arms around her. "It's so good to see you."

Rachel held Jacqueline just a little too tight and Jasmine didn't like it. "Jacquie," she said. "Come on, you don't want to mess up *Miss* Rachel's . . ." She paused and looked Rachel up and down. "You don't want to mess up *Miss* Rachel's jeans, do you?"

"Oh, that's okay," Rachel said, pulling Jacqueline even closer to her. And then she said, "Hi, Jasmine."

Jasmine squinted, studying Rachel, trying to see if there was any deception in her eyes. But Rachel had been such a liar for so long, she knew how to hide behind eyes that pretended to be genuine.

Jasmine knew this whole Jacqueline's Hope thing was a ploy. Oh, of course, there was really a building — Jasmine had checked that out. And there was really a staff that had been hired to help them get started, including one of Rachel's aunts — Jasmine had checked that out, too. But even though Rachel had promised, Jasmine knew this was all about getting her down to Smackover during Rachel's family reunion.

Jasmine had wanted to tell Rachel that she could never outslick a slickster. But she kept all her plans to herself. She planned on losing herself, Hosea, and the kids in the city so that Simon would never even catch them at the hotel. And she planned on telling the front desk and the concierge to alert her if anyone came by asking for her — at least for tonight. While she was on the plane, she'd come up with another plan. As soon as Rachel dropped them off at the hotel, she was going to check them into another hotel and not tell Rachel where they were.

Jasmine still hadn't greeted her when Hosea hugged Rachel and then Rachel embraced Zaya. When she pulled back she said, "So, where's Mae Frances?"

"Here I am!" Mae Frances waved her hand high in the air as she sauntered over from the escalators. "I had to take care of my business in the restroom." When she stood in front of Rachel, Mae Frances added, "So you missed me, Roberta? Is that why you asked?"

Jasmine expected Rachel to roll her eyes, suck her teeth, or do one of her ghetto rolls with her neck. But she did none of the above. Just gave Mae Frances a small smile and answered, "I'm glad to see you, Mae Frances." Then she looked at Jasmine, Hosea, and finally, the children. "I'm glad to see all of you."

"Well ain't you something?" Mae Frances said. "Now that you got yourself a sis . . ."

Before Mae Frances could finish, Jasmine punched her in the arm.

"Owww! Jasmine Larson. What's wrong with you?"

Jasmine stroked her hand against the matted fur of Mae Frances's coat. "I'm sorry. I thought I saw something crawling up your arm. Anyway, Rachel, where's baggage claim?"

"Right here."

Jasmine hadn't noticed that they were practically at the baggage claim area. This airport was almost as small as the one she'd flown into in Mobile. Only Jasmine had expected a little bit more from Little Rock. After all, wasn't Little Rock the capital of Arkansas?

At the baggage carousel, Hosea stood on one side of Rachel and Mae Frances stood on the other as Rachel held on to Jacqueline and Zaya as if they were . . . long-lost relatives. When had this happened?

First of all, Hosea hardly knew Rachel, so why was he over there chitchatting? And her children. Sure, they'd seen Rachel far more than Hosea had, especially when they were in Atlanta filming their reality show. But when had they become so close to Rachel that Jacqueline, who hardly let Jasmine kiss her in public, had to be all up under Rachel now?

And finally, there was Mae Frances, who just needed to change her name to Judas. She was the ultimate betrayer, standing and chuckling as if Rachel (and not Jasmine) were her best friend. Really? Mae Frances could hardly remember that child's name and now they were friends?

But this wasn't her family's fault. This was all Rachel with her fake self. They didn't even realize that they were being sucked into Rachel's web. Well, Jasmine had something for her.

"Okay, these are all our bags, right?" Hosea asked.

Jasmine hadn't even noticed that the bags had rolled around. She counted. "Yes." Then she glanced around. "Uh . . . where are the porters?"

Rachel smirked. "You'll have to carry your own luggage here."

"What? Surely . . ."

"That's okay, darlin'," Hosea interrupted, handing both Zaya and Jacqueline their bags. "We can carry our own bags just this once." When her husband smirked at her the same way Rachel had, Jasmine wanted to smack both of them. "It'll be an adventure!" he added.

"Yeah, an adventure," her children chimed in together.

"And anyway, the car is parked right outside." Then Rachel marched away, followed by Hosea and the children. Mae Frances lingered behind.

"You really need to fix your face," her friend said when the others were far enough away. "You look like you don't want to be here."

"How high does your IQ need to be to figure that out?"

"Look, Jasmine Larson, don't get snarky with me. It's not my fault your mama got around."

She chuckled and Jasmine glared at her. "I thought you were my friend."

"I am."

"Why did you come down here, anyway?"

"That's a good question, because I could've been home working on the outline for my book. But you need me for moral support."

"Well, your support is not working."

"It would work if you would let it. Here's my advice: you have to be here anyway, so let's enjoy it. Have you ever been to Arkansas?"

"No."

"Me either. And that means that you've never been to Smackover. So I say let's have a good time while we're here. Let's do what Preacher Man said. Let's make this an adventure." Then she strutted off, ahead of Jasmine as if she wanted to catch up with Hosea and the kids . . . and Rachel.

Jasmine pouted. But then she stepped out into the July heat of Little Rock and she melted. "There is no way I can walk in one-hundred-degree temperatures." Looking at Rachel, Jasmine added, "Can you just get the car?"

"The car is right over here, Jasmine," Rachel said in a way-too-nice voice. "Just a couple of steps and you'll be right there."

Less than a minute later, the trunk of the Escalade was open and Hosea was stuffing their bags inside. Rachel opened the doors and the kids piled inside before Jasmine could get into the backseat. Well, at least she would still be able to sit in the second row.

But then Hosea whispered, "You sit up front with Rachel."

He didn't give her a chance to respond before he jumped in next to Mae Frances. Jasmine could have squeezed in with them, but then Rachel would've looked like she was driving Miss Daisy.

Not that she had any problem with that, but Hosea certainly would have. So she climbed into the front seat, secured her seat belt, and kept her eyes on the road ahead.

"So, how far is Smackover, Rasheda?"

"It's about two hours south," Rachel answered as if Mae Frances had addressed her properly. "Right down 167."

Two hours? What am I supposed to talk about for two hours? But as they rolled out of the airport, Jasmine realized that she wasn't going to have to say too much. It seemed like Rachel was going to play tour guide.

"So, do y'all know anything about Little Rock?"

"No," everyone sang. Everyone except for Jasmine.

"Well, Little Rock is the capital and largest city in Arkansas. It has a population of about seven hundred thousand, and is actually in central Arkansas . . ."

Really? Did she think anyone cared?

Rachel went on and on about the hills and the lakes, the mild winters and humid summers — all the things that no one in the world would be interested in. So why was her family oohing and aahing with every word that passed from Rachel's lips?

After about fifteen minutes, once they'd

hit the two-lane highway, Jasmine wanted to tell Rachel to just shut up! But she let her talk to Hosea and Mae Frances and Jacqueline and Zaya because that meant that she didn't have to talk to her.

Actually, Jasmine didn't want to talk to anyone. All she wanted to do was think about Smackover and her mother.

She closed her eyes and imagined her mother, all those years ago, rolling down this road on one of those rickety church buses. The first year, her mother didn't know what awaited her. But Jasmine could imagine her mother's excitement each time after that as Doris headed toward the city where Jasmine had been conceived.

This is where I was born, she allowed herself to think. Of course, she'd actually breathed her first breath in Los Angeles. But if it weren't for Smackover . . .

At least, she should be grateful to Simon Jackson for that — for giving her life. Not that she wanted to give him any kind of credit, lest it took away from the man who really loved her.

She leaned back in the seat and let her mind continue to wander. It was just so hard to believe that the woman she'd called Mommy had done all the things she'd told Jasmine not to do.

The only way to keep the boy is to keep the boy waiting, her mother had told her when she was twelve years old.

You don't want to grow up too fast, Jas. Grown-up acts are for grown-up people, she'd said when Jasmine was fourteen.

But all her warnings had really kicked in when Jasmine was sixteen.

Be careful because boys only want one thing.

She had been trying to pass on the lessons she'd learned, and Jasmine didn't even know it.

Jasmine's mind drifted with memories, long-ago situations that she had long ago forgotten. The times when it was just her with her mother, the times when her mother had told her that she was her special girl, the times when her mother had loved on her as if she was the most precious girl in the world.

Jasmine had been right — coming here did help her to feel closer to her mother.

And that made her smile.

"Okay, here we are."

Finally! Jasmine opened her eyes just as the car came to a stop, and she blinked. And then blinked. And she blinked again. Then she wiped her eyes to remove the sleep that was causing her to hallucinate. And finally, she frowned. She looked around at the parking lot, and then once again glanced up at the marquee above the hotel: super 8.

"Uh . . ."

Trying to appear innocent, Rachel glanced at Jasmine. "We're here."

"Yay!" Jacqueline and Zaya cheered.

Even though Hosea opened the door, Jasmine would not move. "You know we're not staying here, right?"

"Yes, we are," Hosea said, giving a quick glance to Rachel. "You told her to make the arrangements."

"Well, then she'll just need to make new ones."

"We can't ask her to do that."

"Why not, Hosea. This is the Super 8," Jasmine said, thinking that maybe Hosea hadn't seen the sign.

Rachel came around to the passenger side and folded her arms. "What's wrong?" she asked, still wearing that half smile.

"Okay, I get it," Jasmine said to her. "You're trying to get back at me for telling you to pay my expenses."

"That was foul, but I'm not trying to get back at you for anything."

"So what is this about?" Jasmine asked. "Because you know I don't stay in Super 8 hotels."

"Well, that could be a problem," Rachel said. When Jasmine hardened her stare, Rachel sighed. "Okay. If you don't want to stay here, you can stay with our aunt Ruby. She's Daddy's sister and Daddy will be staying there. I'm staying with my cousin Linda. She has a nice four-bedroom home, but me and my brothers and our kids are there, so it's not enough room, but Aunt Ruby could make you a pallet on the floor . . ."

"Rachel! I'm not playing with you."

"And I'm not playing with you! This is the only hotel in Smackover, so you're either staying here or you'll be with Aunt Ruby. So which one is it?"

"The only hotel?" Jasmine whispered.

Rachel nodded.

"In Smackover?"

She nodded again.

"Welp!" Mae Frances said, jumping out of the car. "Guess we're about to lay our burdens down at the Super 8 tonight!"

As everyone else piled out of the car, grabbed their bags, and strolled into the hotel, Jasmine stayed in the front seat, staring up at the three-story building. Maybe it wouldn't be that bad. After all, it wasn't a motel. That would've been completely unacceptable. And this looked like it could've once been a Holiday Inn or a Ramada

Inn . . . once. A long, long time ago.

But whatever it was in the past, it was a Super 8 now. There was no way she could stay here.

"Mama!" Jacqueline came dashing out of the hotel. "You have to come in and see. I've never seen a hotel like this. They don't even have a lobby! It's just this little space," she said, excited. "And the lady behind the desk said that we can have three towels, but any more will cost us extra. But she said they have a pool!"

Oh my God! I can't stay here.

Jacqueline grabbed her mother's hand. "Come on, you've got to see this."

Once again, the heat was stifling, but this time it wasn't the one hundred degrees that was going to make her faint. Right before Jasmine stepped through the sliding door, Rachel stepped out.

"Oh, I was looking for you!" she said, her voice filled with cheer. "So, I gave Hosea the keys, he paid for the extra towels, and I'll see you tomorrow." Then Rachel walked — almost skipped — away. Over her shoulder, she shouted back, "Just call me if you need anything. Smooches!" Rachel slid into her car and pressed the pedal to the metal, leaving a little stream of exhaust behind her.

Jasmine swore she saw Rachel laugh.

Swore that Rachel had leaned her head back and let out a good one. She wanted to run behind that car, drag Rachel out, and choke her until she couldn't take another breath. Rachel could've told her that there was only one hotel in Smackover. No wonder she didn't mind making the reservations and paying for it. It probably only cost her two dollars for three rooms.

"Come on, Mama," Jacqueline said, tugging her arm. "Come and look inside. This is going to be an adventure."

An adventure? Weren't adventures good things? So why did Jasmine feel like crying?

CHAPTER 20

RACHEL

Simon Jackson had better be glad he was a loved man. That was the only reason Rachel was going through all of this — she really and truly wanted her father to be happy. And if she was being honest with herself, a part of her hoped Jasmine could reconcile whatever feelings she had and maybe, just maybe, they could have a real sister relationship. Rachel didn't know why she was suddenly longing for that. Of course, she still felt some kind of way about her father's fascination with Jasmine, but her desire to have a real sister was perhaps overtaking that.

It took Rachel all of three minutes to get to her aunt Ruby's house, where the family was gathering for the Friday fish fry. Ruby lived in a wood-frame home that had withstood decades of wear and tear. According to Simon, he and his eight siblings had all been born right there in that house, which his father had built from the ground up.

Rachel smiled as she pulled into the dirt driveway. Several of her cousins were sitting on the front porch, laughing and joking around. The mosquito zapper hummed and the music blasted.

There was something about being here that gave her peace. She'd spent summers here, running up and down the dirt road, playing kickball, dodgeball, and hide-and-seek on the two acres of land. Rachel didn't make it back often, but when she was here, she relished her time. She didn't feel the need to be fabulous, and despite the craziness, there was no shortage of love.

"What's up, cuz?" her cousin Wanda said, greeting her first. She was sitting in her usual spot on the front porch, in a metal chair that looked like it would collapse at any minute. She *always* sat in that metal chair, watching the comings and goings of Smackover. Wanda was three years older than Rachel, but country living had worn her down and she looked about twenty years older.

Some guy Rachel had never seen stood in front of Wanda, his oversize CD case spread out on the ground.

"Hey, pretty lady, I got that new Tyler

Perry movie," he said, pointing toward the case.

"Aww, naw, she ain't the Tyler Perry type," Wanda said. "She's more Meryl Streep." They all busted out laughing like something was really funny.

"No, I'm more 'I don't do bootleg,' " Rachel replied.

"You got to excuse my cousin: she's siddity." Wanda chuckled.

"I got three movies for ten bucks. You can't beat that," the guy said.

"I. Don't. Do. Bootleg," Rachel replied. "And I report people who do." She rolled her eyes and turned to go inside to find her father when she bumped right into her cousin Sky.

"See, Rach, you need some of this right here. It'll help you relax," Sky said, lifting a small joint up in her direction. Sky was in a perpetual state of highness (hence the name Sky). Ever since he was thirteen years old, he began and ended each day with marijuana.

"Boy, you can't be offering the first lady no dope," her other cousin, Big Junior, said. "So, let me hit it."

Wanda shot them both chastising looks. "Put that out before Mama come out here and kill us all," she said, referring to her mother, Ruby.

They both took one last quick pull and mashed the joint out.

Rachel simply shook her head as she stepped over them to head inside. But Wanda stopped her. "So, unc said we got some new fam we're going to meet. Where she at?" Wanda asked.

"She's in the hotel resting." Rachel hadn't considered it before, but seeing her cousins scattered all over the front porch reminded her of something: "Look, I need to lay some ground rules."

"You know I don't do too well with rules," Big Junior said, chuckling.

Rachel ignored him and continued talking. "This visit means a lot to my dad and I just want to make sure y'all get it together. This is hard on Jasmine as it is, so can we keep the jokes and wisecracks to a minimum?"

"Why should we change who we are?" Wanda asked, leaning in so Big Junior could high-five her. "She needs to love us or leave us."

"That's just it. She'll definitely leave," Rachel replied, matter-of-factly. Jasmine was only here by the grace of God. One wrong move and she'd be heading back to the Big Apple. "This is really difficult and giving her a hard time will only exacerbate the problem."

"Exact what?" Big Junior said.

"You know she siddity. She know all them big words," Wanda replied to him before turning to Rachel. "Yo, cuz, I get what you trying to do, but this is us. You run from us, you move to the big city, trying to forget your country roots, but we all got the same blood running through our veins. At the end of the day, we're all family. And that includes your new sister."

Wanda was right, but there was no way Rachel would be able to convince Jasmine of that.

"Baby girl!" Simon said, swinging the screen door open. "I didn't know you were back." He stepped out on the front porch and looked around. "Where's Jasmine?"

"She's at her hotel. Dad, we have to give her a minute. She brought her whole family with her and I told you, you're going to have to take this slow."

Aunt Minnie appeared in the doorway right after her brother. "Well, she got three hours," Minnie announced. "The fish fry starts at five and all family needs to be here."

"Well, I don't know if that's going to happen, Aunt Minnie," Rachel replied. "They've been traveling and they're tired.

So I doubt if they'll come down to the fish fry tonight."

"So, the way Simon been in here going on and on about this girl, and she don't even want to see him?" Minnie's nose was turned up as she crossed her arms in disgust.

Rachel debated trying to explain Jasmine's point of view to her aunt, but she knew that would be useless. She focused her attention on her father.

"Daddy, we talked about this," Rachel said.

"I know," Simon finally said. "David and Jonathan will be here in an hour or so, and I want her to get to know us all. I just want to meet her and my grandkids."

"You will."

"She got kids?" Minnie said.

"I told you that," Simon replied. "But you don't listen."

"Hmph. You don't listen. I told you to stay away from that Doris girl all them years ago. If you had listened, you wouldn't be here 'bout to meet some secret daughter." Aunt Minnie turned back to Rachel. "Well, since she won't come, go get her kids. Teeny 'bout to take the kids fishing down at Calhoun Creek."

The thought of Jasmine allowing Jacquie or Zaya to fish brought a smile to Rachel's face. She'd pay good money to see that.

"You think she'd like that?" Simon said.

"Uh, yeah, I know she wouldn't. Y'all call me bougie. She's on a whole 'nother level," Rachel replied.

"Lord, one siddity child in the family is enough." Minnie stepped her hefty frame closer to Rachel. "So, y'all 'bout to give her my daddy's building for her charity, and she can't see fit to come see my brother?"

"Minnie, Ruby owns the building. She bought you out twenty years ago. So it's hers to do with as she sees fit," Simon reminded her.

"It was my daddy's building. That's the bottom line. And Ruby don't see fit to give it to some ungrateful, uppity illegitimate child. She's only doing that because all she ever wants to do is make her big brother Simon happy." Minnie growled her words. That was obviously a source of contention between them. Rachel hated that Jasmine was giving her cantankerous aunt any ammunition.

"Anyway, Minnie. This doesn't even concern you." He turned back to Rachel. "I understand."

"No, you don't. You been talking about that child since you set foot on this red dirt," Minnie snapped, pointing to the front

227

yard. "Now I get she got some issues, but shoot, we all do. So she needs to put on her big-girl panties and come face her family." Aunt Minnie turned to her sister, who had followed her siblings outside. "Ruby, where are the keys to that building?"

Ruby looked over at Simon, then back at Minnie. "Right here, in my pocket," she said, patting the pocket on her housecoat.

"Hand 'em here," Minnie demanded.

Before anyone could protest, Ruby had the keys in her outstretched palm. Minnie took them and dropped them in her double-E bra. She glared at Rachel. "Now, you tell *my niece* that we got her some TV and newspaper coverage and everybody is looking forward to her opening her little charity. But if she wants those doors to open tomorrow, she's gonna have to come get the keys from me, *after* she talks to my brother." Aunt Minnie clapped her hands to let everyone know she was done talking. She turned to Wanda. "Wanda, go run out to the deep freezer and get me another pack of those ham hocks, then come on back in here and help me finish cleaning these mustard greens."

Oh, God, Rachel thought. Ham hocks, mustard greens, crazy cousins, an overanxious father, and now Aunt Minnie was holding the keys hostage. No, Jasmine wasn't ready. Shoot, Rachel wasn't even sure if she was ready.

ing the keys hostage. No, Jasmine wasn't
one. Should Rachel wrap Jasmine and the sys
was death.

Chapter 21

Jasmine

The tattered washcloth covered Jasmine's forehead as she lay with her eyes closed. But she wouldn't be able to rest for too long. Soon she'd have to get up and wrap the washcloth around fresh ice cubes. Even the ice in this hotel was cheap; it kept melting faster than any ice she'd ever used before.

This ice pack on her forehead wasn't doing a thing, though. She still felt like she was going to faint, even though she was lying on this twin bed, which was covered with a hideous floral bedspread.

When was the last time she'd seen a bed with a bedspread? She was used to beds with silk duvets that were as soft as any cloud in the heavens. And sheets that were at least eight hundred thread count. She'd peeked at the sheets on this bed and she doubted that they had any thread count at all.

"Ohhh," she moaned. Really, there was no way that she could stay here. But what was she going to do? Her children already saw this as an adventure, running from Mae Frances's room to their own, which was connected to hers and Hosea's. And then there was the fact that Jacqueline's Hope would open tomorrow. She had to stay — at least for one night.

The hotel door opened then closed, but Jasmine didn't move. And though no one spoke, she knew those were her husband's heavy steps that she heard, then his calming presence that she felt standing over her.

The only thing was that this time not even Hosea could quiet her spirit. That little devil who from time to time stood on her shoulder was there again. Only this time he wasn't encouraging her to do something she shouldn't do. This time that little devil was laughing, cracking up, really. That devil was hootin' and hollerin' and tauntin' her.

You're in a Super 8. You're in a Super 8.

Jasmine had no idea why, but she heard that mantra in her head for so long that she began to sing along.

"I'm in a Super 8. I'm in a Super 8."

"Jasmine," Hosea said as he sat down on the edge of the twin bed. "Darlin', are you okay?"

Just that quickly, she'd forgotten that Hosea was there. It was official. Rachel had driven her to the brink of insanity. She needed to call her and congratulate her. Tell her she'd won.

As she tried to lift her head, the washcloth fell off, plopping down into her lap, and right away a water spot began to spread across the front of her white linen dress.

With tears in her eyes, she said, "Hosea, I don't think I'll ever be okay again. We can't stay here."

Hosea lifted the washcloth and tossed it onto the nightstand. "Come on, darlin'. Just like you haven't always been saved, you haven't always had money."

"But I've had money for a long, long time now. And even when I didn't" — she paused and her eyes did a slow scan around the room — "I had enough money not to stay in a place like this."

"Well, this is all we got." He stood and removed his watch from his wrist. "And the kids are lovin' it."

"Where are they?" Jasmine asked as she flopped back against the pillows. "Ouch!"

"What's the matter?"

"This isn't a mattress, it's a cement block."

Hosea chuckled. "Yeah, it is a little stiff and hard, isn't it?"

"And we won't even be able to sleep in the same bed," Jasmine whined.

"Who said?" he asked before he turned around and climbed into the bed with her. "See, we'll just snuggle like this . . . all . . . night . . . long."

This was the first moment of peace that she'd felt since she'd landed in Arkansas. And if she could stay in Hosea's arms, maybe she'd be able to handle this hotel.

"Where are the kids?" she whispered.

"With their Nama. She took them down to the pool."

"So, then, we can stay here like this? For at least a little while?"

"For at least a long while," he said, pulling her even closer.

The moment she closed her eyes, there was a banging on the door.

"Ugh!" Jasmine groaned. "Who is it?"

"Rachel!"

"What do you want?" Jasmine shouted.

"Can I come in? I need to talk to you."

"About what?"

"Jasmine!" Hosea glanced at her as he rolled out of the bed. "You can't have a conversation while she's standing in the hall."

Jasmine wanted to ask Hosea why not. She never planned to let Rachel into any part of her life ever again. After the opening, she was going to (politely) ask Rachel to stay away from Jacqueline's Hope and her and her family forever.

She knew Rachel would have no problem with that. Her sister . . . she stopped that thought again. Why in the world did she keep thinking of Rachel as her sister when they would never, ever have that kind of relationship?

When Hosea opened the door, Rachel rushed into the room, then she paused and glanced around the exact same way Jasmine had done about an hour before. And there it was again. That smirk.

"I hope you're enjoying your accommodations."

Jasmine sprang up from the bed. "You know what?"

"Ladies," Hosea said, jumping between them. Turning to Rachel, he said, "You needed to talk to Jasmine?"

And then it was like Rachel just remembered her reason for returning to the hotel, and the smirk she wore vanished. Now her forehead was etched with deep lines.

"We have a little bit of a problem," Rachel said as she lowered herself into a chair. It wobbled as if the four legs might not be even.

Jasmine said nothing; she just stood and crossed her arms.

"What's up?" Hosea asked.

"Well," Rachel began, "and please don't think this is a trick or anything. My father — our father — and I had nothing to do with this."

Now Jasmine's frown matched Rachel's. "What did you do?"

"I didn't do anything. It's my . . . our aunt Minnie." She took a deep breath and blew it out. "She wants you to come ton —"

"No!"

"You have to, Jasmine."

"The only things I have to do are stay black, pay taxes, die, and get the hell out of Smackover as soon as the center is open."

"And you need to add one more thing to the list. You have to come to Aunt Minnie's house for the family fish fry tonight."

"No."

"Or else they're not going to give you the keys to Jacqueline's Hope!" Rachel cried.

Jasmine had her lips poised to say no once again, but then she stopped and glared at Rachel. "Your family never intended to give me that building, did they?" Before Rachel could answer, Jasmine turned to Hosea. "Get the kids; we're flying home now."

"Wait, Jasmine." Rachel jumped up. "I

thought Jacqueline's Hope was important to you."

"You know it is!" Jasmine shouted. "And you're using that against me."

"I'm not. It's my family who's doing that. I mean, our family. I mean . . ." Rachel sank down onto the bed. "I told Daddy your rules, I really did," she whispered. "But he wants to meet you, they all want to meet you," she said, sounding like she was about to cry.

There were tears in Jasmine's eyes, too, when she said, "But I don't want to meet them. I don't want to have anything to do with any of them."

"Why not? They're your family."

"No." Jasmine shook her head. "They're not. And I don't want them to be. Don't any of you understand that?"

Hosea rested his arm on his wife's shoulder. "Rachel, can you give us a moment, please?"

She glanced at Jasmine and nodded before she scurried toward the door. But before she stepped into the hallway, she said, "Please," and then she closed the door behind her.

Slowly Jasmine lowered herself to the edge of the bed and Hosea knelt down in front of her. Using the tips of his fingers, he lifted her chin. He said nothing for a moment; all he did was use his thumb to wipe Jasmine's tears away.

"I don't want to go, Hosea," she said so softly he could hardly hear her. "Not even for Jacqueline's Hope. I can't do it."

"You *can* do it."

"I know, I know," Jasmine said, waving his words away. "I can do it with Jesus."

He gave her a soft smile. "Yeah, Him, too. But you can do it with me, and the kids and Mae Frances. We'll all be there with you."

Jasmine thought for a moment, really considered it. But then she shook her head. "I can't."

"Why not?"

"My heart won't let me" was what she said. But in her mind all she saw were images of her father, her real father. And she would never betray Charles Cox.

"You'll still have the same heart. Only it'll be bigger because it will be filled with more love from more people."

More thought. More images. And again she said, "I can't."

Sitting next to her, he continued, "You know what I think?" He didn't wait for her to respond. "I think somewhere deep inside, you *do* want to meet them."

"You're wrong."

237

"You do want to get to know them."

Her head kept shaking.

"Or else you wouldn't have come here. Because you had to know that Simon was going to find a way to see you."

"I thought he would stay away. I thought he would keep his word. He's a pastor, isn't he?"

Hosea nodded. "But before he was a pastor, he was a man. And a father."

It didn't take her any time to say, "He never wanted to be my father, so why should I want to be his daughter?"

"Well, maybe you need to tell him that. Maybe you need to tell him how you feel."

She sat still, not moving her body, not moving her thoughts. Then she shook her head, and Hosea sighed.

"I'm going to check on the kids."

Jasmine knew that was just his way of leaving her alone. As if her own thoughts could convince her to do what he could not. But no matter how long he stayed away, no matter how long she'd be alone, she wasn't going to change her mind.

She'd get another center for Jacqueline's Hope. She was sure of that. She didn't need this one in Smackover. Jasmine stood and walked to the window. Usually, no matter where she was in the world, there was always a view. At home, she had Central Park. On vacation, snowcapped mountains or the endless wonder of the ocean. But this view right here was nothing but a parking lot filled with pickup trucks and motor homes.

And then there was the huge black SUV parked right in front with a woman leaning against it, staring at the hotel.

Jasmine took in Rachel for a little longer, and then she turned away.

A second later the door opened and Jacqueline and Zaya came bouncing in.

"Mama," Jacqueline said, "we're going to Auntie Rachel's house. I'm gonna see Nia! Yay!"

She glared at Hosea. "We're going home," she told her daughter, even though her eyes were on her husband.

"No, we're not," Hosea said. "We're going over to . . ." He paused. "We're going to see . . . to meet Rachel's family."

Tears sprang to Jasmine's eyes as her children cheered.

"Come on," Hosea said, leading the children to the adjoining room. "Let's change your clothes." Looking over his shoulder, he added, "And you'll be ready when we get back, too, right?"

She pressed her hands to her face and

held back her sobs. She lay down on the bed and when Hosea came back into the room, she couldn't hold back anymore. She cried when he told her that he, the children, and Mae Frances were going with Rachel.

When he stood at the door to leave, she asked him, "Why are you doing this?"

"Because of you. I know that this is what you want, but you can't do it right now, so I'm going to stand in for you. And I'm going to save Jacqueline's Hope at the same time." He paused. "Are you sure?"

She nodded and then watched him walk out the door. And Jasmine had never felt so left behind.

CHAPTER 22

RACHEL

The look in Hosea's eyes said everything without him saying anything.

"So, she's not coming?" Rachel asked. In her heart she already knew the answer to that question.

Hosea shook his head. "She needs more time." He and the children had just walked out to her SUV. The kids were so excited, oblivious to the tension surrounding them. "But we're going and we're anxious to meet everyone."

Rachel contemplated saying more, going in there and demanding that Jasmine get it together and come on, but Hosea was right. It wasn't time. Trying to force anything more would only backfire.

"Well," Rachel said, forcing a smile as she held the back door open for Jacqueline and Zaya. "Let's go have some fun."

"Yay!" Jacqueline said as she and her

brother crawled into the backseat.

"Wait!"

The front door of the hotel slid open and Mae Frances scurried out. "Y'all not about to leave me."

Hosea had just opened the passenger door. "I thought you'd changed your mind, Mae Frances."

"And why would you think that?" she said, pushing him aside and getting in the front seat. "I didn't come all the way to this godforsaken town to sit up in these luxury accommodations."

Rachel smiled as she climbed into the driver's seat. "Mae Frances, it's July. Why do you have on that coat?"

"I'm not leaving my mink in this hotel." Mae Frances pulled it tighter around her.

Rachel wanted to tell her that nobody wanted that tattered old chinchilla, but instead she just said, "Okay, whatever."

A few minutes later, they were pulling up to Ruby's house. More relatives had gathered and Wanda had pulled her '78 Cutlass onto the grass, lowered all the windows, and set the music blaring. Simon was sitting on the porch with his nieces and nephews. They were all laughing as Nia, Jordan, and several of the other children danced to Michael Jackson songs. Rachel chuckled at the

242

sight. Maybe it was best Jasmine didn't come this evening; she would've had a field day with this. She wouldn't have been able to see that beneath the "outrageousness," the over-the-top antics, this was a place rooted in love. This, her family, is what really mattered in life.

Jacqueline was the first one out of the car and Rachel's daughter, Nia, spotted her immediately. Nia raced over and the two hugged like they were long-lost friends.

"Well, if it isn't the great Hosea Bush," Simon said after they had gotten out of the truck. He stood to shake Hosea's hand. "So glad to see you again."

"Likewise," Hosea said. "Hi, everyone," he added, waving to all the people who sat around the porch.

Simon's eyes made their way down to the little boy who stood nervously next to Hosea. "Hi," he said softly, kneeling in front of Zaya. "My name is Simon Jackson. I'm . . ."

"Thrilled to meet you," Rachel said, quickly jumping in. Jasmine would have a straight conniption if Simon told these kids he was their grandfather without her permission.

"Dad, this is Zaya." She motioned for Jacqueline to come over. "And this is Jacquie."

"Hi," both children said at the same time.

"Pawpaw, can they go fishing with us?" Nia asked. She was holding on to Jacquie's hand like she was scared to let her go. "My cousin Teeny is about to take us," Nia told Jacqueline. "He said he's gonna show us how to put a worm on a hook and everything."

"A worm, ewww," Jacquie said.

"I wanna touch a worm!" Zaya added.

"Don't worry, you don't have to touch the worm if you don't wanna," Nia told Jacqueline.

All three children turned to Hosea.

"Daddy, can we go? Please?" Jacquie said.

"Ooh, fishing?" Hosea said, worry lines etched across his face.

"They'll be fine. They're just going up to Calhoun Creek," Simon said. "We don't have enough fish for tonight, so my nephew is gonna go try to catch some more. They won't be more than an hour."

"Please, Daddy?" Jacquie said.

Hosea sighed, but then could barely get his "yes" out before all the kids took off to go find Teeny.

"He's going to catch some more fish? Why don't you just go to the fish market?" Everyone turned to Mae Frances, who had been standing quietly off to the side.

"My apologies," Simon said, turning to shake her hand. "You must be Mae Frances. I've heard a lot about you."

Mae Frances cut her eyes at Rachel. "Lies. It's all lies."

Simon laughed. "Well, welcome to Smackover. And to answer your question, we don't have any fish markets around this place." Suddenly it must've dawned on Simon that one key person was missing. He peered toward the SUV, like he expected Jasmine to still be sitting inside. "Where's Jasmine?"

"She's not feeling well," Hosea said. "The trip wore her out."

Rachel looked up to see Aunt Minnie peering out of the screen door. She shook her head, patted her breast where the keys were, then turned around and went back inside.

Simon looked like he was about to say something else when a loud honking caught their attention. A red pickup truck swung into the driveway, spinning dirt everywhere.

Rachel fanned away the clouds of dirt as her great-uncle Bubba jumped out. He was the patriarch of the family, the last living sibling of Simon Jackson's parents. And even though he just turned eighty yesterday, he showed no signs of slowing down.

"The party can get started now because

I'm here," Bubba said, laughing in his hearty voice. He had on his signature overalls and dusty white T-shirt, which hung on his bony frame.

"Uncle Bubba, you know you're not supposed to be driving," Simon said.

"When they pry my keys from my cold, dead hands, I'll stop driving."

Simon shook his head before turning to Hosea. "This is my uncle, Bubba."

Hosea extended his hand. "Pleased to meet you."

"Where do I know you from?" Bubba asked, studying him.

"He's a well-known preacher," Simon replied.

Bubba snapped his fingers. "Oh, that's right. My Eleanor used to watch you every Sunday morning. God rest her soul. What brings you round here to these par . . ." Bubba's words trailed off when he noticed Mae Frances standing behind Hosea. "Well, Lord be a circus and hand me a clown." He licked his lips, patted both sides of his gray Afro, shined the bald spot in the middle of his head, and stepped over to Mae Frances. "The Lord must've taken me early, cuz I gots to be in Heaven. Who is this beautiful thing here?" He took her hand and kissed it. "I know I'm eighty, but all my parts are in working order."

Mae Frances snatched her hand away, like she couldn't believe he had the nerve to touch her.

"Uncle Bubba, this is Mae Frances," Rachel said.

His eyes roamed up and down her body. Rachel knew Uncle Bubba still had 20/20 vision, but surely he was losing his eyesight if Mae Frances was turning him on.

"Please, please tell me you ain't family," he said.

"No, I'm a friend of the Bushes."

"Well, I don't know who the Bushes is, but I got a few bushes I'd like to go have a conversation with you in."

"Uncle Bubba!" Simon said, appalled.

Several relatives who overheard him cracked up. Rachel just shook her head.

"Shoot, I'm too old to sugarcoat," Bubba said, flashing a toothy grin at Mae Frances.

"Uncle Bubba, would you go on somewhere?" Simon said. "You're going to have this woman thinking we're country."

"We are. Ain't nothing to be ashamed about." He smiled, his pride evident. "See, that's the thang about folks. They move on to the next phase of their lives and they try to forget their roots. They become citified and want to snub the very foundation that made them who they are." He looked over at Rachel and winked. "But it's all good, the Good Lord is keeping Uncle Bubba around to remind them."

It was at that moment that Rachel noticed Big Junior ease up next to Mae Frances. "Is that real mink?" he asked.

"Umm, yes," she said, pulling her coat tighter.

"How much is it worth?"

"Nothing," Rachel said, pushing her cousin away. "Mae Frances, I know you've got to be burning up. Let me take your coat."

Mae Frances looked around. "It is hot. But I'll hang on to it," she said, sliding the coat off and draping it across her arm.

The screen door swung open and Ruby stepped out. "Hi, I'm Ruby," she said, introducing herself to Hosea and Mae Frances. "My sister Minnie is in the kitchen. Why don't you come inside and sit and chat?" she told Mae Frances.

To Rachel's surprise, Mae Frances followed Ruby inside with no protest. Probably just so she could get away from Uncle Bubba.

"Bye, sweetness. You and I will talk later. That's a promise!" Bubba called out after her.

"Uncle Bubba, can you behave yourself?" Rachel asked.

"Shoot, why start now?" He motioned toward Sky, who was sitting at a card table with some other relatives. "Sky, can you come down off that cloud and get this stuff out the back of my truck? Big Junior, Little Willie, come help him."

Rachel watched as her cousins begrudgingly got up and made their way over to the truck, where they started removing coolers and other supplies.

"And hand me my Brut cologne off the front seat," Bubba said.

"This?" Little Willie asked, holding up a small white bottle.

"Yep," Bubba replied, taking the bottle and dousing himself in the putrid-smelling cologne. "I gots to go get that woman." He pointed toward the front door.

"And you think that cologne is gonna help you?" Little Willie asked.

"Boy, what you know about women? Your woman left you because you can't cross state lines 'cause of that thing on your leg." Bubba pointed to the electronic monitoring bracelet on Little Willie's leg. After one too many DUI arrests, he was being forced to wear an ankle bracelet for the next year. It was a sensitive subject for Willie, but Uncle

Bubba didn't seem to care. "I wrote the handbook on snagging a woman. Watch and learn, little grasshopper. Watch and learn."

Uncle Bubba disappeared inside and Simon turned to Hosea.

"Can I talk to you a minute?"

Hosea nodded and they stepped off to the side. Rachel stepped right with them. She wasn't about to let them go at this alone.

"Hosea, I just don't understand why Jasmine won't come," Simon said, ignoring Rachel standing next to him.

Hosea released a heavy sigh. "You have to understand, this is very hard on her. She's feeling like everything she's known is a lie." He paused, like he was deciding just how much he wanted to say. Finally he said, "And, well, she has some issues with you as well."

"Me? What kind of issues?"

"You'll have to talk to her."

"How can I do that if she doesn't want to see me?" Simon replied. "Please. How can I get through to her if I don't understand the root of her refusal to see me?"

"It's not that she's refusing. This is just a lot. And, well, she doesn't understand how you could've abandoned her mother," Hosea finally said.

"Abandoned?" Simon said, getting worked

up. "I would've never abandoned Doris. I didn't know she was pregnant. I would've never abandoned my child."

"Okay," Hosea said, trying to calm Simon down. "Maybe you two will get a chance to talk."

"We sure will because I'm about to go to the hotel right now!"

"No, you're not," Hosea said, gently placing his hand on Simon's forearm. "Reverend Jackson, you know I respect you, but my wife isn't ready, okay? You can talk to her tomorrow." His voice was calm and soothing and he seemed to settle Simon down. "Let's you and me talk some more and get to know each other."

Simon looked to Rachel and she nodded. She was glad Hosea was the man he was, because if it had just been her, there's no way she would've been able to stop her father from going down to the Super 8 and knocking on every door until he found Jasmine.

Simon relaxed but added, "Jasmine has to know, if I had known about her, I would've found her mother. And I would've married her."

Now, that was a dagger through Rachel's heart. Because if he had found Jasmine's mother, then Rachel would never be here.

251

"It's okay," Hosea said. "God worked it out just the way He was supposed to." He looked over at Rachel. "God knew that you and your wife needed to create this beautiful legacy. And tomorrow, maybe God will allow you to have a conversation with Jasmine and open the door to expand that Jackson legacy."

Rachel could only hope that it would be as easy as that.

And then Rachel got an idea. She knew exactly what to do. She only prayed that it would work.

CHAPTER 23

JASMINE

"You're kidding me!" Jasmine exclaimed. "This is where we're eating?"

"What else do you want us to do?" Hosea asked. "We didn't rent a car, the kids have to have breakfast." Hosea glanced to the left and then to the right. "This is the only place to eat that's close enough to walk. And you need to eat, too. You haven't had anything since yesterday afternoon. And with the opening of Jacqueline's Hope today, you need your strength."

And I'll starve for a few more hours if I have to eat here.

But even though those were her thoughts, she followed a bouncing Zaya and Jacqueline into the Waffle House. The moment she stepped inside, she scrunched up her nose.

What is that smell?

Then she heard the crackling sounds from

253

the kitchen, which appeared to be in the open right behind the counter. And she knew the smell — that was nothing but grease.

She shuddered.

"Let's sit over there," Jacqueline said, pointing to the only empty booth across the room.

"No, we have to wait for the hostess to seat us," Jasmine said.

"Oh, y'all don't have to wait!" a woman standing behind the counter shouted out. "Ain't no hostess here, just seat yourself." She waved them inside.

The woman had barely gotten the words out of her mouth before Zaya dashed to the vacant booth. Jasmine slid onto the hard seat next to her son while Jacqueline and Hosea sat across from them.

Jasmine glanced around at this place that she could only think of as a dive. Even though they were in the Deep South (at least deep to Jasmine), this diner seemed to be no respecter of persons. All kinds of folks filled the seats: black and white, young and old, some sitting together at the counter, all seeming to enjoy their fat-filled meals of waffles, eggs, and sausages.

"It smells good in here!" Jacqueline said, taking an extra-deep breath like she was inhaling the finest perfume.

"Yeah!" Zaya chirped.

"How y'all doing today?" The woman who had greeted them at the door slapped four plastic-covered menus onto the table.

"We're blessed," Hosea said.

"Hmph," the lady said. "I can see that. Y'all here with all your fancy clothes."

Fancy clothes? Jasmine took a quick glance down at the jeans and rhinestone-studded T-shirt she was wearing. There was nothing fancy about what she had on, nothing fancy about what any of them were wearing. All four of the Bushes were in jeans.

"Where y'all from?" the woman asked.

"New York," Hosea answered.

Jasmine picked up the menu, glad that her husband was doing all the talking because she wouldn't have been so gracious. The next words out of her mouth would've been "Mind your business." And since this lady would be serving them their food, Jasmine kept that thought to herself.

"Oh, New York," the lady said as if she were impressed. "I ain't neva been there, but I'm hoping to go up there one day. I got a cousin, Butch, who's up there working on Broadway."

"Oh, is he an actor?"

"Nah!" She laughed. "Butch ain't a he. Her real name is Gertrude, but she's up there in New York working in one of them fancy restaurants on Broadway. Anyway, I hope to get up there once she sends me money for a bus ticket. It's been something like seven years now, but she made a promise, so . . ."

Why is she still talking?

"So, what y'all doing in Smackover? Y'all visiting your people?"

"No!" Jasmine said, uttering her first word. "We're here on business."

"Business?" She laughed. "Smackover ain't got no business." Then, with a side-eye glance, she whispered, "Unless y'all into pharmaceutical sales."

Hosea chuckled, but Jasmine's eyes widened. "You know, all you need to do is take our order," she said, forgetting all about the fact that this woman was in control of their food. "We don't need all this extra conversation."

"And you don't need to talk to me like that." The woman looked to be in her fifties, maybe even sixties. But she rolled her neck like she was twenty-five.

"You know what? May I speak with your supervisor, please?"

"Jasmine," Hosea said, placing his hand

over hers.

"No, this two-dollar-an-hour chick needs to learn —"

"Who you calling two-dollar-an-hour? I make more than that. I get tips, you know! And you just need to —"

"I apologize for my wife," Hosea said, giving Jasmine a stare, then turning to the waitress with a smile. "Just give us a few minutes and we'll be ready to order."

The waitress glanced at Jasmine and waited for her to look up before she rolled her eyes (like she was twenty-five) and stepped away.

When Hosea stared at Jasmine as if she'd done something wrong, it was her turn to roll her eyes.

She didn't care what Hosea thought. He should have been more concerned with the way that woman had insulted them. Pharmaceutical sales? Really?

"Okay, let's order our food," Hosea said, more to the children than Jasmine.

But when he finally did look over at her and asked, "What do you want to have?" she just shrugged.

"I'll order a waffle for you."

Hosea raised his hand and the waitress came back. Jasmine pressed her lips together, willing herself to say nothing. But she kept her eyes on the woman, glaring as hard as she could, hoping to burn a hole that would go right through to her soul.

"Thank you, sir," she said to Hosea as she gathered the menus. Once again she rolled her eyes at Jasmine before she turned from them. But she'd taken only two steps before she looked back over her shoulder. "And for your information, I am the supervisor!" Then she swished away.

"Mama," Jacqueline said, before Jasmine could give the waitress another piece of her mind. "You should've been there yesterday with us and Auntie Rachel."

"Miss Rachel," Jasmine corrected, ignoring Hosea's glare.

"Auntie Rachel's cousin took us fishing!" Jacqueline kept on as if Jasmine's words didn't matter.

Jasmine stiffened and now she glared at Hosea. "Really?"

"Uh-huh, and it was fun," Jacqueline said, oblivious to the storm that was brewing.

"Except Jacquie was scared of the worms," Zaya added.

"No I wasn't!"

"Yes you were. That's why I had to put the worms on the hook for you." Then, with pride on his face, he turned to Jasmine. "Grandpa taught me how to do it before we got in the boat!"

"Grandpa?"

"Yeah," Zaya kept on. "Auntie Rachel's dad told us we could call him Grandpa like all the other kids."

"Don't call him that," Jasmine snapped. "He is not your grandfather."

"But Auntie Rachel's kids call him that," Jacqueline said.

"And she is not your aunt!" Jasmine shouted, turning heads in the eatery. "She is nothing to you. Call her *Miss* Rachel or don't call her anything at all."

For a moment, her children sat there with wide eyes, then they both fell back in their seats. While Zaya looked like he was about to burst into tears if his mother said anything else, Jacqueline folded her arms, pouted, and glared at her.

Then Jacqueline added, "Daddy, I'm not hungry anymore." She spoke to Hosea, but she didn't stop staring at her mother. "I want to go back to the hotel."

"You have to eat something."

"I want to go back, too," Zaya added in a whisper.

It was Zaya's words that made Jasmine regret her outburst. Jacqueline was always over-the-top, the drama queen who sometimes tested Jasmine's black-mama card membership. But Zaya rarely did. Her sensitive son was so much like her husband, just calm, always cool.

Right now, though, Jasmine could see he was just seconds away from tears and she wanted to put her arms around him, but she couldn't. If she did, then the children might believe that it was really all right to accept the Jacksons as family. And she would never.

"Okay, let's get out of here," Hosea said.

"But . . ."

It was the way Hosea looked at her that made Jasmine stop speaking. Jacqueline and Zaya slipped out of the booth, and scurried as fast as they could to get as far away as they could from Jasmine.

Jasmine stood between Hosea and the children as he signaled the waitress, then whispered something to her. The woman nodded, glanced over Hosea's shoulder, and shook her head as she stared at Jasmine. When Hosea handed the waitress a twenty, she grinned. "Guess I just got a raise. Ain't did nothing and made more than two dollars an hour." She laughed. "Y'all have a great day."

Jasmine wanted to snatch the money from the woman's hand, but she knew she'd pushed her husband just about as far as he could go today. Once outside, the four walked to the street corner in silence and once they crossed, the children dashed to the hotel. Silence stayed with them as they rode to the third floor, and then when the elevator doors parted, the children dashed down the hall, passing by their hotel room as well as their parents'.

Jacqueline banged on Mae Frances's door as if she'd just made a prison break. "Nama! Nama! Let us in."

A second later the door opened and the two ran inside. Jasmine stood in the hall, debating whether she should get the children. She needed to talk to them. Yes, she'd upset them, but she needed to explain to them her good reasons.

Before she could go after them, though, Hosea said, "Can I talk to you for a minute?" He unlocked their hotel room, opening the door wide for her to enter.

She took another glance at Mae Frances's room and then followed Hosea inside. He had barely closed the door when he started in: "What is wrong with you?"

She held up her hands. "I'm sorry. I shouldn't have talked to the children that way."

"Damn straight."

His words made her take two steps back.

In all the years that she'd known her husband, had he ever used the word *damn* in her presence?

He kept on: "Jasmine, I have had just about enough of you."

"What?"

"This has gone beyond ridiculous. We all know that you're upset and miserable, but why are you trying to make the rest of us miserable, too?"

"I'm not . . ."

"You are and I'm tired of it. I get that this is upsetting for you; it would be upsetting for anyone. But you know what? It is what it is. Simon Jackson is your father and now you have only two choices — you either accept it or you don't. That's it. You either say, 'I'm going to be part of this family,' or you say, 'I don't want to have anything to do with them.' But this thing that you're doing . . . this way that you're playing the middle . . ."

"I'm not doing that."

"Then why are you even here in Smackover?"

Jasmine frowned. "Because of Jacqueline's Hope. I wanted another center."

"You could've opened another one anywhere."

"Not for what this is costing us. This is

almost free."

He paused, and then brought his voice and his attitude down. "It's not free at all, Jasmine. This is costing us a lot. Because now you're taking your hurt out on your children. You're taking it out on me. And I don't know what to do about it anymore. But I know I'm not going to take this. So you need to find a way to get it together."

"What do you expect me to do?" she cried.

"I don't know; you figure it out. But you need to give it some serious thought and work it out."

When he turned away from her, she asked, "Where are you going?"

"I'm going to get the kids and call Simon or Rachel or one of the other many wonderful people we met yesterday to come and get us."

"I'm not going over there."

"I didn't ask you to," he said.

And that made tears spring to Jasmine's eyes.

"Mae Frances may want to rest up some more, so she'll be here, but the kids and I will hang out over there before it's time to go to the ribbon cutting." He paused and added, "Look, I'm not trying to hurt you any more than you're already hurting. But I've tried to help you figure this out. Now you've got to do the rest, you've got to take the next steps on your own."

He walked out of the door before she could tell him all that she was thinking. That she couldn't do this on her own. That she needed him because she was so confused and so scared.

But she didn't get to tell Hosea any of that. Because he had walked out.

And once again, she was all alone.

An hour passed, and then another, and another.

And Jasmine still sat, on the edge of the bed, her eyes on the door that Hosea had closed. What was she supposed to do?

She knew what Hosea wanted — for her to suck it up, go to Rachel's family, and accept them as her own. But didn't he understand that if she did that, it would wipe away who she was? It would negate all that she knew and believed for the forty-something (or maybe fifty-something) years of her life? It would erase everything that Charles Cox meant to her.

Hosea was right . . . maybe she had come to Smackover to at least meet them under the guise of Jacqueline's Hope. Yes, she'd wanted to see the place that Aunt Virginia said her mother loved so much. She did want to know if she'd feel any connection with this newfound side of her family.

But, except for the few minutes when they were on the road to Smackover yesterday, she didn't feel anything. And not only did she not feel a thing, she didn't want to.

Truly this had been a mistake and all she wanted was to go home, put this behind her, and pretend that she'd never heard this news. Hosea would just have to understand. And in time, he would. She'd just have to keep reminding him of how he would feel.

But it did hurt that right now, while she was sitting alone, her family was bonding with the Jacksons. She needed to get them all out of Smackover and that's what she would do. They would definitely leave tomorrow and not the day after like they'd planned.

She grabbed her iPad. She'd change their reservations now and explain it to Hosea later.

But the moment she powered up, there was a knock on her door. She smiled with relief. Hosea had come back for her.

She ran toward the door, swung it open, and stood staring there for a moment without saying a word.

"Aren't you going to say hello to your favorite person in the world?" Serena asked.

Jasmine scooped her sister into her arms and squeezed her so tightly that Serena gasped for air.

"I can't breathe," Serena kidded.

Jasmine loosened her grip and pulled her sister into the room. "Thank God, Hosea called you," she said. "How did you get here so quickly?"

"We're sisters, Jasmine. I'd move Heaven and earth for you." Serena sat on the bed and Jasmine lowered herself next to her. "So, what is going on? I thought you were coming to Smackover to meet your family?"

"I never said that."

"I know, but I thought since they would all be here . . ."

"I just wanted to do Jacqueline's Hope. But now there's so much pressure for me to embrace these people I don't even know."

"I think maybe you're making this bigger than it has to be. It's not like you have to make a commitment to anyone here. Just meet them. Free yourself a little bit."

Jasmine thought about her sister's words. "Free myself? If I do that, I'll be freeing myself from you and Mama and . . . and especially . . . Daddy."

Serena took her sister's hand and squeezed it. "Is that what's stopping you? What was in your past will always be there. Mama was your mama, I will always be your sister, and Daddy died as your daddy. Nothing will ever change that. But now you get a chance to meet another man who loves you."

Jasmine stood, folded her arms, and paced in front of her sister.

"Seriously, Jasmine. You're all tied up emotionally. The best thing you can do for yourself is at least talk to Simon. Really. Free yourself."

Before Jasmine could tell her sister all the reasons why Simon didn't deserve and would never get a chance with her, there was another knock on the door and Serena jumped up.

She placed her hand on the doorknob, but then paused. "Jas, I know you can't do this alone. That's why I'm here. But I'm not by myself. There's someone else who really cares about you, who really wants to help you." She opened the door and added, "It's your other sister."

And there stood Rachel.

"She's the one who called me," Serena said. "She bought my ticket and made sure I got here. Because she knew that you needed me."

Rachel stepped over the threshold, but didn't move any farther into the room.

Serena kept on: "And you need her. To

figure this out, Jas. We're both here to help you."

Jasmine looked at the women standing side by side. *My sisters.*

"I really do want to help," Rachel said. "It's not easy for me, either, because I'm no longer the only girl. And I don't even know . . ." She paused and then took a deep breath. "I don't even know if I'm the apple of my father's eye anymore. But even though I hurt, I love him. And sometimes, I kinda, sorta like you, too. So, anything that I can do to help get the two of you together . . ." She stopped and then glanced at Serena.

Serena smiled, nodded, then finished for Rachel: "Anything that we can do to help, we're gonna do. Right here, right now, we're gonna work this out." She took Rachel's hand and then reached for Jasmine's. "We're gonna figure this out like the sisters we are."

Jasmine stared at her sister's outstretched hand and then she looked at how Rachel was holding on to Serena. Her lips trembled, but Jasmine finally took hold of Serena and then the three of them sat down in that hotel room, together.

CHAPTER 24

RACHEL

Never in a million years did Rachel think she'd be sitting here doing this — holding hands with her *sister.* And her *sister's sister.* It had been easy enough to get Serena's number (she was listed), but Rachel hadn't been so sure that she'd be able to get Serena to hear her out, let alone jump on the first flight to Arkansas to help Rachel get through to Jasmine.

Rachel smiled as she replayed that conversation. She'd been bracing herself for a full-scale pitch.

"So, you want me to come to Smackover and convince my sister to meet your father?" Serena asked after Rachel had introduced herself and explained why she was calling.

"Meet *our* father," Rachel corrected.

"So she hasn't seen him?" Serena asked.

"She won't leave the hotel room, so she hasn't seen anyone."

That elicited a chuckle. "That is so my sister."

"Serena, this is really hard on her. I mean, I see it tearing her up." Rachel took a deep breath and braced herself. "Serena, I hate to ask this, but I think Jasmine could really benefit from having you here. There's a six a.m. flight out in the morning. I know it's short notice, but —"

"I'll be on it," Serena said, cutting her off.

"What?" Rachel was surprised that she hadn't had to deliver her long spiel on why Serena just had to come.

"I said I'm coming," Serena said. "I knew my sister was struggling with this and if I had been thinking, I would've come with her from the jump. But if you can just text me the address, I'll be there."

"Well, you'd have to fly into Little Rock. You'd get in about nine. Then you'd have to rent a car and drive about two hours to Smackover." Rachel paused, waiting for Serena to say "forget it."

"Okay," Serena said.

Wow, Rachel thought. *Is that what a sister bond was all about?*

"Well, of course, I'm paying for your ticket," Rachel continued. "It'll be booked, so you just pick it up at the airport."

"Okay. I'll see you tomorrow."

Rachel held the phone for a moment then said, "Serena, thank you."

"No, thank you for calling me," Serena replied.

And just like that, she was here.

"So, we really need to get moving," Rachel finally said. She'd been pretty quiet as Serena talked to Jasmine and finally, it seemed like she'd made some progress. "The ribbon cutting is at two." Rachel didn't tell Jasmine about the family reunion program at six. She'd have to find a way to work that in between now and then.

Serena flashed a reassuring smile and Jasmine seemed to gather up enough strength to stand.

"Okay, fine," Jasmine said. "We'll do this, and then we'll . . ." She let her words trail off. As if part of her wanted to say, we'll get out of town . . . but the other part wouldn't let her.

"We'll play it by ear," Serena said, finishing her sentence for her. Serena turned to face Rachel. "Well, now that you have me in this quaint little town, you'll have to show me around."

"Look out the window there," Jasmine said, pointing to the dusty windowpane. "What you see is what you get."

"And you would know this how?" Rachel

said, with a smile. She wanted to be careful not to agitate Jasmine. She was smiling for the first time since getting to Smackover. Rachel wanted to keep it that way. "You haven't left this hotel room. There's so much to see here. You'd be amazed. This used to be an oil town."

"I saw the sign when we went to that disgusting Waffle House. Eighteen hundred people? We have more than that in my apartment building in New York," Jasmine said.

"I keep telling you, it's the quality that counts, not the quantity." Rachel wagged a finger at her. "And we produce world-famous people."

"Like whom?" Jasmine asked.

"Sleepy LaBeef."

Serena and Jasmine looked at each other and busted out laughing.

"Oh, I guess y'all never heard of Sleepy?"

"Isn't he related to Happy and Grumpy?" Jasmine asked.

"Oh, y'all got jokes. He's a musician. And the most famous person to ever come out of Smackover. Next to me, of course."

"See," Jasmine said to Serena, "I told you she was delusional."

Rachel waved her off as she picked up her keys and headed to the door. "Serena, I'll show you around on the way to the center. Lester got in early this morning. He will come get Hosea and the children. You two and Mae Frances can ride with me."

Rachel said her good-byes and raced to her cousin's to change. Thirty minutes later she was back at the Super 8, parked out front, waiting and praying that Jasmine hadn't changed her mind. But Rachel felt a sense of peace now that Serena was here. Serena wouldn't let Jasmine leave. But whether she'd be able to get Jasmine to open up was the question of the decade.

"All right, let's get this shindig started," Mae Frances said, making her way out of the hotel first. She still had her mink, but the Arkansas heat must've gotten to her, because it was draped across her arm this time.

"Nice dress, Jasmine," Rachel said as Jasmine walked to the SUV in a plum wrap dress with puffy sleeves. "Is that Diane von Furstenberg?"

"I'm impressed," Jasmine said.

"Don't be," Mae Frances called out from the front seat. "She only knows that because they started selling Diane's stuff at T.J.Maxx."

Rachel climbed into the driver's seat. "You know what, Mae Frances? I'm not going to let your negativity ruin this day. This is all about Jacqueline's Hope."

Mae Frances gave her a sideways glance but didn't respond.

"So, the center is downtown," Rachel began as they pulled out onto the main highway. "You'll be happy to know they've installed a stoplight right in front of the center, so it's sort of a local attraction now."

"Did you say a stoplight?" Jasmine asked, leaning forward like she hadn't heard right.

"That's what she said," Mae Frances said, chuckling. "Lord, and I thought Galveston was country."

"We're close to bigger towns. El Dorado is right up the road. Camden is the other way, so it's not like we're isolated," Rachel continued. She pointed out the passenger window. "That field is where I used to spend my summers with my cousins, tipping cows."

"Tipping cows?" Serena asked. "What does that mean?"

"I know this is gonna sound crazy," Rachel answered. "But when a cow sleeps standing up, and you tip them over while they're still sleeping, they can't get back up."

Every eye in the truck was on Rachel.

"And why in the world would you do that?" Jasmine finally asked.

"Yeah, is that supposed to be fun?" Serena added.

Rachel shrugged. "It was funny to us."

"I ought to call PETA on you right now," Mae Frances said.

"Call them, because I'm sure they'd like to know how many mongrels died for that coat of yours," Rachel shot back.

"Look here . . ."

"Okay, okay. Sorry. I was just messing around," Rachel said, quickly trying to diffuse everything. She showed them a few more landmarks, shared a few more stories, and then pulled into a small grocery store. "I'm going to grab a few bottled waters. Do you all want anything?"

"I need to pick up a couple of things for the hotel. Some juice and snacks for the kids for later tonight and then tomorrow," Jasmine said, following her inside. It was amazing the transformation Serena was able to perform. Granted, Jasmine hadn't agreed to see Simon, but emotionally, she did seem to be in a much better place.

"Hello, ladies," a friendly voice greeted them as they walked in the store. "Welcome to Steve's."

"Hi," Rachel said.

Jasmine leaned in and whispered, "Is everyone always this friendly?"

"All the time. I know you guys don't even make eye contact in New York, let alone speak." Rachel laughed.

They gathered a few things and made their way up to the counter.

"Are y'all here for the Jackson Family Reunion?" the clerk asked as she started ringing up their items.

"We are," Rachel said. "We're Ruby Jackson's nieces." Out of the corner of her eye, Rachel saw Jasmine tense up.

"Oh, I just adore Miss Ruby. I think I remember you. You're Simon's girl, right?"

Rachel nodded.

"Yeah, I used to have the biggest crush on your brother David when y'all came here for the summer. Tell him Veronica Andrews said hi."

"I sure will."

Veronica finished ringing everything up and said, "Your total is thirty-six seventy-nine. Will you be paying now or later?"

"What?" Jasmine asked, speaking for the first time since they'd stepped to the counter.

Veronica frowned. "I said: will you be paying now or later?"

"You mean we have an option?" Jasmine asked in disbelief.

Rachel shook her head as she removed two

twenties from her wallet. "You'll have to excuse her. She's from New York City. She doesn't know a thing about the honor system."

"I sure don't. Because if you ask a New Yorker are they paying next week, they'll say yes and you'll never see them again."

"Which is exactly why I like my small-town living," Veronica said as she handed Rachel her change.

As soon as they were back in the car, Jasmine started telling Mae Frances and Serena about the "unbelievable honor system." Rachel was happy to see her focused on something other than the drama with her father. Jasmine was actually laughing and smiling. But as they turned onto Main Street, and the center came into view, Rachel could only pray that Jasmine's good mood would last.

CHAPTER 25

JASMINE

When the tires of Rachel's SUV rolled over the dirt-covered space that looked like it was supposed to be a parking lot, Jasmine frowned. And when Rachel pulled the truck to a complete stop, turned off the engine, and glanced at Jasmine through the rearview mirror, Jasmine said, "What? You're making a U-turn or something?"

"No." Rachel pushed open her door. "This is it. This is Jacqueline's Hope."

From the front seat, Mae Frances leaned her head back and filled the car with her laughter. "Lawd, be an architect, and put this building back together again."

Jasmine would've laughed, too, if she weren't in shock. Slowly, she slid out of the car, walked around to the other side, then moved next to Serena. The sisters stood like twins, with their mouths open in perfectly shaped *O*s and their eyes wide.

"What is this?" Jasmine asked, her gaze still on the dilapidated building.

"I told you, this is Jacqueline's Hope." Rachel pointed to a sign that hung high above the door and looked like it had been written in crayon. "We're going to have a real sign put up next week; this was all that we could get on such short notice."

Jasmine shook her head. She knew it; she knew that this had been nothing but a trick to get her down to Arkansas. Why in the world had she ever trusted Rachel?

When she found her words, Jasmine snapped, "I cannot believe this. I can't believe you played me like this."

"What?" Rachel asked, her expression and her tone indicating she had no idea where Jasmine's rage was coming from.

"I can't believe that you would make a joke out of something that's so important to me."

"What are you talking about?"

"This!" Jasmine shouted, pointing to the weatherworn, aged building with bars covering the windows.

"*This* is the building that belongs to my aunt Ruby and she was kind enough to let us have it for free because she believes in your foundation and . . ." Rachel ended there as if she'd spoken a full sentence.

"It's nothing but a run-down warehouse."

"It's the old Piggly Wiggly."

"And what the hell is Piggly Wiggly?"

"You can't be that bougie, Jasmine." Rachel folded her arms. "Every black person in America knows that Piggly Wiggly is a grocery store."

"Well, whatever it was . . . that was . . . this building isn't fit for my foundation. The Department of Health probably won't even let us go in there."

With a glare, Rachel said, "We can go in." Her neck moved with every syllable. "I've been working in there for the past week, and I can't believe you're so ungrateful."

"And why would I be grateful for this?"

"Yeah, Rolita," Mae Frances said, finally stepping out of the car. "How is Jasmine Larson supposed to feel good about this? This building's got to be one hundred years old!"

"No, Mae Frances," Rachel said with a stiff smile. "One hundred years old — that would be the mutt that you carry around and wear as a coat." Then she glanced at Jasmine, shook her head, whipped around, and marched toward the building.

"You don't want to test me, little girl," Mae Frances grumbled as she stomped behind Rachel. "The last person who insulted me was Stephen Curry, and once I told LeBron about that, you saw what happened," Mae Frances fussed. She was still muttering as she walked into the building behind Rachel, and the door closed on the rest of her words.

Jasmine hadn't taken a step away from the car. "I cannot believe this," she said to Serena. "I can't believe Rachel would try to make a fool out of me with my own foundation."

"I don't think she would do that," Serena said.

"She's *always* trying to do that. From the moment I met her, she's tried to one-up me, tried to bring me down. She's jealous and envious and wishes she were me. Usually I can smell her tricks coming, but I didn't see this one at all."

"Why would she do that now?" Serena asked. "She's trying to get you to accept her and her family. It wouldn't make sense for her to do something crazy like that."

"It wouldn't make sense to you because you have a brain." With her forefinger, Jasmine tapped her temple. "Rachel doesn't have one of these. So she can't make sense of anything."

"Well, we should at least go inside."

"Why?"

"Because everyone will be here soon, and maybe we can figure out what we'll say to them." Serena paused. "That sign says Jacqueline's Hope, and you're the spokesperson so you're gonna have to make this work somehow."

"Ugh!" Jasmine growled. But she knew Serena was right, so she moved across the parking lot, kicking up dust along the way, thinking that it was a good thing that she had those Protect Your Pumps on her red bottoms, and thinking about all the things she could say to the people who were on their way. Then she thought about all the ways she could kill Rachel for even doing this.

Then, she stepped inside and she paused.

Her eyes scanned the huge open room, which was freshly painted bright yellow. But the smell of the paint didn't bother her; how could it? Not when she took in the ten desks neatly lined up and evenly spaced, all polished to a high gloss. Black executive chairs sat behind each one and every desk was set up so that someone could sit down and get right to work. There were telephones on every desk, pads and pencils, too. Along one of the walls there was a long table holding four computers. Above the computers was a whiteboard with three names listed.

And on the adjacent wall, there were three framed photos and above the pictures were the words WALL OF HOPE.

Jasmine slowly walked toward that wall. "Oh, my goodness," she said, pressing her hand against her chest. "Are these children missing?" she asked no one in particular.

Rachel came to her side. "Yes, these three are the ones we were able to find out about in the two weeks it took for us to put this together."

"We've got to bring them home." Then Jasmine turned to face Rachel. "I can't believe you did all this in a week."

Rachel gave Jasmine a small nod and said, "Did you see the wall over here?"

Jasmine turned to where Rachel pointed. There were more gold letters: WALL OF FAITH. Jasmine frowned as she stepped closer to the dozens of framed photos on that wall. Pictures of children she recognized. Pictures of children who'd been found and returned home.

Rachel explained: "I know you don't have a Wall of Faith in your other centers, but I thought of this because Jacqueline's Hope has helped to bring so many children home and I want people to know that. I want people to know that with faith, we can move the children from that wall" — she pointed to the Wall of Hope — "to this one."

Jasmine looked from one wall to the next, then she fully faced Rachel. Before she could think about it, she pulled Rachel into her arms, holding her, squeezing her. But, after a couple of seconds, she took two giant steps back as if she realized that she'd just gotten a little caught up.

"Uh . . . thank you, Rachel." Jasmine lowered her eyes. When she looked up, she added, "Really, thank you so much."

Rachel smirked. "You're welcome. But while you're saying thank you, can you say you're sorry for what you said to me when we were standing out there?"

"But you've got to admit . . ."

"Can I just get an apology?" She held her hand up to her ear.

Not even a millisecond passed. Jasmine said, "I'm sorry."

"And you'll never judge a book by its cover again?"

"I won't. But you have to admit it looks pretty raggedy out there."

"Yeah, Rawanda, I mean, you can at least plant some flowers. Put a couple of plastic ones into the ground. No one will notice."

Rachel rolled her eyes at Mae Frances, but this time she was smiling when she faced Jasmine again. "We are going to get the outside cleaned up, but it was more important to get this all done now. For the opening."

"Okay." Jasmine looked around again. "Wow!" she said. "I'm just so overwhelmed. Thank you again for doing this."

Just as she said that, she heard chatter behind her and in walked Jacqueline and Nia, their heads close together as if they were sharing secrets. They were followed by Jordan; Lewis; Rachel's baby girl, Brooklyn; and Zaya. Hosea and Lester pulled up the rear.

"Look at this," Hosea said, stepping over to Jasmine as he continued to scan the space. "It's set up so people can get right to work."

"My wife did the dang thing, didn't she?" Lester said, his chest swelling a bit. Then he reached his hand out. "You must be Serena; nice to meet you."

"Oh, I should've introduced you two," Rachel said, but then she turned to the door. "There's Mayor Bruce," she said, pointing to a big-bellied man. "Jasmine, I need to introduce you."

She grabbed Jasmine's hand as if that was the most natural thing in the world to do and led her to the door. As they got closer, Rachel said, "No wisecracks. He's only the mayor part-time."

Jasmine took in the man who was wearing a pair of dress pants, a short-sleeve white shirt, and suspenders. "A part-time mayor?"

"Yeah! You'd be part-time, too, if you only earned three hundred dollars a month."

"That's it? So what does he do when he's not being the mayor?"

Right before they stepped up to the mayor, Rachel said, "He's the manager over at the new Piggly Wiggly." Then she greeted the mayor and wrapped him in an embrace.

It took everything in her power to hold back her laugh, but Jasmine did it as she held her hand out toward the mayor; he swiped it away. "We don't do handshakes in these parts." He laughed and his whole body shook. "We believe in hugging." He wrapped his arms around her, lifted her a couple of inches off the floor, jiggled her around a little, then planted her back on her feet. "We're so honored to have you here, little lady," Mayor Bruce said.

Jasmine felt as if she'd just gotten off a roller coaster. It took a couple of moments to regain her balance once her stilettos were back on the floor.

The mayor said, "No one cares about our kids, certainly not down here. With this here Jacquie's Hope, we'll be able to take care of our own."

Jasmine didn't even bother to correct him.

Two councilmen stepped through the door and from that moment, Jasmine was caught up in a whirlwind of introductions as Rachel took her from one person to the next. The room was festive, filled with chatter and laughter; it was a celebration.

As she met the guests, everyone thanked her, told her how they'd made donations of five, ten, twenty dollars. And as they thanked her, Jasmine thanked them all back.

By the time Rachel told Jasmine that the program was going to start, Jasmine was beaming. She was ready to get this center open.

"You'll have a few more interviews after we speak, but we want to start the official part of the program now," Rachel said.

Jasmine whispered the signal to Mae Frances, "It's time," and Mae Frances led the children to one of the rooms in the back of the center, since Jasmine never liked talking about the reason for the foundation in front of Jacqueline.

Once they were out of the room, Jasmine, Hosea, Rachel, and Lester gathered in the corner behind the podium that had been set up. They were surrounded by several of the city's dignitaries. One of the city councilmen spoke first, next came the mayor, and finally, Rachel stepped up to the podium.

"I really want to thank everyone not only for coming out today, but for supporting me as we put this center together. Jacqueline's Hope is really important for our children and I'm so glad we now have this center here in this town that's so close to my heart. I'm not going to take all the time talking because I want you to hear from the person who started Jacqueline's Hope." She turned to Jasmine. "Ladies and gentlemen, I'd like to introduce you to my . . ." Rachel cleared her throat. "Introduce you to Jasmine Cox Larson Bush."

Jasmine stepped forward, hesitated for a moment, and gave Rachel a halfhearted embrace. Turning to the crowd, Jasmine said, "I want to add my own gratitude to Rachel's and thank you all so much for coming to the opening of Jacqueline's Hope.

"This foundation means so much to me. Back in 2010, I had the worst experience of my life. My daughter was kidnapped, and for days, I didn't know if she was dead or alive."

The group was stone silent now, listening to her words.

"But I held on to hope. That was all I had.

Just hope and the Lord. My hope came from deep inside of me. And thank God He put that hope there because my husband and I and our family received very little support from the outside. When it's our children who are missing, there is little media support."

"Amen!" the mayor shouted and held up his hand as if he were about to testify.

"When it's our children it may seem as if no one cares."

"That's right!"

"But we care!" Jasmine stated, as she got worked up. "We have to care. And we have to do everything we can to bring our babies home. I never gave up hope. No matter how dark it looked, I never did." She paused. "And my baby came home!"

It was as if they were in church. Because the people started dancing and shouting, all in step as if they heard some kind of organ music. They did their praise dances and when Jasmine glanced at her husband, he was dancing, too.

She laughed and joined in.

Some shouted and some raised their hands to the heavens.

Through the hallelujahs and amens that rang out, Jasmine continued, "My baby is right back there . . ."

Just as she said that, the door opened . . . and in walked Simon Jackson.

For a couple of seconds, Jasmine was covered by the shouts that still filled the center. But once they quieted down, her silence became evident.

Rachel frowned and followed Jasmine's gaze, her eyes widening. Quickly, she stepped away from the podium and rushed to the door as Jasmine stood, frozen, with her eyes locked on the door.

Hosea moved to his wife's side. "As you can see," he began, "this is really emotional for my wife."

"That's all right!" someone shouted.

As more words of encouragement came from the crowd, Jasmine watched as Rachel dragged her father out the door. But even though Simon was gone, he'd taken the joy of the afternoon with him.

Why had he shown up? Why did he have to ruin this day for her?

As Hosea spoke to the crowd and closed out the speech, Jasmine prayed that Simon would be gone by the time this was over. That all she had to do was make it from the center to the car. Then from the car to the hotel. And once in the hotel, she'd be safe. Because now she was sure. She didn't care what Hosea had to say.

The Bushes would be leaving Smackover, Arkansas.

Chapter 26

RACHEL

Rachel had never moved so fast. She'd darted across the room and whisked her father out the front door. She didn't want to ruin Jasmine's mood and from the look on Jasmine's face the afternoon was about to quickly spiral downhill.

"Daddy, we talked about this," Rachel said as soon as they were outside. "You were supposed to meet us at the church."

At that moment, both Ruby and Minnie walked up.

"We told him to come on," Minnie said, shifting her handbag to her other arm as she defiantly placed her hands on her hips.

"Aunt Minnie . . ."

"No. That little girl doesn't need to come around here and start running things," Minnie said.

"She's not a little girl. She's like almost sixty," Rachel replied. She knew Jasmine

292

wasn't really that old and made a mental note to scale back the disparaging remarks.

Minnie waved off her comment. "My brother wants to see his other daughter and we think she should see him."

Ruby nodded in agreement.

Rachel didn't have the energy to deal with her aunts so she focused all her attention on her father. "Daddy, I understand your sisters want what's best for you. *I* want what's best for you. But I'm telling you, I know Jasmine. She's not going to let you force anything."

Stress lines covered Simon's face. "What do you want me to do, baby girl? Just sit at the house? I'm going crazy. I need to talk to Jasmine."

Minnie shook her head. "And poor Brenda. Your daddy been snapping at her so, had her in tears."

Simon lowered his head in shame. "I have to apologize to my wife." He turned to Rachel. "This all just has me so stressed out. I don't understand why she won't give me a chance."

"I'm working on that, Dad. I want you all to sit down and talk, but *at the church*. I'm going to bring her over to the tree where you met her mother and maybe she'll feel

293

some type of connection and open up to you."

"Hmph," Minnie muttered as she jabbed her finger in the direction of the building. "She can open up right now. All those folks in there, she's not going to act a fool."

"Maybe not, but she will leave," Rachel said. She let out a heavy sigh. "Dad, just please go on to the church, get things ready for the dinner, and we'll be there in a little while."

Simon looked unsure, but Rachel could tell she was getting through to him. "This is all going to work out. I just need you to trust me."

He finally nodded then took her hands and squeezed them. "I trust you, Rachel. And I'm sorry if I've been insensitive to you. You will always be my number one girl."

For the first time, Rachel believed that. "Aunt Ruby," Rachel said, "can you please take Daddy on to the church? I know you all have a lot of work to do and really the only reason you're even here is to be nosy."

"You know your aunt," Ruby replied.

"Can't I just go peek inside?" Minnie asked.

"Bye, Aunt Minnie."

Minnie huffed. "Fine. But I'm telling you now, if that girl gets over to the church acting out, I'm gonna tell her about herself."

Rachel made a mental note to keep Jasmine away from Minnie.

Crisis averted, Rachel thought as she watched them climb back into Ruby's 1980 Buick. She waited until they drove off before she turned to go back inside.

Rachel could feel Jasmine's eyes on her as soon as she walked back in. She gave her a reassuring nod to let her know everything was taken care of. When Rachel closed the door behind her, Jasmine seemed to relax.

Rachel eased into a corner until the last person finished speaking. When she saw Jasmine deep into an interview with a newspaper reporter, Rachel pulled Serena and Mae Frances aside.

"What is wrong with you?" Mae Frances asked, her eyes going to the grip Rachel had on her arm. "You obviously don't want that hand."

"Sorry," Rachel said, dropping Mae Frances's arm. "I'm just trying to hurry up before Jasmine finishes her interview."

"Hurry up for what?" Serena asked.

"Look, I know both of you have done a lot to get Jasmine here, but this is only half the journey," Rachel began.

"What in the world are you talking about?" Mae Frances snapped.

"I mean, I know she doesn't want to, but Jasmine needs to talk to my . . . to our father. If for nothing else, to get some closure on all the questions I'm sure she has."

"I agree," Serena said.

"Good, then that means you'll help me get her to the church."

"What's happening at the church?" Serena asked.

"We have a family dinner there. It's like the culmination of our family reunion. We don't even have to tell Jasmine the real reason we're going to the church. We just need to get her there."

"Is that old geezer going to be there?" Mae Frances asked.

Rachel raised an eyebrow. "Uncle Bubba? Umm, yeah, I'm sure. But I promise I'll make him stay away from you."

Rachel couldn't be sure, but it almost seemed like a light flickered in Mae Frances's eyes, but she quickly said, "Good."

"Does that mean you'll help me convince Jasmine to go?"

"Nope. I never said that," Mae Frances said. "I'm not in the trickin' folks business."

"Since when?" Rachel asked.

"No, Rachel, I think Mae Frances is right," Serena interjected. "I want to be honest and up-front with my sister."

"But being up-front with *our* sister right now isn't the best thing," Rachel countered. "Please?"

Both Serena and Mae Frances turned and looked at Jasmine laughing as she talked to the reporter. "It is nice to see her smiling with all the crying she's been doing lately," Serena said.

"She ain't gon' be smiling if we trick her," Mae Frances said.

"I'm not asking you to trick her, or lie. Just go along and when we get to the church, make sure she gets out."

Mae Frances stood like she was thinking for a moment. Finally, she said, "Okay, fine. I'll do what I can."

Serena sighed. "Me, too. But I'll be honest. I don't know if it's going to work."

"It might not. But we have to try." Rachel squeezed both of their hands. "Thank you so much." She looked over as the newspaper reporter walked away and Mayor Bruce walked up to Jasmine. "Let me go rescue Jasmine because the mayor will run his mouth all day."

Rachel made her way over to the corner where the mayor had Jasmine hemmed up

"Mayor Bruce, the stoplight looks good," Rachel said. "If you don't mind, though, I have someone else I want Jasmine to meet."

"Sure," he said and laughed. "Lady Jasmine, please know that our door is open anytime you want to come here. Me and the missus have plenty of room, so you can stay with us."

Rachel flashed a smile as she took Jasmine's hand and led her away, leaning in and whispering as they walked off, "Yeah, that's one place you don't want to stay, since he lives in the same plantation house where his grandfather owned slaves."

"Yeah, I won't be staying in the big house," Jasmine replied. Once they'd gotten over to the refreshment table, Jasmine asked, "Where's . . ."

"Daddy? I sent him on."

Jasmine's shoulders dipped in relief. "Thank you."

"No problem. You just worry about Jacqueline's Hope. I told you, that's what this afternoon is about. Oh, here comes the lady from the El Dorado newspaper. I'm going to let you do this interview."

"What? You're not going to try and steal my shine?" Jasmine said, finally smiling.

"This ain't *Oprah*." Rachel winked as she walked off.

Twenty minutes later, the crowd had cleared, Hosea, Lester, and all the children had left, and Rachel knew she couldn't avoid the inevitable. It was time.

"Rachel, this ended up being really nice. I mean, did you get the whole town of Smackover to come out?" Jasmine said after the last of the guests had gone.

"Just about. And folks from the surrounding towns, Norphlet, Louann, El Dorado, Camden. The churches helped me spread the word."

"Wow, well, thank you."

"No, thank *you*. I think this is a great charity and I'm happy you brought it to my hometown."

They stood in an awkward silence for a minute. Under normal circumstances, two people sharing such a meaningful moment might hug, but Rachel didn't know if she and Jasmine were there. Yet.

"Can we go now or are we going to shut the joint down?" Mae Frances asked.

"I'm ready. Hosea and the children should be back at the hotel by now," Jasmine replied.

Rachel, Serena, and Mae Frances exchanged glances. "Well, let's go," Mae Frances said. "I can't wait to get back to that luxury hotel and take a nap."

Rachel shot her a sideways glance as they headed to the parking lot. Of course, she would have to try to go overboard.

As they were driving, Rachel pointed out a few more landmarks. "Not that you all will ever need to know this, but that's the Greyhound bus stop."

"Stop? So you don't have a bus station?" Serena asked.

"Nope, the bus slows down just long enough for you to hop on." They chatted some more until Rachel turned down an unpaved road. As dust flew up on both sides of the truck, Jasmine finally spoke up. "Where are we?" she asked as they pulled into the church's parking lot.

"This is my home church," Rachel said, looking up at Jasmine in the rearview mirror. "I wanted to take you guys on the tour of our cemetery."

"Cemetery?" Mae Frances asked. "Why we need to go see dead folks?"

Rachel parked the car and got out. She walked around and opened the passenger door. "Come on, Mae Frances. It's part of our tradition."

"Your tradition. It ain't part of mine," she said, pulling the passenger door back closed. "You didn't say nothing about a cemetery. I'll be at one soon enough. In the meantime, I'm good."

"And I'm going to sit right here with Mae

300

Frances," Jasmine said. "I mean, why do you even have a cemetery in the back of a church? Do you even have a license to bury bodies back there?"

"A license? Seriously?" Rachel asked.

"If you bury bodies in the backyard in New York, CSI will be knocking on your door."

"Well, you're not in New York," Rachel said.

It was at that moment that Jasmine peered out the window. "Wait a minute, why are all these cars here?"

Serena looked away and quickly stepped out of the truck.

"Serena!" Jasmine called out. Then she must've noted the expression on Rachel's face because she said, "What. Is. Going. On?"

Mae Frances went ahead and stepped out of the truck. "Jasmine Larson, I'm sorry, but I didn't come all the way here to sit in a rinky-dink hotel. And you might not want to admit it, but there's a reason that you're here in this town."

"What's happening here?" Jasmine asked, glaring at Rachel.

After a moment's silence, Rachel inhaled deeply and said, "It's our family dinner, Jasmine."

Jasmine's gaze was piercing, like if she hadn't been standing on holy ground, she would've strangled Rachel right then and there. "I don't know why I ever trusted you. You always have been a conniving backstabber. You knew what you were doing all along."

Rachel let her rant. "I wasn't trying to be deceptive, but I —"

"Take me back to the hotel," Jasmine demanded, cutting Rachel off.

"I'm not going to do that," Rachel said. "You have to at least try."

Jasmine slammed the door shut. The window was still partially cracked, so Mae Frances stuck her face in. "You don't think you're being a little dramatic?"

"I want to go back to the hotel," Jasmine repeated.

Mae Frances turned back to Rachel, shrugged, then said, "Oh well, I did my part."

Before Rachel could reply, the front door of the church opened and people started pouring out.

"Oh, no, here comes my family," Rachel said. She could see Jasmine's eyes grow big.

"Come on, Jasmine," Serena pleaded through the cracked window. "We're here now. Let's just make the best of it."

Jasmine ignored her and kept staring forward, pouting like a teenage girl. Rachel knew she was stubborn, but was she that set against meeting the Jackson family?

Several relatives from last night and some new ones from today surrounded Rachel's truck, peering in at Jasmine.

"Is this my new cousin?"

Rachel shook her head as her scrawny thirty-year-old cousin leaned in the window. Rachel stepped up next to him. "Jasmine, this is my cousin Magic Mike," she said.

"Why do they call him Magic Mike?" Serena whispered.

"Because if you lay your purse down, he can make it disappear," Rachel replied.

"You steal a few purses over the years and your family never lets you live it down." Magic Mike laughed, then stuck his hand in the window of the truck.

Jasmine refused to shake it, but Mike didn't seem fazed as he started calling relatives one by one up to the window to say hi to Jasmine.

"Jasmine, this is ridiculous," Serena whispered in between relatives. "Do you know how crazy it looks you refusing to talk to these people?"

"I don't care. I'm not getting out of this truck."

Just then, Uncle Bubba walked up, ignoring everyone as he came face-to-face with Mae Frances. "I knew I should've been coming to church more often. Nobody told me angels were making personal appearances."

Mae Frances waved him off. "You need to go somewhere else with those tired 1970 pickup lines."

"Come on, pretty lady. Why won't you give me the time of day?"

Mae Frances's eyes roamed up and down his body, taking in his dusty overalls, his tattered T-shirt, and his bald spot. "Was that a rhetorical question?"

"Sweet thang, ol' Bubba never made it past the third grade, so I don't know what all those big words mean, but I meant what I said." He wiggled his hips. "Try it, you'll like it."

"I don't do dirty ol' men, number one," Mae Frances replied. "Number two, I've dated prominent politicians, superstars, and civil rights activists."

"But you ain't neva had nobody like me." He tugged on the buckles of his overalls to emphasize his point. "Ask the ladies, Bubba ain't got no stubba."

Mae Frances laughed as she shook her head. "Rachel, get your people." She slapped a mosquito as it landed on her arm. "Oh, I'm not about to get the Zika virus. Jasmine Larson, you can sit out here if you want to. I'm going inside."

"Come in, Jasmine. Just for a little bit," Rachel pleaded.

"Rachel, take me back to the hotel, please," Jasmine said. She no longer seemed mad. She just seemed desperate. Maybe this hadn't been such a good idea after all.

"Ahhhhhhh!"

The sound of screaming caused every head to turn. Jacqueline came bolting from around the side of the church, crying hysterically. Every ounce of stubbornness that was keeping Jasmine in the truck disappeared and she jumped out.

"Jacqueline, are you okay?" Jasmine said, racing to her side. "What's wrong?"

"They killed it," Jacqueline cried, wrapping her arm around her mother and pointing in the direction she'd just come from.

Jasmine, Rachel, and several others raced around to the side of the church and stopped cold in their tracks. Big Junior was standing in front of an old swing set, wearing an apron covered in blood. Hanging upside down from the swing, and dripping with blood, was some type of bare animal.

"Oh my God," Jasmine said, pulling Jacqueline close to her. "What is that?"

Rachel couldn't answer because she had no clue.

"Dang. You city girls kill me," Big Junior said.

"Big Junior, what are you doing?" Rachel asked.

"Skinnin' a deer for dinner. What does it look like?"

"And on that note, we are out of here." Jasmine snatched Jacqueline's hand and pulled her back around to the front.

"But, Mommy, I'm okay. We can't leave. Daddy and Grandpa went into town and they're gonna bring us snow cones," Jacqueline said, trying to dry her eyes.

"He's not your grandpa!" Jasmine screamed, causing Jacqueline to flinch.

"Jasmine, your hysteria is only getting Jacqueline more worked up," Serena said calmly.

It took fifteen minutes for Serena and Rachel to settle Jasmine down once she realized Jacqueline wasn't seriously traumatized. But she made it clear to Rachel that she was done. "As soon as Hosea gets back, we're leaving," Jasmine said.

"Fine, but for now, let's just go inside to the dining center. It's cool back there and you can get something to drink," Rachel said.

Jasmine didn't move.

"Mom, it's really hot," Jacqueline whined.

Jasmine stared down at her daughter, blew out a frustrated breath, and reluctantly followed Rachel into the church, through the sanctuary, down a hall, and outside to a detached center.

Mae Frances was sitting at a table with three of Rachel's relatives. She smiled when she saw Jasmine. "Look, Jasmine Larson. They're teaching me how to play dominoes." She slapped a domino on the table. "Gimme fourteen tricks and a pimp to run them hos."

Jasmine's mouth fell open in horror. Even Rachel had to laugh. Nobody but her cousin Sky had taught Mae Frances that terminology for when she scored fifteen points.

"Mae Frances! We're in God's house!" Serena said.

"Oops," Mae Frances said, glancing upward. "Sorry, Lord."

"Technically, we're not," Rachel's cousin Wanda said. "We're in the multipurpose center. That's not the same as the church."

"Whatever," Jasmine replied. "Come on, Mae Frances. Wrap that up. We're leaving."

"You can leave. I'm having fun," Mae

Frances said, studying the dominoes in her hand. "They said we're playing Penny Spades after this."

"Yeah, and Sweetness is gonna be my partner," Uncle Bubba said, winking at Mae Frances. "I got a feeling we'll make a great team."

Mae Frances let out a small chuckle, but to Rachel's surprise, didn't protest.

"Come on, baby," Ruby said, taking Jasmine's hand. "Sit down and enjoy yourself. I sent the kids up front to play kickball since Big Junior back there scared them all."

"I'm just ready to go," Jasmine said.

"Here, drink this," Little Willie said, handing her a cup.

Rachel snatched the cup. "Boy, nobody wants to be drinking after you." Rachel sniffed the cup. "What's in this anyway?"

"Grade-A moonshine, baby."

Mae Frances raised her cup. "I ain't had none like this since Jasper first started dabbling in liquor and had me trying out all these new recipes."

"Who is Jasper?" Little Willie asked.

Mae Frances laughed. "Jasper Newton Daniel," she replied. "Folks nowadays know him as Jack Daniel."

"Oh, snap! You knew Jack Daniel?" Little Willie exclaimed.

"Excuse me, does anyone hear me when I say I'm ready to go?" Jasmine said. "Hosea isn't back yet?"

"Come on, Jasmine, relax," Serena said. "This is all so entertaining." She guided Jasmine to the window. "And look, Jacqueline is fine. She and Zaya are playing and having a ball. When is the last time you've seen them so happy?"

Jasmine studied her children for a minute and watching them did seem to relax her.

"It's not that bad," Rachel said.

"Really, it isn't. All you have to do is give the Jacksons a chance. I think you'll like us."

Everyone turned toward the soft voice that had eased up behind them. Rachel's first instinct was to whisk her father away again, but she knew this was it. It was time.

"Jasmine," Simon slowly continued, "first of all, thank you so much for coming. It would mean a lot to me if you would just step outside with me and talk for a minute."

"I . . ."

"Just hear me out. Just five minutes. Please."

Rachel wanted to cry at the strain in her father's voice, but she stayed out of it. She'd done her part. She'd gotten Jasmine here. She'd gotten her father to wait. Now it was on them.

"Please, Jasmine?" Simon continued.

Jasmine looked over at Serena, who once again nodded. Every eye in the room was on them. Finally, Jasmine turned her attention back to Simon.

"Fine. Five minutes." She headed toward the front door, Simon right behind her. And it took everything in Rachel's power not to follow them out.

CHAPTER 27

JASMINE

It was a wonder that Jasmine was able to walk, the way her knees knocked together. How in the world had she allowed herself to be tricked like this? Rachel would always be duplicitous. That was just who she was, down to her soul. So getting into that SUV with her and letting her drive around this town was not the smartest decision Jasmine had ever made. Being here now, in this position, was totally her fault — first, for trusting Rachel, and then, for not leaving once Simon had shown up at the center. But she was going to fix this and end this now.

Jasmine left several feet between her and Simon as she followed him down the hall, made a turn to the right, then went out through the heavy double doors. Thank God he'd taken her away from the church. Now she wouldn't have to be concerned with or be responsible for the words that would come from her mouth.

When Simon paused right under the old oak tree, Jasmine was grateful. Walking on wobbly legs in designer stilettos hurt!

Simon turned around, his eyes steady on her. And Jasmine returned his stare. The only difference between them was that as Simon's lips spread into the widest of smiles, Jasmine folded her arms.

"What do you want?" she asked.

Her tone did not deter him. "I can't believe I'm actually standing here talking to you."

"Four minutes."

That took his smile away. "Jasmine, please give me some time. I need time with you."

"Three minutes."

He inhaled, and stared at her for another few moments. "I can't believe I didn't see this the first time I met you at the American Baptist Coalition. You looked familiar then, but now . . . standing here, looking at you. You look just like your mother."

"Two minutes."

He took a step forward and she took two steps back. "However much time you give me, I'm grateful. Because with you standing right here . . ."

"One minute."

"Right where I met your mother."

She was ready to tell Simon that his time was up, but his words had stopped those thoughts. "This is where you met my mother?" she whispered.

He nodded and in the next moments of silence, Jasmine realized that this was the church. This was the church that Aunt Virginia had told her about and the church that she'd planned on visiting, if she had come to Smackover alone. Her plan had been to come to this place, to stand in the church where her mother had stood. To be in the place where her mother had met her father.

She waited for a moment, to see if she felt anything. Any more of a connection to the woman she loved so much. But just like with the rest of this town, with the rest of this trip, she felt nothing.

Simon spoke up again: "When she came to Smackover that first time, her bus stopped right there." He pointed to the spot where Rachel had parked her SUV. "I remember it like it happened just a few hours ago. When Doris got off that bus, I was in love. I had never had a girlfriend, but my heart knew that she was the one that I would love forever. We were only kids . . ."

"Yeah, my mother was just a young girl and you took advantage of her."

313

"No, Jasmine!" Simon exclaimed, shaking his head. "It wasn't like that at all."

"Then why did you leave her?" She held up her hand, her palm just inches from his face. "You know what? I don't want to know. I don't want to hear your excuses and I definitely don't want to hear any lies."

"You haven't given me the chance to tell you the truth."

Her teeth were clenched so tightly, her jaw hurt. But still, she spoke. "You had your chance with my mother; you're not getting a chance with me." There were tears in her eyes when she turned away, but she was not going to cry. Never again would she shed a tear over this man.

She spun around, but she'd only taken one step before Simon grabbed her arm. She paused, looked down at where he held her, and then allowed her glance to move slowly up to his face. With a deathly stare, she growled, "Mr. Jackson, if you don't get your hands off me . . ."

He looked like he'd just been stabbed and now Jasmine wished she had called him Mr. Jackson before. If she'd known it was that easy to hurt him, she would have called him Mr. Jackson all day long.

"I'm sorry," he said, dropping his hand away from her. "I just don't understand why you won't give me a chance. Why you won't listen to me?"

"There's no need to. I don't want to hear anything and I never want to see you again."

"But . . ."

Jasmine kept walking.

"Please . . ."

She didn't miss a step.

"I need to tell you the whole story." His words followed her, though he did not. "I want you to know the truth."

She slammed the church doors on his last words and marched back into the center. From the hall, she heard the chatter, as if there was a celebration, but the moment she stepped inside, the joyful noise stopped. Now all that was heard was the heels of her pumps tapping against the wooden planks of the floor as she stomped across the room.

Jasmine didn't look to her left or her right. Her plan had been to go directly to Serena or Mae Frances and find a way to get out of there. But when she walked through the doors, she spotted Hosea. He must've entered the church through another door, but that didn't matter to her right now. She had one mission, one purpose.

When she stopped in front of Hosea, she said, "I need to go now."

Gently, he placed his hands on her shoulders, looked into her eyes, and nodded. "All right. I'll get Rachel."

"No!" Jasmine shouted. She felt all the eyes on her, but she didn't turn around and she didn't care. "I don't want Rachel taking me anywhere. I just want to go back to the hotel and get out of Smackover."

"But we don't have a car," Hosea said. "How else am I going to get you back?"

"I'll take you, Jasmine," Lester said, rushing to their side. "I can take you to the hotel."

"Thank you," she said, her voice lower now. "Please, can we leave now?"

Lester looked at Hosea and he nodded. "We can't all fit in one car, though . . ."

"You take Jasmine back," Hosea said, "and the kids and I will get a ride . . ."

Before he could finish, Jasmine had already turned toward the doors. Without giving anyone a single glance or a good-bye, Jasmine marched out the same door that she had entered. She was ready for Simon if he dared to approach her again. But she didn't see him, and really, that was a good thing — for him.

Lester ran in front of her, opened the door to his Yukon, and she jumped inside. The door was barely closed before she leaned back and closed her eyes. She could feel the tears right there, fighting to get out. But she was stronger; she pushed them back. She was not going to cry.

That was her vow. There was no need for any more tears. She'd come to Smackover and faced Simon, and now she was ready to go home.

It was over.

The door to the SUV opened again and Jasmine's eyes widened. She was ready to fight, physically if she had to. But it wasn't the man who was her father. It was just her sister. Her real sister.

"Oh, Jasmine, I'm so sorry," Serena said. And when she held open her arms, Jasmine leaned into her sister's embrace. And then, she did what she didn't want to do.

Jasmine wept.

God was on her side. That was the only way she could explain that just three hours after she told Simon Jackson that she never wanted to see him again, she and her family were on the last flight out of Arkansas to New York City.

Her only regret was that she'd had to leave Serena behind to catch a flight in the morning.

"That's okay," her sister had told her. "I'll stay here and make sure you didn't leave anything in your hotel room since you packed like you were in the witness protection program and had to get out of dodge."

What her sister said was true. From the moment she'd left that church and Lester had taken her back to the Super 8, she hadn't stopped moving. By the time Hosea and the children had returned, she'd packed, called the airline, and paid the almost four thousand dollars that the new tickets had cost for the five of them to travel back to the city.

And to Jasmine, it was worth every dollar.

As the plane floated upward, Jasmine leaned back in her seat. Zaya had snuggled against her, already in a deep sleep. She held her son a little tighter and glanced out the window.

Silently she bid good riddance to the place she should have never visited, and the place she would never return to. It would be easy enough to train the staff of Jacqueline's Hope through Skype sessions, and if they ever needed on-site support, Hosea would just have to be the one to make the trip.

As the plane sailed above the Natural State, the events of the past few days scrolled through her mind, but her thoughts stayed on the memory of the last few hours and her face-to-face with Simon. If he had just acquiesced to her wishes and had given her the space she'd asked for, he would still at least have Hosea and the children there in Arkansas.

But he hadn't listened, and Rachel hadn't learned that Jasmine always meant what she said. So they had to go. And because of the way it had all gone down, none of the Jacksons would see any of the Bushes again.

The seat belt sign chimed off and Mae Frances tapped Hosea on the shoulder. "Preacher Man, let's change seats," she said from across the aisle. "I need to talk to Jasmine Larson."

As the two switched places, Jasmine closed her eyes. Maybe Mae Frances would get the hint. But of course, her friend did not.

"Are you okay, Jasmine Larson?"

"I am now," she said without opening her eyes.

"You know, it's such a shame this didn't work out."

Now Jasmine opened her eyes. She twisted in her seat, careful not to disturb her son, and faced her friend. "Did you know that Rachel was going to take me to that church? Did you know that Simon was going to ambush me?"

"Yes and no. I did know about the church, but I didn't know your father . . ."

"Simon."

"I didn't know your father, Simon, was going to be there. But really when you think about it, that was the perfect place for the two of you to connect. At church."

Jasmine shook her head, turned away, and studied the clouds as if she were a storm chaser.

"Why are you so hell-bent against having a relationship with that man?"

"Why?" Jasmine responded, her eyes still on the clouds outside. "Why should I have a relationship with him? What can he do for me now?"

"If all he can do is say I love you, that's a gift."

"I have enough people telling me they love me."

"No one can ever have enough."

"Well, I don't need to hear that from Simon Jackson. I don't need him trying to come into my life and wipe away my past."

"Is that what you think he wants to do? That doesn't even make any sense. Your past is your past. Nobody has a delete key over their life. He can't take anything away; all Simon can do is add to all the wonderful things you already have."

Jasmine said nothing.

"You know how many women out there

would love to have a man come into their lives and claim them?" Mae Frances paused, but Jasmine didn't turn back.

"Maybe you don't understand," she continued, "because you were raised by a good man. But there are so many women who would give anything to have a father, no matter how old they are."

Jasmine still had nothing to say.

"Simon's just a man who's trying to live his life right."

"And that has nothing to do with me," Jasmine said, though she still didn't face Mae Frances. "I'm grown. I had a wonderful daddy. I don't need a new model."

After several moments of silence, Mae Frances said, "All right, but I think you're going to be sorry."

Jasmine whipped around, now facing her friend. "You know the only thing that I'm sorry about? I'm sorry that I didn't ask you to change the test." And then she paused as she thought about those words. "Oh my God. Why didn't I think of that? Mae Frances, I could have had you just change the test and then I wouldn't have had to go through any of this."

"Well, it's a good thing that you didn't ask me to do that because you would've missed out on all of that love down there . . . not that you got any of it because your heart is so hard, you won't let anyone in. But my prayer is that one day the Lord will show you the light."

"I've seen the light," Jasmine said, leaning back once again. "And that light has nothing to do with the Jacksons."

Jasmine closed her eyes and twisted her body away from her friend, telling her without words that the conversation was over. She heard Mae Frances's heavy sigh, but Jasmine didn't care. She'd told Simon, now she'd told Mae Frances, and when they landed in New York, she was going to make sure that Hosea knew, too. None of them were to bring any of this up to her ever again. She was tired of it and she'd made her decision.

Simon Jackson would never be more than a sperm donor and they all just needed to get that. The sooner they did, the better it would be for all of them.

CHAPTER 28

RACHEL

The mood of the Jackson Family Reunion had definitely shifted, which was pretty hard for it to do. Rachel's family had seen their share of ups and downs, triumphs and tragedies, so it took a lot to rattle them. But from the silence that filled the room, Jasmine had done just that. The solemn expression on Simon's face bothered everyone. If Rachel didn't know better, she would've thought her father was about to cry. She'd only seen that look twice in her life. Once, when he almost lost his church. And again, when he lost his wife.

Because Simon was so revered in the Jackson family Rachel guessed everyone hated to see him so sad. That's why everyone was mulling about. Even the domino game had come to a halt.

"Simon Louis Jackson, if you don't pull it together," Minnie said, coming out of the kitchen. She must've had enough of the silence because she muttered a curse word, then stomped over to the table where Rachel and Simon were sitting. She pointed a chubby finger in his face. "You've gone all your life without knowing that child and the way I see it, she isn't even worthy of knowing you now, let alone of having a relationship with you. If she can't see you for the wonderful man you are, then it's her loss."

"Simon, I agree with Minnie on this one," Ruby said, appearing on the side of her sister.

"So do I," Big Junior chimed in from the domino table. "We don't need any mo' snobs in this family anyway."

"I don't like her, either," Uncle Bubba added. "I know my Mae Frances was just about to give me a chance till that gal went and ruined things."

"Uncle Bubba, that woman wasn't about to give you a chance," Minnie said. "Matter of fact, you probably had as much chance with her as you do of getting with Michelle Obama."

"How you know I ain't already been with Michelle?" he cackled.

That seemed to lighten the mood and everyone, little by little, returned to their normal selves.

Once the attention was off Simon, Rachel took her father's hand. "Daddy, I think Aunt Minnie may be right. You might need to let this go," Rachel said. She felt a small pang in her heart. She had started to look forward to being Jasmine's sister. But after what Jasmine had just done, the way Jasmine had hurt Simon, Rachel didn't care if she ever saw Jasmine Cox Larson Bush ever again.

"I can't let it go, baby girl." Simon's voice was just above a whisper, and his words carried the weight of his sadness.

"Daddy, she doesn't want to get to know you."

He looked Rachel in her eyes. "If I lost you, would you want me to give up on finding you?"

Rachel sighed. "I just don't know what else you can do."

"I can keep trying."

"Trying, smyring," Minnie interjected. Rachel hadn't realized she was still standing over them. "You know she wasn't raised by us because she'd know better than disrespecting grown folks."

"She's not disrespectful," Rachel replied. "She's hurt and trying to deal with it."

"Hmph," Minnie muttered, rolling her eyes. "Pain is no excuse to be a prick. Come on, Ruby. Help me bring the food out."

Minnie was done and Rachel felt defeat set in even more. Even if they did get through to Jasmine, now her family didn't like her, so becoming a part of the Jackson family would be even more of a challenge.

"Maybe Reverend Bush could help," Simon said, snapping Rachel's attention back to him.

"He was here, Daddy. Even he couldn't get through to Jasmine."

"Not Hosea. Reverend Samuel Bush, his daddy."

"Oh." Rachel frowned. "Help how?"

Simon threw up his hands in frustration. "I don't know. He has a way with people. It's the only in I have." Simon turned to Brenda, who was sitting across the table from him, worry lines etched in her face. "It's a good thing you spent all those years working for Delta, because we can fly anywhere, right?" Simon asked her.

"Yes." Brenda frowned like she was trying to figure out what he was saying.

"Including New York."

"Daddy, what are you thinking about . . ."

"I've always wanted to go to New York."

Suddenly, it dawned on her what her father was trying to do. He was really going to try to follow Jasmine to New York! "Seri-

326

ously, Daddy? You cannot go to New York."
Rachel was shocked. As much as her father
hated flying, the fact that he was ready to
board a plane without a second thought
spoke volumes about his determination to
get through to Jasmine.

"Why not? I'm not going to be able to rest
until I get Jasmine to hear me." And as if he
were reading her mind, he added, "I'm just
going to have to take me a sleeping pill to
make it through the flight."

Rachel released a defeated sigh and turned
to Brenda. "Can you get two tickets to New
York?"

CHAPTER 29

RACHEL

If Samuel Bush was not an esteemed preacher, he definitely could've been a college professor, because at this moment, Rachel felt like she was in somebody's classroom. A regal man, Reverend Bush commanded the room, looking more like a Hollywood legend than a minister. He could be intimidating, were it not for the warm and genuine smile.

"Well, I imagine you all must be pretty tired," Reverend Bush said after he'd gotten Rachel and Simon settled in his office.

"We're fine," Simon replied. "This was a last-minute trip, so we really appreciate you making time to see us."

Rachel couldn't believe this time last week she was in Smackover, Arkansas. Now, she was in the Big Apple attempting to do the impossible. After Simon made the decision to go to New York, the tension seemed to lift from the family reunion and they'd had a wonderful time. When everyone returned to Houston, Rachel was hoping — no, praying — that her father would just let the issue drop. Of course, she should've known better. Rachel had even tried to get her father to talk to Reverend Bush over the phone, but he was insistent that they do this in person. Once Simon got in touch with Reverend Bush and secured a meeting date, he had Brenda immediately get tickets, and here they were.

Rachel had been a bit frazzled because she didn't have a good feeling in her gut. But sitting here in front of Reverend Bush brought her a sense of peace. Maybe he could convince her father that it was time to let go of the delusion of them being one big happy family.

"I can't apologize enough for calling you and asking for a favor," Simon continued.

"Nonsense. I'd love to help however I can. But I'll tell you," Reverend Bush said, taking a seat behind his desk, "I'll admit, I was a bit taken aback when Hosea first told me that you're Jasmine's father. How long have you known?"

"Just recently," Simon said. "After I saw Jasmine on TV several times, I just had this feeling. Then I prayed about it because I didn't want to disrupt Jasmine's life. And the Lord revealed to me that she's my daughter." Simon said it with finality.

"And the tests confirmed it," Rachel added. She didn't want Reverend Bush thinking her father was some psycho who randomly heard from God.

"Yes, I know," Reverend Bush said. "So Jasmine and I haven't talked about this at all, but what are your thoughts; why do you think she isn't receptive to this news?"

"I don't know. She won't even talk to me."

"And you came to New York *because*?"

"Because I have to talk to her. I have to get her to hear me out."

Reverend Bush nodded. "That's understandable. And what role do I play in this?"

Rachel knew it was time for her to speak up. She would make her father's pitch — ask for Reverend Bush's help — but then she would pull him aside and ask him to help her convince her father to let this dream go. "As you know, Lester greatly admires you. We all do. But Hosea told Lester that you have a special relationship with Jasmine. You're one of the few people in the world who can get through to her."

He nodded as he continued listening.

"And we need her to hear him out."

That caused Reverend Bush to shake his

head. "I don't know about this."

"Please, Reverend Bush," Simon said. "If you had a long-lost daughter, wouldn't you move Heaven and earth to see her?" He paused for a brief moment. "She has a lot of animosity. She doesn't have to ever talk to me again, but what she's feeling is not going to go away. It's just going to fester."

"And we know unresolved anger only creates issues down the line," Rachel felt the need to add. "And we know you wouldn't want your grandchildren subjected to that," Rachel threw in for good measure.

"Of course, I want only the best for my grandchildren, but this is a completely separate issue." Reverend Bush sat in silence for a moment before saying, "I understand where you're coming from, but let me talk with my son, then I'll talk to Jasmine. I can't make any promises, but I'll see what I can do."

Simon smiled as he shook Reverend Bush's hand. "Thank you. Thank you. That's all I need."

"Okay, but if I get her to talk to you, you'll have to take it from there."

Rachel didn't have to see her father beaming. She knew that was all he needed to hear.

CHAPTER 30

JASMINE

It had been a week. A peaceful week. A week without any conversation about Simon Jackson. It was as if when they landed in New York, the nightmare had stayed behind in Smackover. She hadn't even had to say a word to Hosea; he didn't mention their trip. And except for the few snippets about their fishing expedition and that close encounter of a strange kind with the skinned deer, Jacqueline and Zaya had pretty much moved on to the next part of their summer.

So when her father-in-law called and said that it was time for them to have their quarterly lunch, Jasmine felt like that was the cherry on top of a sweet week.

As the taxi rounded the corner onto Central Park West, Jasmine leaned back against the hard leather seat. She blocked out the video that was playing on the machine in the back of the cab, and instead

turned her attention to the towering build-
ings that stood in the historic district known
as Central Park West.

The two-way thoroughfare was packed
with all kinds of cars, primarily cabs, but
the New York traffic didn't bother Jasmine
today. She relished taking in the sights and
loved hearing the music of New York City.
After spending those days in Arkansas, she
felt blessed to call New York her home. So
even though her cab jerked to a stop, then
started again over and over, it was fine with
her.

She would've broken out into a song if
she didn't think the cabdriver might pull
over and demand that she, a crazy woman,
get out. That's just how happy she was. It
was her father-in-law who had made her
feel that way from the moment he called
this morning.

"So what are you doing today?" he'd
asked her after he'd spoken to Jacqueline
and Zaya.

"Nothing. Mrs. Sloss is taking Zaya to a
friend's party and Jacqueline is going with a
couple of her friends from school to the kiddie spa."

"The kiddie spa?" Reverend Bush chuckled. "Only in New York."

"Yup, she's going to have a manicure and

pedicure, so while she's being pampered and Zaya is out partying, I'm going to chill since Hosea is in Queens at that prayer luncheon."

"Well, instead of staying home by yourself in that big lonely apartment, why don't you have lunch with me? We haven't had one of our father-daughter lunches in a while."

Jasmine's heart had swelled when he'd said those words. See, this was just another reason why she didn't need Simon Jackson in her life. She'd been raised by the best man and now Samuel Bush gave her everything that she needed as a grown woman.

They'd made plans to meet at the church in a few hours and Jasmine was really looking forward to this time. It still amazed her that she had such a special relationship with Hosea's father. It had been almost ten years since they'd met and when she and Hosea had started dating, no one could have told her that she and Reverend Samuel Bush would ever like each other, let alone get to the point where she loved him like a father.

She remembered how she'd first gone to City of Lights at Riverside Church to hook up with the senior pastor. But Samuel Bush had not only made it clear that he wasn't interested in Jasmine, he'd let her know that he didn't think she was anything more than a common hoochie. So when she had turned her attention from the father to the son, the senior Pastor Bush was not having it. To him, the girl was just not good enough.

But once Hosea had fallen in love with her, Reverend Bush had opened his heart, too. And once he did, he was all in. Jasmine knew he had a great deal to do with saving her marriage when Hosea had found out that he wasn't Jacqueline's biological father. And any other time when their marriage had been strained, Reverend Bush was always there, helping them to put the pieces back together again.

They had all settled down, and now she had a wonderful life and a greater than wonderful family — which was just another reason why she didn't need Simon Jackson.

"Ugh!" she moaned softly. Why in the world did her thoughts continue to turn back to that man? No matter what, he kept rising up in her mind.

The taxi rolled to a stop in front of the church, and she pressed two twenties into the driver's hand, then slipped out of the car. Trotting up the side steps, she opened the door and called out the moment she stepped inside.

"Dad?"

"I'm in my office, Jasmine."

She walked by the empty desk where Reverend Bush's longtime assistant, Mrs. Whittingham, usually sat. Even though it was Saturday, Jasmine was a little surprised that Mrs. Whittingham was not here, though she didn't miss her. They'd gone through so many peaks and valleys in their relationship that Jasmine always felt like she was on the world's greatest roller-coaster ride. Right now they were in the middle of a truce — they said hello, then good-bye, and stayed out of each other's way in between.

Reverend Bush met her at the threshold to his office. "How is my favorite daughter-in-law?" he asked as he kissed her cheek.

Jasmine laughed. "I'm your only daughter-in-law."

"That doesn't matter to me," he said as he led her to one of the two chairs in front of his desk. "You would be my favorite even if I had ten." Chuckling, he then added, "So how are you, baby girl?"

Jasmine beamed at the love she felt from this man. "I'm good."

"And my favorite granddaughter?"

"You talked to her this morning; can't you tell that she's getting grown?" Jasmine said, then paused. Her heart always wanted to cry — in a good way — when Samuel Bush talked about Jacqueline. Though there was not a single drop of Bush blood in her veins, to Samuel, Jacqueline was his firstborn grandchild. He loved her and doted on her as if she carried every bit of his legacy. It was the love this man had for her child that made Jasmine love him even more.

"And my favorite grandson?"

"He's just like you. He's sweet, and kind, and patient, and always so concerned."

"I have the best grandchildren."

She laughed. "You do."

"We're all so blessed," he said. "So, Hosea told me it was a little rough for you down in Arkansas."

Jasmine sighed. How did the conversation make that left turn? If this were anyone else, she would shut this down right now. But this was her father-in-law, a man who could not be turned off. The only way to get to the end of this conversation was to begin. And then move through it as quickly as she could.

"Hosea told me that he shared my . . . news with you."

Reverend Bush nodded. "He did. And I know it's been rough on you."

"It was at first, but I'm fine now."

"I'm glad about that. I want you to be fine." Then he added, "But, Jasmine . . ."

She groaned without meaning to.

He continued, "No matter how hard it's been, what I can't figure out is why you're so against even sitting down with Simon. Hosea said you won't even talk to him."

"He doesn't want to just talk. He wants me to accept him as my father. And how can I accept him when I have so many questions about my life?"

"Questions?"

"Yeah. Now I have questions about my own fa— questions about the man who raised me. I mean, did my dad know I wasn't his daughter? Or did he know and then he adopted me? Was he fine with that? Did he ever look at me and regret it?"

"Jasmine, you know that didn't happen."

"How do I know that? How do I know anything anymore? My dad could have had moments when he looked at me and didn't see me as his daughter. All of those are questions I have now, and I won't ever be able to get the answers."

He nodded. "I can understand you having questions. But how do they matter? The only one that matters is: did your dad love you? And from what I know about you, from what I know about Serena, that man loved you and then some."

In an instant, another memory of the man she loved so much: her father standing, clapping, cheering when Jasmine crossed the stage to receive her college diploma, then meeting her afterward with tears still streaming down his cheeks. He'd kissed her, hugged her, and kissed her again. Told her a million times in thirty seconds just how proud he was of her.

That was the man who was her father.

Reverend Bush broke through that memory with, "And now, you have a chance to have another man love you."

"How could he love me when he didn't even love my mother?"

His eyebrows rose, as if he were shocked by that question. "Well, first of all, I could tell you that there are lots of men out there who love their children but don't have too many fond words to say about their children's mothers. That's a whole 'nother sermon. But how do you know that about Simon and your mother?"

"Because he just left her, pregnant."

"Do you know the story behind that?"

Jasmine shook her head. "But I don't need to. I'm not interested in hearing any more stories. I had my dad, I have you, I have enough fathers in my life."

"And I feel blessed that God gave me you as a daughter. But having Simon in your life will never take away from me and you.

339

And it won't take away from the man you know as your dad."

Jasmine shook her head slightly.

"Three men, Jasmine? You're going to turn down the chance to be loved by three fathers?"

That was enough for her. "So where are we going for lunch? I'm starving."

He looked at her for an extra moment, chuckled a little, then stood. "I have to take some of these folders to Brother Hill," he said, referring to the man who'd been his armor bearer for more than a few decades. "He's in his office. I'll be right back."

When he closed the door behind him, Jasmine breathed. Thank God she'd gotten out of that. Prayerfully that would be the last conversation she'd ever have to have about Simon Jackson.

A few minutes later, the door opened behind her and she turned around. She smiled when she saw her father-in-law, but he was not alone, and that took every bit of her joy away.

"What is he doing here?" she snapped, pointing to Simon.

"I had to come," Simon said, taking a stiff step forward. "I couldn't let you just go away. We have to talk."

"Dad!" She pleaded with her father-in-

340

law as if she expected Reverend Bush to rescue her from what she saw as madness.

But all Reverend Bush said was, "Just talk to him, Jasmine. Listen to what he has to say." Then he gave Simon a soft tap on his back before he left the room, closing the door behind him.

Jasmine had never felt so deserted, so alone in her life.

"Why don't you leave me alone?" she shouted. "You're acting like a stalker."

"I can't just walk away. I know that's what you want me to do, but I can't. Not until we sit down. At least once."

"Why are you trying to be my father when I don't want to be your daughter?"

Simon flinched, but his head was still high when he asked, "Why would anyone be against speaking to their father, even once?"

"Because I don't even know if you're really my father."

He looked at her, his eyes filled with pity.

"Really," she continued. "I don't know."

"We had the test . . ."

"It didn't come back that you were one hundred percent absolutely my father."

"Jasmine . . ."

"And I never saw the test being done."

He shook his head.

"And I have no idea who had their hands

on them before the results got to me. They were delivered from the clinic to a courier and then to my concierge. And he didn't even bring it up to me. He gave the envelope to Mae Frances." Jasmine stopped. Mae Frances! The words in her head were jumbled, as if they were trying to find their way to making a single thought. But as the idea formulated in her mind, she calmed down. Her voice was more controlled now when she said, "Who knows what could have happened to that test since it was handled by so many people."

"Are you serious?" Simon asked. "So you really think that the results could change just from the paper being handed from one person to another?"

"All I know is that I haven't trusted those tests from the beginning," she said, thinking that her words weren't totally a lie. She never wanted to believe those results. "That's why I never wanted to talk to you." Before he could answer she said, "It's because I don't even know if you're my father." A beat, and then, "I don't think that you are."

He shook his head.

It was a full-fledged idea when she said, "Look, I'll make a deal with you."

His eyes brightened, as if he thought she

was willing to give him a chance.

She said, "Let's have another test."

He frowned. "Why? We already know . . ."

"No, we don't know. Let's have another test and this time, let's all be there, right there in the center when the results come back. So the results will just go from the technicians to us. Period."

"You know this isn't necessary. I can look at you and know . . ."

"That's the deal," Jasmine interrupted him. "Another test."

After a moment, he said, "Fine. And if the tests come back that I am not your father, I will go away and never bother you again."

"All right."

"But" — he held up his finger — "if the test once again comes back that I am your father . . ."

"It won't . . ."

"Then you have to sit down with me. Just once. And after that, I'll let you make the decision about what kind of relationship you want to have with me. But just once, we'll sit down and talk." He held out his hand. "Deal?"

Jasmine looked at the hand hanging there, but she didn't touch him. "Deal, Mr. Jackson."

Once again, she watched as her words

caused pain to spread across his face. But all he did was lower his hand and smile. Awkward seconds passed and Simon made a move as if he wanted to embrace her. But then, he stepped back.

"I'll stay in New York until we have this done. Just call Rachel. Let us know where you want us to be and when."

Jasmine nodded.

"I'll be there," he said. He waited another moment before he turned and walked out the door.

Jasmine felt like she was just taking her first breath when she was finally alone. But she didn't give herself any time to recover. She snatched her cell from her purse and tapped Mae Frances's name.

As the phone rang, Jasmine thanked God for this woman who was her friend. From the moment they'd met, Mae Frances had saved her from one crisis after the other. And this was going to be one of the most important ones.

When her friend answered, Jasmine said, "Mae Frances, I need a huge favor."

"What is it now, Jasmine Larson?"

She took a breath. "Remember on the plane when I said I wish that I'd asked you to change those test results?"

"Yeeeeeaaaahhh," she said, dragging out

the word.

"I'm going to take the DNA test again to determine if Simon is my father."

"Oh, Lawd!"

"And I need you to use your connections. I need the test to come back negative."

"Simon Jackson is not going to fall for that. He'll just make you take the test again and again and again."

"I don't care how many times I have to take it. You just have to make sure that it always comes back the way I want it."

There was a long moment of silence.

"Mae Frances?" Jasmine finally said. "Please. Please, I need you like I've never needed you before."

After more silence Mae Frances sighed. "Okay, Jasmine Larson. I got you. You know I always got you."

"Thank you," Jasmine said. And when she hung up, she'd never been more grateful for her friendship.

CHAPTER 31

RACHEL

"She wants you to do what?" Rachel immediately lowered her voice, reminding herself that she was in this shi-shi poo-poo boutique hotel. Since she'd had a taste of the good life, Rachel didn't do Holiday Inns anymore, and she took full advantage of the luxurious experiences every chance she got. She'd just returned from a full spa experience while Simon had gone back to Reverend Bush's church. Rachel hadn't held out much hope that Reverend Bush would make progress with Jasmine, but she'd never expected *this*.

"She wants me to take another test," Simon repeated. "She didn't trust the first one."

Rachel didn't know what kind of game Jasmine was playing, but another test was a complete and utter waste of time. "Daddy, that's ridiculous. It's just a stall tactic."

"Whatever it is, if it makes her feel more at ease, I'm doing it." The expression on Simon's face told her no amount of protesting would change her father's mind.

Rachel plopped down on the sofa in the suite that connected their adjoining rooms. Samuel Bush had called first thing this morning and told Simon to come to the church for lunch. He hadn't said whether Jasmine would be there, but Rachel figured she would be. "I don't know why you're even entertaining this," she added.

"Because I have to. And you said you understood that." Simon removed his jacket and hung it in the hall closet.

"Fine. If you want to subject yourself to more heartache, then so be it." Rachel reached for her cell phone, which was on the coffee table. "But just like she doesn't trust us, I don't trust her."

"What are you doing?" Simon asked as she scrolled through the phone in search of Jasmine's phone number.

Rachel stopped when she got to "Big Sis," the name she'd changed Jasmine's number to. She made a mental note to change it back to "Old Troll." "I'm calling Jasmine."

"Rachel, you're not going to change my mind about this," Simon warned.

Rachel held up a finger to cut her father

off. "Hello, Jasmine?" Rachel said when Jasmine answered. "This is Rachel."

"What, Rachel?" At that moment, it dawned on Rachel that Jasmine was always acting irritated with her. Why in the world did Rachel keep trying?

"My father told me you want to have another test," Rachel said.

"Yes, that's right."

"Why?"

"Not that I have to explain anything to you, but for all I know you could've tampered with the test."

"Don't flatter yourself. I was trying to do you a favor by inviting you into our family. But trust, now, I want that *not* to happen just as much as you do."

"Then we're in agreement."

With every word she spoke, Rachel was reminded of why Jasmine had few friends. This woman was just evil and bitter.

"This isn't about me, though. It's about my dad. Our dad. You can test till the cows come home, but it's not going to change that."

"We'll see." There was cockiness in Jasmine's voice, almost like she was sure of a different outcome. It gave Rachel pause.

Finally, she said, "Unh-unh, something isn't right."

"Rachel, I really don't have time for your paranoia."

"It's not paranoia. I didn't train as an investigative reporter for nothing."

"I'm sorry, your three classes at community college hardly qualify as training."

Rachel was fed up with Jasmine's condescending attitude. "You know what, Jasmine? You think you're too good to be a part of our family. Well, I've got news for you, you're not. My family — from my daddy to my ratchet cousins — have more love in their pinky toe than you have in your whole body."

"Are you finished?"

"Naw, we'll be finished when we take the test again, prove you're just a butthole, and give my daddy peace of mind."

"Rachel!" Simon said.

Rachel stood and moved into the bedroom. She wanted to get away from her father and tell Jasmine how she really felt. "So, here's the way this is going to go down. I'm picking the testing facility."

"You picked it last time."

"Well, I don't trust you."

"The feeling is mutual."

"So, we'll pick one together. I'll call and schedule the test for tomorrow."

"I want one that gives immediate results. I

don't want to drag this out any further than we have to," Jasmine said.

"Fine by me. I'm ready to get out of this concrete jungle anyway." Rachel reached over, grabbed her laptop, and logged on. "I'm googling DNA testing in New York City." As soon as she typed in the search engine, several facilities popped up. "I should make you go to this one," Rachel said, clicking on the first link. " 'Who Da Daddy.' "

"Girl, please."

Any other time, Rachel would've laughed. "Fine. It looks like there are three that do instant results," Rachel said, scanning the list. "I'm picking DNA Center in Queens."

"Fine."

She said that a little too fast. "No, make that Identigene in the Bronx," Rachel corrected.

"Fine, Rachel. See if can you set it up for in the morning."

It was settled. She'd call, pray they could get in, and get this over with. "Before I let you go, Jasmine, in all seriousness, what are you going to do when this test backs up the first one?"

"It won't. I know in my heart Simon is not my father."

Rachel was quiet for a moment. She was

ready to get off the phone, but she had one more thing to say. "Do you know when I was growing up, my father made me so mad. He gave everything to his church and all I wanted was his love. It's why I rebelled. It's why I caused him major headaches. I just wanted his love. And when I got it, when he realized his little girl was truly hurting, he stepped up to the plate. And he's shown me the power of a father's love. I feel sorry that you'll never know that."

Jasmine hesitated, but then said, "I know a father's love."

"You don't know *my* father's love." For the first time since they began this journey, Rachel didn't feel inclined to refer to Simon as *their* father. If Jasmine didn't want him, it was time to move on. "My dad isn't try-ing to replace the man who raised you. He knows that man is your father. My father is just trying to add to your life." She sighed, tired of the same argument. "I promise you, if the first test was wrong and you aren't his daughter, I'll make sure he stays out of your life. I'll make sure we both do."

Rachel wanted to add a "but . . . ," but she didn't really care anymore. In fact she *hoped* that the test came back negative. Then they could return to Houston and forget that they ever knew Jasmine Cox Larson Bush.

CHAPTER 32

JASMINE

Jasmine took a deep breath and willed herself to be calm. Really, she didn't know why she was anxious. She'd made it through the week; there was nothing to be nervous about now. She'd climbed over every obstacle, dodged every bullet, broken through all the walls. But she was here, even though it didn't seem that way when she and Mae Frances had met to discuss the plan.

"You want to have the test where?" Mae Frances had asked when Jasmine told her which clinic Rachel had chosen. "And why in the world would you let Rasheeda pick out where this would be done?"

"Because I didn't want her to think I was trying to pull a fast one."

"You *are* trying to pull a fast one and you need me to do it. I don't know anyone at that clinic." Mae Frances had shaken her head. "I'm sorry, but I don't think I'm going to be able to do this, Jasmine Larson."

Jasmine had felt her blood pressure rising. "What do you mean?" She didn't understand what Mae Frances could possibly be saying — that she couldn't help her? There had never been a time when Mae Frances hadn't rescued Jasmine. "You've got to do this, Mae Frances."

"I'll try; let's just hope I can deliver."

So for the next few days, Jasmine had had to dance, giving Rachel one excuse after another for why they couldn't take the test right away.

"You're just stalling," Rachel had protested.

She was right, but couldn't prove it. And Rachel didn't press too much since Jasmine kept using her children as an excuse — Jacqueline was home with a cold, Zaya had to have an emergency dental procedure. And the whole time, Jasmine had been patient until Mae Frances had found a connection who knew a connection who had a connection.

And the plan was set in motion.

But that didn't end Jasmine's angst. Because even once Mae Frances had told her connection what she needed, she still tried to convince Jasmine that this was one hookup that was wrong.

"It doesn't make any sense," she kept telling Jasmine. "No matter what we make the test say, Simon is still going to be your father."

"He won't know that."

"But you will. Can you sleep knowing what you're doing?"

"I've been sleeping just fine all these years."

"All right," Mae Frances had finally agreed, though it felt to Jasmine that Mae Frances was just giving up.

Now, they sat in the waiting room of the clinic with Jasmine shoulder-to-shoulder with her human savior. And the two of them sat across from Rachel and Simon.

This was the first time Jasmine noticed just how much Rachel looked like her father, though right now there was little that was similar about them. Simon sat, leaning forward with his elbows resting on his knees, wearing that smile. That same smile he had on his face whenever he looked at her. That smile that never went away except for when she called him Mr. Jackson.

Right next to him, Rachel sat, glaring at Jasmine like she had never hated her so much. And that was quite a feat since over the years the two had known each other they'd shared many moments of hate.

That part hurt Jasmine's heart just a little. Not that she wanted to be Rachel's sister, but she'd kind of grown fond of her. And except for that trick Rachel had pulled dragging her to the church when they were in Smackover two weeks ago, Rachel had treated her. Rachel had handled her with a porcelain kind of care, as if she understood what Jasmine had been going through. She hadn't tried to push her, at least not too much. And Jasmine really appreciated that.

But it was better this way, with all ties broken. She couldn't ever see herself forming any kind of friendship with that girl anyway. Because Rachel wasn't anything more than a country-ghetto superstar who'd been able to clean herself up a little bit with some money. But class was bred, not bought, and Rachel would never be able to rise to Jasmine's level. If she'd had any doubts about that before, Jasmine knew that for a fact after having spent time in Arkansas.

"Jasmine Larson, would you calm down?" Mae Frances whispered.

"What?"

She tapped Jasmine's leg and only then did Jasmine realize how much she'd been shaking. Uncrossing her legs, she smoothed out her skirt and tried to inhale peace.

Still she leaned forward, and using her hand to cover her mouth, she whispered, "You're sure everything is taken care of, right?"

Mae Frances stared at Jasmine for a moment, then rolled her eyes. "You must've forgotten who I am," she grumbled.

"Okay." Jasmine sat up, satisfied. All she had to do now was wait. Though waiting was the hardest part. She just wanted these results so that they could all go home — Jasmine back to the luxury that was her life and Simon and Rachel back to the deepest part of Texas.

The door to the back offices opened and all four of them looked up. "Mr. Jackson," the woman in the white lab coat said.

Though only one of them carried that name, all four jumped up and said, "Yes."

The woman looked from one to the other before her glance settled on Simon. "Well, since you're the only man here, I'm going to assume that you're Mr. Jackson." She handed him the packet.

He held it with the tips of his fingers, like he was holding precious cargo. And Jasmine kept her eyes on the envelope that was about to free her.

Simon asked, "Is there a place where we can go? To open this?"

Again, the woman's gaze swept over the four of them before she said, "Follow me."

Simon was first, followed by Rachel, then Jasmine and Mae Frances. The woman led them to a conference room and ushered them all inside. "You can talk in here." When they were seated, she left them alone.

"Well," Simon said, still wearing that silly smile.

"Go ahead," Jasmine said. "Open it."

Rachel narrowed her eyes. "You seem so anxious."

"I just want to get this over with," Jasmine told her. Then looking at Simon, she added, "Once and for all."

As Simon gently tore the top of the envelope open, Mae Frances took Jasmine's hand and squeezed it. That calmed Jasmine down even more.

Still, she held on to Mae Frances because she didn't have anyone else. She purposely hadn't told Hosea about this retest because she knew her husband would be suspicious, just as Rachel was now, and would be even more in a moment when Simon read the results.

But Hosea wouldn't have let her get away with this; Rachel would have no choice.

She took a final deep breath as Simon pulled the single sheet from the envelope.

And then Jasmine waited for his silly smile to fade away, like she expected. But his smile was still in place when he glanced up at her and said, "Just like before . . . you are my daughter."

It took a moment for those words to settle in before she shouted, "What?" Ripping her hand away from Mae Frances's grasp, she snatched the paper from Simon. "That's impossible," she said as her eyes scanned the paper.

She didn't understand all the numbers, just like before, but she understood enough — there was a 99.9 percent chance that Simon Jackson was her father.

"No!" she yelled again and turned to Mae Frances. "What is this?" She waved the paper in her face.

"This is the right thing," Mae Frances said, her voice level even as Jasmine shouted.

"No!" Jasmine cried, shaking her head. "No! You were supposed to fix this."

"What?"

Suddenly, Jasmine remembered she and Mae Frances were not alone. She couldn't see her clearly, though. Not through her tears.

"What do you mean Mae Frances was supposed to fix this?" Rachel demanded to know. "Fix what? How?"

Jasmine ignored her, keeping her eyes on Mae Frances. "You said you had my back."

"And that's exactly why I didn't do anything, Jasmine Larson." She reached for her, but Jasmine scooted away. Mae Frances continued anyway, "I know you're upset by this now, but I promise you in a few days, in a few weeks, it might even take months or years . . . I didn't want you to have any regrets. And changing those results would have been something you would regret for the rest of your life."

Jasmine shook her head. "I can't believe you betrayed me like this."

"It feels that way now, but I know I did the right thing. I did it because I love you. And I'm not going to let someone I love miss out on any kind of love."

Then, Mae Frances scooted her chair back and with her eyes on Rachel, she gestured with her head toward the door. Rachel jumped up, but glanced at her father. When he nodded, she followed Mae Frances toward the door.

Rachel paused, though. "Jasmine . . ."

But all Jasmine did was look the other way.

Mae Frances led Rachel from the room and closed the door.

It was as if their leaving gave Jasmine permission. She covered her face with her hands and wept, though no tears fell from her eyes. She was cried out, but the pain she felt was still the same. Now this would never end.

She lowered her head and thought about what it would be like now, having Simon around all the time when she didn't want him. She stared at her hands folded in her lap, and wondered what else she had to do. Was there another way to end this?

There was nothing but silence; so much so that for a moment Jasmine thought she was alone. But when she looked up and across the table, Simon was still sitting there. Now, that smile was gone.

His face was etched with pain once more, only this time it was deeper than when she'd called him Mr. Jackson. Jasmine could tell he was hurt down to his soul.

Still, he said nothing for a few moments. Just looked at her with eyes filled with deep sorrow. Finally he said, "Jasmine, if this is causing you this much . . . anguish, then I will respect your wishes. I will just go."

She swallowed and through glassy eyes studied Simon.

"I will just go," he repeated, sounding like he was a broken man.

Jasmine waited a moment before she said, "And . . . you'll leave me alone? You'll never bother me again?"

He shook his head. "You'll never hear from me. I loved your mother too much and I love you. And now . . . to see you like this." He pushed back his chair. "I'm sorry," he said before he turned away.

Jasmine watched him walk from the table and she wondered if this was really over. Would he keep his word? Would he leave her alone?

She had a feeling he would. She had a feeling she would never see him again. She had a feeling she would never get to know . . . her father.

And that made her happy.

And that made her sad.

She watched each step he took. She watched as his hand gripped the doorknob. She watched as he took that first step out the door and then closed it behind him.

That was when she jumped up and ran. Swinging the door open, she said, "Simon! Wait!"

He turned around.

She inhaled, exhaled, and said to him: "Just for a few minutes. Can you stay? Can you tell me about my mother?"

He hesitated as if he thought she might change her mind. Then his smile was as slight as his nod as he came back into the room. Together they sat down, this time on the same side of the table. And then another moment of hesitation passed before he took her hand.

"Let me tell you about Doris Young. Let me tell you about the beautiful, wonderful woman who was your mother."

EPILOGUE

ONE MONTH LATER

Mae Frances reached for her cell phone, and with just one eye open, she peeked at the screen for the identity of the incoming call. Scooting up in the bed, she tugged the sheet up to cover herself and clicked on the phone.

"Yes, Jasmine Larson?"

"Is that any way to greet your favorite person?"

"Well, Jesus isn't on the other end of this line, you are. So, what's up?"

Jasmine laughed. "Okay," she said. "Remember, you wouldn't even know Jesus if it weren't for me."

"Was there any reason in particular that you called in the middle of my vacation? Or did you just call to torture me?"

"If there's any torture going on . . ."

"Jasmine Larson . . ." Mae Frances said, with a warning in her tone.

"Okay. Well, I was calling to see how you were doing and to tell you what's been going on." She paused. "With me and Simon."

"Simon." Mae Frances said his name with a smile spreading across her face. "At least you're not calling him 'that man' anymore."

"No, he's graduated to Simon."

"So, how has it been?"

"It's cool," Jasmine said, though Mae Frances could hear the little bit of hesitation that was still in her voice. "I'm sure Simon would like it to go faster, but he's letting me take my time — if you can call talking on the phone just about every day taking my time."

"Now that makes me happy. So you call him every day?"

"You know me better than that, Mae Frances. I haven't called him once. But maybe I will soon. Maybe tomorrow. Or the next day."

"Well, I'm sure he'd like that. I think he's a really good man."

Jasmine paused as if she wasn't sure that she wanted to agree with that just yet. "Well, the one thing I do know is that he really did love my mother."

Even though Jasmine couldn't see her, Mae Frances nodded because that was the truth. She and Hosea had been with Jasmine the day that Simon finally told her the whole story: How he and Doris had been writing each other, but then her letters suddenly stopped coming. How he didn't know what had happened and how he'd been devastated. How he'd even bought a ticket to take a bus to Mobile, but once his parents found out, they'd shut that down. Still, she let Jasmine repeat the story, knowing there was some kind of therapeutic relief in there for her.

Mae Frances said, "Every time I think about Simon and your mother, I think about that Raymond and Joanne story."

"Raymond and Joanne? You mean Romeo and Juliet?"

"I mean what I said. Raymond was this dude I grew up with in Galveston and his mama hated his girlfriend, Joanne. But even though they were only fifteen, they were in love and tried to sneak off to get married. But then his mama found out and showed up at the courthouse with a shotgun. 'Cause they'd gone to the courthouse with some fake papers. Anyway, his mama pointed that gun straight at Joanne's face. I'm telling you, Joanne ran outta that courthouse so fast and no one ain't heard from her since. That was fifty, sixty, seventy years ago, I don't know. But no one ever saw Joanne again."

Jasmine chuckled. "Are you making that up?"

"I'm serious. Just be glad that didn't happen to Simon and your mama."

"Yeah," Jasmine said. "Simon kinda figures that Mama may have stayed away from him since he was from a family of preachers. She probably didn't want him to be cast aside the way she was."

"True love, I guess. I ain't neva known a love like that before."

"Well, Simon says that if he had found Mama, they would've married."

"Now don't you go wasting your time thinking about what might have been. Shoot, if he'd done that, you wouldn't have had your daddy and your sister and you probably wouldn't have met Preacher Man and had your children . . ."

"Okay!" Jasmine said.

"I have just always believed that everything happens the way it's supposed to. So just be happy with what you got."

"I am," she said. "At least I'm trying to be."

"Good. Now, how's Rachel?"

Jasmine paused for a moment. "Rachel? You actually called her by her name."

"Well, I have to . . . now that she's your sister."

"We're not quite sisterly, but at least we talk . . . sometimes. Simon puts her on the phone and makes us talk to each other. She said that it's gonna take some time for her to get over the way I treated her father . . . our father."

"She'll get over that."

"Whatever; Serena is a great sister, so I'm cool if it's just the two of us for the rest of our lives. Anyway, enough about my crazy situation. How's your vacation?" And before Mae Frances could answer, Jasmine added, "Where are you anyway?"

"My vacation is just fine and you don't need to know where I am."

"Why? You think I'm gonna show up? What? You trying to hide some man?" Jasmine laughed.

"I keep telling you, Jasmine Larson, you don't know who I am."

"Oh, please, I know everything that . . ."

In the middle of Jasmine's sentence, Mae Frances clicked off the phone. And then she powered it off, knowing that Jasmine was probably calling back at that moment. "Hmph! That girl thinks she knows me and she don't know nothin' 'bout me."

"So, what you mean you ain't neva known a love like that before? I bet you know it now."

Mae Frances smiled when she said, "Shut up, you old tyrant."

He stood, stretching as the sunlight beamed through the window of the Super 8. "Hmph, I should've been telling you to shut up last night. I'm sure the folks next door didn't get any sleep." He stood at the edge of the bed in all his glory, not the least bit ashamed. "I told you, the hair may be gone" — he patted the top of his head — "the muscles may be gone" — he jiggled the hanging skin under his arm, then wiggled his hips — "but Big Daddy still got that magic potion that makes the ladies scream his name."

"I don't scream." Mae Frances pretended to pout. She couldn't believe this man had her acting like a giddy teenager.

"Hmph, ask the folks next door. You were acting like you were twenty years old." He moved in closer to her, mimicking her. "Yes, Bubba! Yesssss, Bubba! I ain't neva had it like that, Bubba!"

Mae Frances took a pillow and swung it at him; he jumped out of the way, then dove on top of her. He couldn't have weighed more than 140 pounds so she easily pushed him off. He rolled to lie beside her, out of breath, like their two-minute tussle had really worn him out, which was strange because she knew for a fact that he could go much longer than two minutes.

"Mae Frances, you some kind of woman. Just fine. And you got all your teeth. Don't find that around here often." He chuckled. "I don't know what I did to deserve a woman like you," he said, his tone turning serious.

"You don't have me," she replied, turning over on her side to face him.

"Not yet. But I will." He flashed a confident smile, which Mae Frances couldn't help but return.

She couldn't believe she was back in Smackover . . . but Bubba was right. He had some kind of magic on her. It was strange because she'd had her fair share of men — powerful, handsome, charismatic — but there was something about Bubba Jackson that kept drawing her to him. And it wasn't the fact that he gave her a Viagra-style night without popping a pill. Bubba made her feel young again. He made her feel special. He made her smile inside. Even though they were from two different worlds, he wasn't intimidated and his confidence turned her on.

"So, when we going public?" Bubba asked. "I'm eighty. I can't be spending years as a secret sidepiece."

"Hush. I told you, I don't let the world know my business."

"You know I googled you," he said.

"You don't even know how to spell 'google'!" She laughed.

"My nephew helped me. He bought me one of those contraptions that you can google on."

"You mean a computer?"

"Yeah. But I didn't have any need for it. Till I met you. I wanted to know more."

"Hmph. So you went digging?"

"That's just it. I went digging, but I didn't find anything." He sat up and looked at her strangely. "How you gonna be . . . How old are you again?"

Mae Frances gave him a serious side-eye.

He continued. "How you gonna be however old you are and I can't find nothing about you?"

"And what makes you think I'd be on Google anyway? Maybe I'm just an ordinary woman."

"Ordinary women don't know everyone from Al Sharpton to Colin Powell."

"How did you know I know Colin?"

"I didn't. But see what I mean," Bubba said. He stood and walked around to the edge of the bed, facing her directly. "All those connections and nothing about you nowhere?"

She flashed a sly smile. "You know what you need to know."

"But I want to know more." He crawled toward her on all fours. Mae Frances couldn't help it; she giggled. "What I got to do to get you to tell me more?" he asked. "Tickle your fancy?" He ran a finger across the bottom of her foot. "Find your sweet spot?" He lifted her arm and kissed the inside of her forearm. "What's it gonna take?"

Mae Frances stared at him. She'd never before wanted to tell her story and had only taken the book deal because the price was right. The truth was she'd been unsure if she ever really planned to deliver her life story. But it was time. Jasmine connecting with her newfound family made Mae Frances think about her own. Being here with Bubba made her remember all the loves she'd lost.

"You want to know my story, Bubba Jackson?" She reached over, pulled his boxers off the lampshade, and tossed them to him. "Get dressed, I'm going to give you a sneak peek of my soon-to-be blockbuster book . . . and it's a doozy, because do I have a story to tell . . ."

■ ■ ■ ■

READERS GROUP
GUIDE:
A BLESSING
& A CURSE

RESHONDA TATE BILLINGSLEY
& VICTORIA CHRISTOPHER MURRAY

■ ■ ■ ■

INTRODUCTION

A Blessing & a Curse continues the collaboration between ReShonda Tate Billingsley and Victoria Christopher Murray, following the beloved First Ladies of the Baptist Church and sworn frenemies Rachel Jackson Adams and Jasmine Cox Larson Bush.

After seeing Jasmine on their outrageous reality TV show, Rachel's father, Simon Jackson, makes a shocking revelation — with her eerie resemblance to his first teenage love, Simon is almost convinced that Jasmine is his daughter.

Throughout their storied past together, Rachel and Jasmine have been there for each other through trauma and tragedy, despite their outward hatred of each other . . . in that way, their relationship has always been sisterly. Nevertheless, Rachel and Jasmine are furious with Simon's theory, intent on seeking out anything they can to debunk it. Eventually, Rachel convinces Jasmine to come along to the Jackson Family Reunion in Smackover, Arkansas, in search of a DNA test and the truth.

TOPICS & QUESTIONS FOR DISCUSSION

1. When Mae Frances "tricks" Jasmine into taking a real DNA test, instead of skewing the results in her favor as promised, Mae Frances claims she's doing what is best for her. Do you think this is true? Is Mae Frances being a good friend in this moment? Why or why not?

2. If you've read Victoria Christopher Murray's previous books about Jasmine, are you surprised by how stable Jasmine and Hosea's relationship is? Would you have guessed that their marriage would be as strong as it is currently? Why or why not?

3. Think about the tragedy that Jasmine and Hosea have undergone since Jacquie's disappearance previously in this series. How can tragedy create rifts in relationships? How

can it make a bond stronger? Reflect on how it has seemingly affected Jasmine and Hosea's marriage, especially considering their devotion to Jacquie's foundation.

4. Jasmine and Rachel seem like polar opposites, divided by North and South, differences in class, and upbringing. How do you think these ladies could learn from each other? What qualities do you think they would most benefit in learning from the other?

5. Did you understand Jasmine's resistance to getting to know her new family, or were you frustrated with her stubbornness? What would you have said to Jasmine if you had a chance to convince her to meet Simon, attend the Smackover family reunion, and accept Rachel as her sister?

6. Discuss the ending of *A Blessing & a Curse*. Where do you think Rachel and Jasmine's relationship will go from here? How about Simon and Jasmine's?

7. *A Blessing & a Curse* was written by both Victoria Christopher Murray and ReShonda Tate Billingsley. Did

you notice any indication of the two authors? How do you think they collaborated in the melding of these two beloved characters?

8. Do you have a "frenemy" relationship like Rachel and Jasmine's? Describe this relationship and how it may be similar or different from the one in the book.

9. Do you think Mae Frances is as connected as she says she is? To Bubba, she's an intriguing woman of mystery — what other secrets do you think she has up her sleeve? Come up with a whole backstory for her and how she might have met this slew of celebrities and public figures!

10. Why do you think ReShonda Tate Billingsley and Victoria Christopher Murray decided to bring their respectively beloved characters together for this series? Who do you relate to more? Can you find qualities you respect in the women you relate to less?

11. Discuss the role of faith, God, and prayer in this novel. How does it help Jasmine and Rachel, respectively, in their journeys?

12. Put yourself in Jasmine's and Rachel's shoes. If you found out you had a new member of your family who you didn't previously know about, how would you react?

13. Jasmine's loved ones try to convince her that the father who raised her will still be her daddy, even if Simon is her biological father. How much do you agree with this statement? Are genes the only things that define a family? Why or why not?

ENHANCE YOUR BOOK CLUB

1. Are you on Team Jasmine or Team Rachel? Make T-shirts showing your loyalty like the ones Victoria Christopher Murray and ReShonda Tate Billingsley made for *Sinners & Saints*!

2. Many characters in this book use prayer to help them through difficult times and hard decisions. Have a Bible on hand and give all participants the opportunity to share their favorite scripture passage, prayer, or personal motto. What kind of help do you need throughout the day, especially when

you have a difficult choice to make? Share with the group.

3. For more information on the novels of Victoria Christopher Murray and ReShonda Tate Billingsley, visit the authors' websites, www.reshonda tatebillingsley.com and www.victoria christophermurray.com. If you'd like a chance to meet the authors, be sure to check the tour dates. Both tour extensively and could be reading and signing at a bookstore near you!

ABOUT THE AUTHORS

ReShonda Tate Billingsley's #1 national bestselling novels include *Let the Church Say Amen, I Know I've Been Changed,* and *Say Amen, Again,* winner of the NAACP Image Award for Outstanding Literary Work. Her collaboration with Victoria Christopher Murray has produced three hit novels, *Sinners & Saints, Friends & Foes,* and *Fortune & Fame.* Visit ReShondaTateBillingsley .com, meet the author on Facebook at ReShondaTateBillingsley, or follow her on Twitter @Reshondat.

Victoria Christopher Murray is the author of more than twenty novels including: *The Ex Files, Lady Jasmine, The Deal, the Dance, and the Devil,* and *Stand Your Ground* which was named a *Library Journal* Best Book of the Year. Winner of the African American Literary Award for Fiction and

Author of the Year (Female), Murray is also a two-time NAACP Image Award Nominee for Outstanding Fiction. She splits her time between Los Angeles and Washington, DC. Visit her website at VictoriaChristopher Murray.com.